ABSOLUTION

DANA K. RAY

eLectio Publishing

Little Elm, TX

For Tom, Madison, Keaton, Lydia, and Collins
who may have been somewhat neglected
while I wrote the Luciano Series!!

Love you, guys!!

ACKNOWLEDGMENTS

Thanks to my hubby and kids for cheering me on

To my family who read the very first rough draft and claimed they loved it

To fictional Antony for being…Antony

To all the readers who will fall in love with the Lucianos

To God for giving me the movies in my head

And to Linda Robinson, Beatrice Fishback, and Irene Onorato, Towanda!

ONE

BEADS OF SWEAT FORMED on Antony's forehead as he looked down at the disintegrating parking lot of Kansas City's waterfront district. Carlo's death flooded his mind. The fight. The gunshot. The guilt. He ran his hand through his short black hair. *Guilt?* It was something he prided himself in never feeling.

A silver Porsche skidded to a stop, spraying his black leather shoes with gravel and small shards of glass. Spencer Romeo Nunzio climbed out, took off his sunglasses and suit jacket, and tossed them into the car.

"You thinking about Carlo?" He loosened his tie.

"I'm thinking about how stinkin' hot it is." Antony grinned to camouflage his inner turmoil. Twenty years later, Carlo's empty eyes, the warmth of his blood, and the stench of his death still haunted him.

Spencer extended his hand in a friendly gesture.

"It's good to see you, man." Antony took Spencer's hand, pulled him into a hug, and gave him a hard slap on the back. "Thanks for meeting me."

Antony pointed to a large sign. *Coming Soon, Nunzio's Hotel and Casino.* "Carlo would've liked this. He always said, 'One day the Midwest will embrace gambling.'" Farther down the bank, a riverboat casino sat. "Looks like they have."

Spencer pulled out a cigarette and a gold-plated lighter. He inhaled and released the smoke as he talked. "You need absolution. I need cash. Why don't you invest?"

Was he serious? He needed no absolution. Heat crept up his neck and face. *Easy, Antony. Stay cool.* With great effort, he took steady breaths and loosened the fists that formed, forcing himself not to react.

As much as he'd like to exonerate himself, no one could extract his allegiance like his family. He had confessed to killing Carlo for one reason. To protect his brother, Sonny. Loyalty was more important than life itself. That allegiance had not wavered over the past twenty years, and it wouldn't now.

Spencer kicked the loose gravel. "I heard when your ol' man took you back you got twenty-four shares of Renato's and a seat on the board."

"No thanks to him. Aunt Cecilia left it to me in her will." Antony turned toward the Missouri River and its fast, flowing current. The water sucked an unstable log from the bank and washed it away as quickly as eight years of living on the streets had choked out the last of his innocence.

"I wouldn't exactly say Papa took me back. I didn't give him a choice."

"I would've liked to have seen that." Spencer raised a brow. "The great Lorenzo Luciano taking an order. I heard you've made him millions over the years. He's gotta be happy about that."

"Papa hasn't been happy since I killed Mama, put him in a wheelchair, and ended his life as the Midwest's most feared loan shark."

At least that was Papa's take on the events following Carlo's death. Reality had a different version. When they found the crashed car his father had been driving, Lorenzo was unconscious, cradling his dead wife. Carlo's parents were in the back seat. They had been killed on impact.

Antony rubbed his left temple. Reminiscing always caused a dull pounding in his head. He hadn't come back to rehash the past. He wanted information, and the sooner he got it, the sooner he could leave.

"You heard Dimitri moved out to Ventura?" Antony pulled a toothpick from his pocket, placed it in his mouth, and rolled it across his tongue. He'd rather be smoking, but he'd quit, and failure was not an option.

"I heard."

"You know why?"

Spencer flicked the cigarette then leaned over, picked up a rock, and chucked it hard at the five-story building, shattering a window on the first floor. "You're asking me if Dimitri's out for revenge?"

"It is his duty." Antony never could forget Dimitri's fourteen-year-old eyes. Almost as instantly as they had grieved for his brother, they had reeked of hate and revenge.

"I thought you two were pretty tight when you lived on the streets?"

Tight wasn't what Antony would call it. He tolerated Dimitri because he had to. Papa had always said, *Keep the enemy close.*

Dimitri claimed their families had suffered enough and he would never seek revenge, but Antony never quite bought into it. If Dimitri was anything like his father, he'd play it cool until the opportune time. Antony couldn't help but wonder if that time was now.

"We hung out and had a few laughs." Antony tossed the toothpick to the ground.

"And now you think he's out for revenge?" Spencer lit another cigarette. "After all these years?"

"He claims to need my help, but he is a Romeo."

The veins on Spencer's temples pounded. "So am I."

"But you understand. Carlo pulled the gun on me. I was only protecting Elisa's honor. I loved her. You know that."

"Yeah." Spencer looked away. "You'd have been a great brother-in-law. She married that lowlife Enrico and moved to California. He used to beat her." Their eyes met. "Did you know that?"

"Yeah, I knew." Antony not only knew, he'd tried to help her more than once, but she always went back to the piece of scum. His love for her never completely died, but it hardened his already calloused heart.

"At least someone had the sense to put a bullet in his head."

"Glad someone was watching out for her." Antony winked. It hadn't been his bullet, but letting Spencer think it had might just get him the information he needed. By the satisfying grin that spread across Spencer's face, he knew it had worked.

Spencer took a long drag on the cigarette and slowly released the smoke, running his hand across the sweat on his forehead. "You're right. It's stinkin' hot out here." He looked at Antony and shook his head. "I never could say no to you."

Antony grinned.

"Dimitri's never mentioned revenge." Spencer dropped the cigarette and crushed it out with his shoe. "He's washed up. If he claims he needs your help, he probably does. I heard that what he didn't waste on broads he's gambled away." The lines on Spencer's forehead deepened. "But if I were you, I'd keep a close eye on him. Revenge is in his blood."

Antony gave him a nod. "Planned on that. There's only one Romeo I trust."

Spencer smiled. "Why don't you stick around for a few days? It'll give me time to talk you into investing in my casino."

"No, thanks." Antony placed his hands deep into his pant pockets and rolled back on the heels of his shoes. "I'm on my way to the Bahamas. I've got a dinner date I can't miss."

"With that model? Lauren? The one the tabloids say you're secretly engaged to?"

"You actually read that trash?"

"Only when you're on the cover."

Antony laughed. "Good thing they haven't dug up any real secrets."

Not that he cared if they learned about Carlo's death. It had been deemed accidental, and thanks to missing evidence, he never went to trial for the dead guy in the dumpster.

He could live with the world knowing he had been accused of murder. But the world knowing he was still in love with Victoria was something he couldn't let happen. It was a love as forbidden as the fruit had been to Adam and Eve, yet he was drawn to her by a force he couldn't fight.

He wasn't proud that he secretly loved his brother's wife. In fact, when he thought about it rationally, it was pathetic, but there's nothing rational about love.

"Yeah." He forged a grin. "I'm meeting Lauren."

Meeting Lauren was a means to an end. Victoria and Sonny took a vacation in the same place Lauren had scheduled a shoot. Antony had planned it perfectly. Tonight, he wouldn't just be with Lauren or Sonny but with Victoria.

TWO

THE BAHAMIAN SUN HID behind a large cloud that ascended heavenward, forming huge peaks. Each peak sent white sun rays through the orange and red sky. Gulls and herons flew low over the ocean.

Victoria sat in the outdoor restaurant on the beach and pushed the peanuts around the small bowl with her finger. She looked at her watch and sighed. Cool lips and hot breath whispered against the nape of her neck and sent a chill throughout her body.

"It's about time." She smiled and turned.

"Words I never thought I'd hear." Antony winked.

Her brother-in-law stood before her in perfectly creased khaki trousers and a short-sleeved polo. His short black hair gelled flat, his arrogance only added to his attraction. "Antony? What are you doing here?" She stood and gave him a hug.

Antony kissed her cheek before sitting next to her. "Lauren has a shoot. Thought I'd tag along."

"Tag along? That doesn't sound like you." Far from it. Antony never did anything without a specific purpose.

"Where's the ol' ball and chain?" Antony asked.

"A business call." At least that's what she'd call it. Nothing could extract her husband's allegiance like his father, Lorenzo.

Antony ordered a drink and shooed the waiter away. "How's the vacation going?"

"Good." She shrugged.

Antony smiled his killer smile. Dimples that made hearts melt, including her own if she wasn't careful.

"I sense disappointment," he said.

"You know Sonny." Victoria ran her finger along the beaded water on the outside of her glass. "He drops everything when Lorenzo calls."

"Feeling neglected?"

Her eyes met his. "Sometimes." When a smug smile lit his face, she pointed her finger at him. "But it doesn't mean I love him any less."

Antony leaned back in his chair, and his grin deepened. "Did I say you didn't?"

"I just know how you think."

"What?" He sipped his drink with a satisfied grin.

"Would you stop?" Heat filled her face. "I love Sonny."

"I believe you."

Was Antony reminding her of how she almost chose him? Did he know that deep down, in a place she didn't like to go, she still had feelings for him? Worse yet, would those feelings ever go away?

"Seeing Lauren again?" she asked with a cheerfulness she wasn't feeling. By the way Antony's eyes searched the restaurant, she expected Lauren would join them soon.

She reached into her leather handbag, pulled out a small mirror and a tube of lipstick. Rolling it across her lips, she looked over the compact at Antony.

He crossed his leg and let his ankle rest on his thigh, exposing a small silver Derringer. The hint of danger that surrounded him was as intoxicating as the warm, woodsy scent of his cologne.

She snapped the compact closed, slid it and the lipstick into her purse. "How does Lauren always suck you back into a relationship?"

"I wouldn't call what Lauren and I have a relationship." Antony pulled a toothpick from his jacket, placed it in his mouth, and rolled it across his tongue.

"On and off for years," she added. "Don't you get tired of the fighting?"

"It's the making up that's fun."

His innuendo brought the heat back to her face.

"Speak of the devil." Antony gave a nod toward the entrance as Lauren paraded in. Her strapless cotton dress and red high-heeled shoes were topped off with a red brimmed hat. Her porcelain skin contrasted with the perfect amount of makeup, and her long, straight blond hair fell on her bare shoulders. Her flowery perfume reached the table long before she did.

She sashayed to Antony, ran her fingernails along his neck, then sat on his lap. She wrapped her arms around him. Lips parted, and they kissed passionately for a long time. Antony held the small of her back and pulled her closer to him. Victoria wasn't easily embarrassed, but the shock of their public affection made her shudder.

Lauren pulled away and laughed. She wiped the lipstick off Antony's lips with her finger then stood, looked down at Victoria, faked a smile, and sat next to Antony. She snapped her fingers at the waiter, who quickly came to her aid.

"A bottle of Dom Perignon." Her eyes met Antony's. "You need a refresher, love?"

"No." He rested his arm on the back of her chair.

A gentleman approached the table. His shaking hands grasped a napkin and a pen tightly. "Miss Bauman?"

Lauren looked up.

"I thought that was you." The man smiled wide, exposing a mouth full of yellow-stained, crooked teeth. "Oh. Wow. No one will believe this. You're more beautiful in person than in any of those magazines."

Lauren removed her hat, flipped her hair off her shoulders, and leaned closer to the standing man. "Thank you."

The man gawked.

Lauren rolled her eyes and reached for the napkin and pen. When he stood motionless, she snapped her fingers at him.

"Oh, yes." He handed them to her. "Can I have an autograph? Can you make it out to Walter, with love? That's me."

"Of course." Lauren scribbled something illegible across the napkin then handed it back.

The man stood, mesmerized by the fashion model.

Lauren glared at him. "Was there something else?"

"Oh, no. I'm sorry. Thank you." He bowed then backed away, using every last second to stare at her.

Lauren leaned into Antony. "Where's your bodyguard?"

Antony laughed, patting the Derringer. "I don't need one." He pointed to a table. "I brought Bosco because he needs some R & R. He's over there."

Bosco sat at the table with Doc, Victoria's curly-haired bodyguard. Doc was a present from Sonny when they got married years ago. Bosco gave Antony a single nod.

Both men were solid muscle and sat in white t-shirts with jackets to conceal their Glocks. Bosco had a buzz cut and standard US military-issue sunglasses. Both were ex-special forces.

"Can't you tell them to keep my fans away? You should've just rented the entire dining room like I asked. I won't get a minute's peace. I'll be signing autograph after autograph."

"I doubt you'll be mobbed." Antony's tone was dry, his expression indifferent. "If you think it's going to be a problem, I'll just meet you back at the room." He tossed some peanuts in his mouth as the waiter brought the Dom.

Victoria turned to Lauren. "Antony tells me you're doing a shoot?"

"Yes." Lauren sipped the sparkling champagne.

"You look good."

"Hmm, yes." Lauren's eyes wandered the restaurant.

"Who's the shoot with?"

Lauren smiled and nodded at a young man. "Um, what?" She glanced back at Victoria. "Did you say something?"

"I'm glad to see you working after such a long hiatus." A hiatus was putting it nicely. Victoria had heard that no one in the industry wanted to hire Lauren. Her selfish, childish actions had brought her career to a near standstill. *Difficult* was what the press called her. The photographers, makeup artists, and hairdressers described her with names Victoria wouldn't repeat.

"Yes, it's nice to see someone still has good taste in models," Lauren said. "It's not easy walking down a runway next to a fourteen-year-old."

Victoria was glad to see Sonny walk in. A few strands of his black hair fell forward and hung above his left eyebrow, softening his dark, sexy eyes. The lines on his forehead deepened, and she knew he was annoyed to see Antony.

"Sorry I'm late." Sonny leaned over and gave Victoria a kiss, took off his navy jacket, and hung it on the back of the chair. He turned to his brother, his eyes narrowed. "What brings you here?"

"Lauren finally got a job." Antony laughed.

Lauren smacked Antony in the chest and gave him a hateful smile. "I'm doing a shoot."

She raised her hand to Sonny who took it and gave it a gentle shake. "You look beautiful."

"I do, don't I?"

Victoria rested her elbows on the table and clasped her hands. "How'd it go?"

"Taken care of, I hope. Papa is getting way too uptight about the purchase of this shipping company."

"That's because my name is on the deal." Antony gulped the last of his drink.

"In a few more years," Sonny said, "he'll be so senile he won't know what's going on. Then I'll give you half the company."

"Only half?" Antony snapped. The two brothers glared at each other until Sonny was forced to look away. Antony lifted his empty glass at the waiter.

Victoria avoided the impending argument by pulling the menus from the metal stand and handing them each one. "Let's order some food. I'm hungry."

"Half of Renato's. What would that be worth?" Lauren eyed the menu.

"Why does it matter?" Antony said. "It's money you'll never see."

"You're so conceited." Lauren slammed the menu on the table. "Like I need your money."

"You want to remind me what I see in you?"

Lauren stood and placed her hands on her hips. "You're looking at it."

Antony grabbed her arm and pulled her back to him. One side of his mouth went up into a grin. "Where're you going?"

"I've lost my appetite."

Antony pulled her closer. "You're beautiful when you're angry."

Lauren rolled her eyes. "I'll meet you later." She gave Sonny and Victoria a quick goodbye, replaced the straw hat on her head, and left the room with her hips wiggling, turning the head of every man in the place.

Sonny sighed. "There's never a dull moment when Lauren's around." He placed the menu on the table, waving the waiter over. "How about dinner?"

"Yes, food." Antony grinned.

Victoria stared into Antony's dark eyes. She couldn't tell if he was annoyed or happy that Lauren was gone.

***

Antony glanced around the restaurant before his eyes finally rested on his fourth drink. The dinner crowd had long gone except for a tightly embraced couple swaying to the soft music, a man at the bar, and Bosco and Doc.

Victoria patted Sonny's leg. "I'll meet you upstairs." She leaned in and kissed him.

"I won't be long."

She looked over at Antony. "See ya."

Antony gave her a nod and stared at her while she lazily walked out of the regatta with Doc by her side. When she disappeared from his sight, he looked over at Sonny, who glared at him. "What? I can't admire your wife?"

Sonny rolled his eyes. "Clay called earlier. He told me you purchased the land out from under the developers I was working with."

"Yup. I'm going to build the largest and most expensive residential tower in Los Angeles."

"Those developers were trying to do something good for the community."

"How does a low-income housing development help them? You saw how the people were fighting it."

Sonny gazed at him steadily. "I wonder why the people who once supported this changed their minds."

"Are you accusing me of something?" Antony pulled the napkin from his lap and threw it on the table. Yeah, he'd fed the press and the fears of the community, but not before he'd already purchased another piece of land to relocate the development. Now would be the perfect time to tell his brother. Sonny's pious face kept him silent.

Sonny raised an eyebrow and leaned back. "I wasn't accusing you, but if your conscience is troubling you—"

"My conscience?" Antony blurted out, annoyed that such an absurd statement angered him. "The developers were the ones who ran out of money."

"They were waiting for a grant to come through."

"My development will skyrocket the surrounding property values. Think of it as a spiritual rebirth. It's what you claim Renato's means." Antony's mouth curved into a mocking grin. "Do you think that was Great Grandma's intention when she named her son, Renato?"

Sonny sighed and rubbed the back of his neck. "I have no problem with your towers. I just wish you would've chosen another spot to build on. LA needed that development."

The past swirled through Antony like a huge tornado. "Yeah, let's keep those types off the streets. Don't want to be reminded of what the homeless live like." Something Antony would never forget. He knew firsthand what it was like to eat out of trashcans, stuff balled-up newspapers in your clothes to keep warm, and fight for a dumpster to sleep in.

Being disowned at the age of sixteen while his family moved to California was something Antony hid in the deepest, darkest place in his heart. When allowed to emerge, it only brought out an anger he found to be useless. "You need a penance so bad, why didn't you fund the development yourself?"

"A penance?" Sonny sat staunchly. "I need no penance to live with what I've done."

Antony's anger and resentment gave way to the undeniable love and loyalty he felt for his brother. "Then quit acting like you do. You want another piece of land? I'll take care of it. I always have."

Silence fell over the table. Finally, Sonny asked, "Why are you really here?"

"I thought you should know Dimitri came by Renato's yesterday." Antony picked up his tumbler and sipped the drink. "He bought a place in Ventura."

Sonny's face was unreadable. He leaned back, his elbows resting on the arms of the chair. "Did he say what he wanted?"

"What do you think he wants?"

"You trying to scare me?" Sonny's voice was strong. "Don't you think if he was going to avenge Carlo and his parents, he'd have done it by now?"

"Maybe." Antony swirled the alcohol in the tumbler before taking another sip. Sonny didn't understand anything. It was Dimitri's duty to avenge Carlo and his parents. Loyalty was more important than life itself.

When Antony had confessed to accidentally killing Carlo years ago, it was to protect Sonny. He was never sure if Dimitri had bought into the lie. He'd lived on the streets with Dimitri and had worked jobs with him, but he'd never trusted Dimitri no matter how many times he claimed their families had been through enough.

"He did ask us to lunch," Antony said.

"You came all the way to the Bahamas to tell me that?"

"And to be with Lauren," Antony said with no conviction. He wasn't about to admit he was there to protect them. "Why are you here?" Antony asked.

"I came to spend some time with my wife."

"Then I suggest you do that."

Sonny stood. "You're right."

Antony gulped the drink. "Yeah, go spend time with your wife." He gave a harsh laugh of frustration as Sonny walked away. Even though it had been his idea to lie about who killed Carlo, he couldn't help but envy his brother. Sonny had not only taken over the business Antony was destined to run, but he'd married one of the only two women Antony had ever loved.

Bosco came up to the table and sat. "Sonny's fishing tomorrow. Victoria's shopping."

Antony nodded, his face hard. "Join him. He thinks you're here on vacation."

"Got it." Bosco left.

Antony swallowed the last of the drink, stood, and threw some money on the table. He sighed. Lauren was waiting. She wasn't Victoria, but she would do, for now.

THREE

VICTORIA STROLLED THROUGH the tall, red, Japanese-style gate at the entrance of the International Bazaar. A refreshing breeze held the hot sun at bay. Voices of tourists and natives bartering over goods skipped through the air.

Doc's narrow sunglasses sat on his somewhat large nose. His baggy white shorts and short-sleeved navy shirt hung untucked to conceal the gun he always carried. Doc had once been a mercenary and was given one order when assigned to Victoria—protect her at all costs. Over the years, he had become more like a brother than a bodyguard.

They stopped in the marketplace where a hair braider stood over a woman, finished a braid, then slid a bead on the end. "What do you think?" Victoria asked. "Should I get my hair done?"

Doc smiled, his grin crooked but cute. "All you talked about on the ride over was looking at those artifacts and finding Sonny a Cartier Tank watch, but hey, you want to indulge yourself, go right ahead."

Victoria sighed and pointed to a small building at the end of the street. An associate at Speranza Art Gallery in Monterey had recommended the shop. It carried jewelry and both native and foreign artwork.

They walked to the front counter where an assortment of women's rings sat in a glass case. A beautiful two-and-a-half-carat diamond and sapphire ring caught her attention. "What do you think of that?"

Doc leaned against the glass case, his arms crossed. "Think. Cartier Tank watch and artifacts."

Victoria smacked his arm.

Doc rolled his eyes, smiled, then leaned over the case. "You want me to tell Sonny you want that?"

"Would you?" she said in a playful voice.

"Maybe, but it would cost you."

"Cost me?" She grinned. "Cost me what?"

"Fix me up with that new associate you hired."

"Autumn?"

"Yeah." His grin widened.

"You don't need my help to get a girl. You're a nice guy."

"Nice? Wonderful." He gave her a deep eye roll. "Girls always love the nice guys."

"And handsome," she added, making his ivory skin flush. "Now, if you'll quit distracting me, I can find that watch."

"Me, distracting you?" He pointed to the next case over. "The watches are down there."

The fifty-something owner of the store rubbed his hands together as he approached them. A native who eyed them like a fatted calf at a wedding feast.

"I'll be by the door," Doc said.

Victoria grabbed his arm. "I could use your help."

"No, thanks. I'd rather pay sticker price." Doc looked toward the door. His eyes narrowed. "You got company."

"What?" Victoria turned.

Antony walked in. He stopped in front of two women and gave them his killer smile. "Beautiful."

The women giggled. One pulled a pen and piece of paper out of her purse, jotted something on it and slid it in Antony's shirt pocket. His grin deepened as he leaned back on his heels, turned, and walked toward them.

"Do you think he's following us?" she asked Doc.

"You, not me." Doc winked. "I'll be over there if you need me."

Antony wrapped his arm around her shoulder and whispered in her ear, "My brother abandon you again?"

Chills ran through her body. "Not for work." Antony's expression said *I told you so,* so she added, "He's fishing." She brushed off his hand, angered that he could still stir feelings in her.

"That's convenient."

"It was my idea." She turned back to the glass case, irritated that she felt the need to explain herself. "Besides, I'm shopping for artifacts for the store and a watch for Sonny."

"In the ladies' ring section?"

"I was just looking." She brushed past him toward the watch case. "If you don't mind."

"By all means." Antony tipped his head, the dimples deep from his grin. "But you know, that ring . . . it would look good on you."

She stopped. "You think?"

He nodded.

Her irritation melted. "I thought so, too. It'd match perfectly with the dress I designed for the reception at the new store."

"Then try it on." Antony motioned to the owner to open the case. "That one, right?" He pointed.

"Yes."

"I have a necklace to match." The owner unlocked the case and reached for the ring.

"We'll see it, too." Antony grinned.

"I shouldn't."

"Indulge." Antony took the ring and slipped it on her finger.

She held her hand out and admired the stunning diamonds and sapphires. "It is beautiful, but I can't." Victoria took it off and handed it back to the owner. "I called earlier. I'm interested in the Chinese artifacts and a Cartier Tank watch."

The owner replaced the ring and necklace. He locked the case and motioned to the watches. "I'll be right back." Moments later, he returned with a bronze pitcher and beaker.

Antony picked up the beaker. It stood ten inches tall and resembled an ancient wine goblet. The bottom half of the stem was bronze, and from the middle rim to the lip, the beaker was black and smooth. "You're going to put this in the new store?"

"Yes." Victoria took the beaker from him and ran her fingers along the funnel-shaped lip. "They're replicas from the Shang Dynasty. I'm going to display them in the lobby, next to the coffee shop."

Antony made an annoyed face.

"You question everything I do, don't you?" She handed the beaker to the owner. "I'll take them both."

"You may own Francesca's, but Renato's has a lot of money invested in it. It's my job to question you."

His job? It was more than that, and they both knew it. She turned her attention back to the watches.

A man wearing a brown leather jacket and a dark baseball cap entered the store. He looked around before walking toward Doc and the two women.

A second man came in and walked straight to the counter where Antony and Victoria stood. "I'll be right with you," the owner said to the man then pulled out a velvet-lined tray of watches for Victoria.

The man reached into the front pocket of his hooded sweatshirt and pulled out a Smith and Wesson. "Hands in the air, now." He aimed the gun at Antony, pushing them both up against the wall.

Victoria turned to Doc. His hands were in the air, and there was a long-barreled revolver in his back. He glanced over at her. If he was panicked, he didn't look it.

He tilted his head. Was it a hidden message? She couldn't tell. Doc grabbed the two women, pushed them against the wall, then stood in front of them, using his body as a shield. One woman let out a hysterical scream.

"Quiet," the man yelled, which silenced her.

Fear filled every part of Victoria. It knotted in her stomach. Her chest heaved with every forced breath. Her eyes met Antony's.

He leaned into her. "Just relax. It'll be okay."

The owner of the store reached under the counter. Victoria hoped it was to hit the panic button. The silver gun was waved in his face. "Do it, and you're dead." The robber tossed two black hip pouches on the counter. "Fill 'em up, cash and jewelry."

Victoria's heart pounded, but she couldn't fight the ache in her arms and the tingling in her fingers. She lowered her hands to seek relief. The robber pointed the gun back at her. "Up," he said then turned to the owner. "The loose diamonds. Get 'em."

The robber glared back at them. "Your jewelry. Give it to me, both of you." His gun swung from Antony to her then back to Antony.

Antony lowered his hands to pull off the Gucci watch and black onyx ring. He placed them in the robber's open palm. The man turned toward Victoria, who placed her watch, wedding band, and bracelet on top of Antony's.

The man waved the gun back at Victoria. "The other ring."

Victoria clutched the simple blue topaz ring her mother had given her a few days before she'd disappeared. "No."

He pointed the gun directly in her face. "The ring."

Antony leaned in. "Give him the ring."

"I can't." Her voice shook as badly as her hands.

Antony grunted a laugh. "Man, you can't do anything simple, can you?" Antony, his hands now level with his shoulders, turned toward the man. "I'll get the ring from her, just relax. Point that thing away from her face."

Victoria clutched tighter to the ring. Her heart pounded so hard she knew she would either faint or have a heart attack.

"Just give him the ring," Antony insisted. "He won't make it out of the store with it. Trust me."

"What?" The robber's eyes were wide and crazy. He cocked the gun. "We'll see who makes it out."

Antony cut his eyes to the robber, his mouth tightened. "Give me the ring, Vic."

Victoria clutched her hands closer to her chest and continually shook her head.

Antony cocked his head. "Then I suggest you start praying."

"This is taking too long," the other robber yelled and pushed the gun harder into Doc's chest. "Forget the ring. Get the bags."

The robber grabbed Victoria by the hair, swung her around, and locked his arm tightly around her neck. The gun pressed against her temple. "It's a matter of respect."

The stench of his breath made her stomach churn.

"The ring. Now." His grip tightened.

Antony's chest heaved. His eyes grew dark and intense. He looked over at Doc and gave him a single nod. At the same time, Doc pulled his Glock and pounded the butt of it on the man's head, and Antony lunged at the man who held Victoria.

The force of both men's weight knocked her to the ground. The robber attempted to escape, firing one random shot in the air before Antony stripped the gun from his hand and held it to his face. "Call the police," Antony yelled above the screams of the other two women.

Antony's eyes met Victoria's. "You couldn't just give him the ring, huh?"

"No." She leaned against the wall. Her body shook. "I couldn't."

***

Victoria leaned against the counter. Antony stood by the door and nodded at the police officer. He walked to her and handed her a hot coffee. She ignored his piercing eyes and blew on the steaming drink then took a sip.

"Crap."

"What was that?" The veins on Antony's temples pulsated.

"I burned my tongue."

"That wasn't what I meant."

"I know what you meant."

"It was a stupid ring, Vic. He could've killed you."

"It was my mother's. It's all I have left of her." When she set the coffee on the counter, some of it to splashed out and burned her finger. She shook off the coffee and stared out the window at the gathering crowd. "I don't need a lecture from you."

Antony's lips pursed. He placed both hands on his waist and glared. "You're right, it wouldn't do any good, would it? You're as tenacious as I am."

Tears flooded her eyes.

He tipped his head back. One side of his mouth went up into a grin. "Next time, give him the ring and trust me to get it back for you."

Victoria smiled, forcing the tears from her eyes. "Okay." She wiped them away, lowered her head, and took deep breaths to calm down.

"Vic." Antony brushed his hand on her shoulder. "Sonny's here."

Sonny pushed his way through the crowd but was stopped by the police. Their eyes met as he talked to the officer. Finally, the officer nodded and pointed toward her.

Sonny jogged to her and cupped her face. Her tears fell on his hands. "You okay?"

Victoria nodded.

Sonny wrapped his arms around her shaking body. "Sh, sh, it's okay." He kissed her. "Thank God you're okay." He pulled her into a tighter hug.

"Police are done with her," Antony said. "You two get outta here."

"Thanks." Sonny led her through the crowd.

***

Sonny drove them to the villa, his grip tightening around the steering wheel until his knuckles turned white. He killed the ignition and stared at the waves crashing against the beach. Heat crept up his neck. The battle between relief and anger had been raging since Doc had called. Anger won. "You were almost killed. Do you realize that?"

"Yes."

He squeezed the steering wheel tighter, swallowed hard, then turned to her. "Why couldn't you just give him the ring?"

"It was my mother's. It's the only thing I have left of her."

Sonny looked away, muttered something indiscernible in Italian before turning back to her. They didn't argue very often, but when they did, they tended to be explosive.

"Did you think of me?" he snapped. "What about the kids? Did you think about them?"

"Yes, of course I did."

"Don't you get it? You could've been killed."

"How could I not get it? I was the one with the gun pressed against my head."

Her confession only angered him more. He got out of the car, slammed the door, then ran his hand through his hair, turning as she got out.

The wind blew her long auburn hair, and the setting sun radiated from behind. Her eyes begged for compassion, but it was something he couldn't give her. At least not now.

Looking away, he kicked at the loose gravel on the concrete then picked up a rock. He wound up to throw it then stopped, silently praying to somehow place his anger inside of it so he could throw it away.

He pitched it toward the vast ocean, watched it momentarily hang in the air. It landed yards from the shoreline. Shaking his head, he breathed deeply then turned toward her.

Victoria dropped her head and walked away.

Sonny quickened his stride to catch up. "Look, I'm sorry, but I can't bear the thought of losing you."

Victoria nodded.

He pulled her into his arms, his anger evaporating. "I love you." He kissed her. "Let's go inside."

***

The breeze picked up the aroma from the large vase of gardenias that sat on the balcony outside the villa. It carried it through the half-opened window and danced with the thin white curtains before the room filled with their sweet fragrance.

Waves rolled against the beach. A single candle flickered on its last inch of wick, surrounded by the dinner dishes. Music played in the background.

Sonny sat on the couch with Victoria resting against him. Pulling his arms tighter around her, she relaxed in his embrace.

He kissed the top of her head, reached down, and pulled a blanket over her. "You're sure you're okay?"

"Yes."

"Want to talk about it?"

"No." She closed her eyes.

"It'll make you feel better." He scooped up her long hair and let if fall gently through his fingers. "You should've just given the guy the ring."

She sat up, looking directly at him. "You of all people should understand why I couldn't. You never take off the crucifix your mother gave you."

"If a gun was pointed at my head, I'd rip the thing off." Anger and love churned inside his stomach and formed a huge knot. She turned away, but he placed his fingers under her chin and turned her head to face him. "Don't you understand? I couldn't live without you. You're my life."

"Maybe I was wrong." She looked into his eyes, a small smile on her face. "I'm sorry." She leaned in and kissed him.

Sonny took the hint and pulled away. She wasn't ready to talk about it, if she ever would be. He picked up the jeweled cross that hung from the ornate chain. "You like the necklace?"

"Yes. Did Doc tell you I wanted this?" She stretched her hand out to admire the matching ring.

"Antony mentioned it. He had the artifacts sent to the store."

"Oh, he did?" She wrapped her arms around him. "That was nice of him."

Sonny's body tensed. "Yeah. Lucky he just happened to be following you."

"You're not jealous of your brother, are you?" She rested her hand on his chest.

"Me, jealous?" He pressed his lips against hers. "Maybe a little. I'm glad he was there to save the day. Otherwise, I might not be doing this." His lips made their way to her ear and playfully nibbled.

Victoria giggled.

A knock on the door stopped him. "You expecting someone?"

"No."

Sonny opened the door and a room service attendant handed him a bottle of the resort's finest champagne.

"Thanks." Sonny shut the door and read the card. "Antony." He picked up a cold piece of steak, tossed it in his mouth, then leaned against the windowsill.

"That was nice of him." Victoria picked up a strawberry and dipped it in the chocolate.

He stared at her.

"What?" Her forehead wrinkled.

"I'm concerned about you."

"I'm fine." She licked her fingers, strutted over to him, and grinned. "Don't I look fine?"

Sonny pulled her to him and kissed her. "You look more than fine." His hands tangled in her hair and then stroked the slender column of her neck.

Victoria looked into his eyes. "I love you."

"I love you, too."

***

Justice placed a cigarette between his teeth, brought the lighter up, and lit it. He stared at the smoke as it mingled with the shadows inside the car.

The six-inch scar on his neck was a present from a fellow inmate years ago. It had severed his vocal cords. He could still talk, but his voice was raspy—his words were few.

Pulling the phone from his pocket, he dialed Dimitri's number

"She bought it." He reached into a velvet bag and pulled out the ten-inch bronze beaker stolen during the Boston Museum heist in 1980. It was worth millions.

He sensed Dimitri's smile.

"Is it being shipped?" Dimitri asked.

"Tomorrow."

"Good. Make the switch tonight."

"Done."

Justice slid the phone into his pocket then slipped the beaker back into its velvet bag. The Lucianos would never know the new Francesca's would front the stolen artifact. Finally, after all these years, retribution would come.

FOUR

CALIFORNIA'S BRISK AUTUMN AIR danced around Fresh Grill, a fast-food restaurant three blocks from Ventura High School.

Christian Luciano leaned into the rearview mirror of a parked car, tilted his head, and checked out his spiked, coal black hair. Satisfied, he nodded at himself. His father had insisted on the haircut as soon his parents had gotten back from the Bahamas and at first, Christian hated it. But with a little gel, he decided it made him look cool.

He tucked his hands into the pockets of his black bomber jacket. The street buzzed with cars, and random horns honked. He scanned the lot and saw Liz standing with a group of kids. A girl leaned in and said something to her that made her look around. Christian knew she was trying to find him. He took a step away from the parked car so he was sure to be in her line of sight.

When their eyes met, the left side of Christian's mouth curled up into a grin. A smile spread across her face, but it wasn't until he winked that her face flushed.

His heart skipped a beat as she tucked her strawberry-blond hair behind her ear then turned back to the other girls.

He looked around then stopped abruptly and glared at Bruno, his personal babysitter.

Christian was the first to admit that bringing the Smith and Wesson airsoft gun to the private school was stupid, but the no-tolerance rule got him kicked out. The principal used him to send the other students a message. A message that skyrocketed his popularity. He was addicted to the rush of defiance. The problem was that his rebellion had led his parents to give him a gift that kept on giving—Bruno.

Uncle Tony said a bodyguard made him look cool. A two-hundred-pound GI Joe in cowboy boots didn't make him look cool. It only made him more determined to do as he pleased. Losing Bruno became a daily lunchtime routine, but his oversized bodyguard was getting good.

Bruno leaned against the black Jeep Cherokee, his arms crossed. Their eyes met, and Bruno gave him a quick nod.

Christian turned away and craned his neck to see over the crowd of other tenth graders that filtered into the lot.

"Christian!" Ned yelled from across the lot.

"It's about time."

Ned grabbed a kid's shoulder as he passed in front of them, reached around, and swiped a handful of fries off the red tray.

"Come on," the kid whined.

"Thanks, man." Ned shoved the fries into his mouth.

"Whatever." The boy hurried off before his hamburger became Ned's lunch.

Ned leaned against the car next to Christian and pulled out a pack of cigarettes. "Want one?"

"Naw."

Ned quickly lit it. The smoke escaped as he spoke. "Russ should be here any minute."

"What about Tex?"

Both boys looked over at Bruno, who stared at them and repositioned himself against the car. The silver tips on his cowboy boots glistened in the sunlight.

"Russ will lose him," Ned said.

Russ's dark blue pickup pulled into the lot. Ned walked around and climbed into the passenger side. Christian would have to play it cool. He leaned into the driver's side. "You got a plan?"

"Always." Russ laughed. "Get in."

Christian looked over at Bruno, who now stood at attention.

Christian walked around the truck. The same time he jumped in, Bruno climbed into the Cherokee. Russ peeled out of the lot. No sooner had Bruno gunned the engine, he had to slam on the brakes, inches from a yellow Camaro that pulled out in front of him and blocked the drive. Bruno threw the car into reverse, but a silver Camry sat directly behind him.

Russ stopped. All three boys turned back as Bruno got out of the Jeep, waved his arms and yelled at the drivers who blocked him in.

Christian hung his head out the window, laughed and gave the side of the truck two swift pounds. "Let's roll."

Russ cranked the stereo full blast and floored it. The tires squealed in delight. Christian glanced in the side mirror. Bruno was pacing, his cell phone to his ear.

Thirty minutes later, they pulled into the parking lot of the new Francesca's that overlooked the ocean. It would be his mother's second store.

The large glass front of the store was covered in black plastic to keep the paparazzi's cameras out until the grand opening. Russ pulled around the large parking lot and headed toward the loading docks.

"Stop here." Christian chewed on his thumbnail. The front of a semi jutted around the corner of the building.

"You ain't chickening out, are you?" Russ asked.

"He ain't chickening out." Ned turned to Christian. "Are ya?"

Christian spit the chewed off nail out the opened window. "Me, chicken? This will be the easiest money we'll ever make." He jumped out of the truck and shut the door. "Stay here."

Christian slipped his hands into the pockets of his jacket, got to the corner of the building, and peeked around. He could see men sitting on the loading dock eating their lunches.

He walked back to a side entrance and pulled out a key he'd taken from the top drawer of his father's desk. His heart pounded and his hands shook as he slid it into the lock and turned it. He peeked through the cracked door, scanned the place, and went inside.

The empty rooms had textured walls painted a mustard yellow. Looks like baby poop, he'd told his mom, but she loved it. In a few weeks, the clothing store would be open for business. It was projected to outsell the competitors over the Christmas season.

He'd gotten the idea to steal some of the sculptures when he listened to his parents talking about them over dinner a couple of nights ago. He'd only take two or three, enough to get cash for Russ to buy some pot.

Christian knew Russ was trouble, but since the recent tabloid articles claiming his grandfather was a small-time gangster, all his friends had ditched him. Even the kids at church looked at him differently, unsure what to believe. Their indecision hurt more than the rumors.

He slipped into one of the rooms on the main floor. According to his mother, the shipment would arrive today, and by the looks of the boxes and crates in the far corner, it had.

Christian quickened his pace and began to search through the opened crates. "Crap," he whispered. "Paintings?" He needed the small stuff. Things he could tuck in his jacket.

A box-cutter lay on the floor. He grabbed it, slit the box open, and sifted through the packing. More paintings. He moved to another box and pulled out an ancient votive vase. The pawnshop wouldn't give him anything for that. He laid it back inside then pulled out a tiger carved in jade, gave an unsure nod, and slipped it in the inside of his jacket. He zipped the jacket farther up, hoping the elastic waist would hold the tiger and anything else he found.

Digging deeper into the box, he pulled out a small alabaster box and a bird broach with some feathers overlaid in a blue stone. He shoved them inside his jacket. *I hope we can get enough money out of them.*

Reaching into a smaller box, he pulled out a beaker. Looking at it, he wondered what his mother saw in the small, useless object.

Voices sent his heart pounding. *Get a grip.* He tucked the beaker into his pocket, pushed the straw-like packing back in the box, closed it and crouched down.

Two men walked into the store. Christian crept around the boxes and made his way to the front of the room. He took long deep breaths before he slipped into the next room.

Relieved, he stood.

"Christian?"

Christian held his breath. He turned to Frank, who was more like a friend than a foreman. He had built their house, remodeled the old Francesca's, and was now building the new one.

The muffled chatter of workers began to fill the building. *Think of something quick.* "You seen my mom?"

"I didn't think she was coming by today. Let me check." Frank whistled.

The building fell silent, and Christian knew everyone could hear the blood pounding in his veins. His stuck his hands in his coat pocket and gripped the objects through the material to keep them from hitting against each other or falling out. His eyes were drawn up to the cathedral ceiling then around the three-story balcony where men were now looking down at them.

"Any of you seen Mrs. Luciano?" Frank yelled.

No's echoed throughout the atrium.

"Sorry."

"Thanks." Christian's heart pounded. He hurried through the loading dock, down the concrete stairs, around the corner and jumped into the truck. "Let's go, quick."

Russ floored it. "You get some stuff?"

"Yeah." Christian reached inside his coat and pulled out the tiger, the box, and the broach and tossed them on Ned's lap. "They saw me. They know I was there."

"Who?" Ned ran his fingers over the smooth jade of the tiger.

"Mom's foreman and about thirty other guys."

"They find out you stole this stuff, I wasn't with you," Russ shouted. "You hear me?"

Christian looked around Ned at Russ. Heat crept up his neck, and his fear turned to anger. "Yeah, I hear ya. It's just like you. Let me stick my neck out while you sit in the car."

Russ reached around Ned and hit Christian's shoulder. "I'm the one who's gonna hawk this stuff." He grabbed the tiger from Ned's hand then tossed it back in his lap. "If I can."

"Would you both shut up?" Ned said. "Just get pretty boy back to school before Tex sends out the cops."

Christian stared out the window and caught his reflection in the large side mirror. He didn't recognize the face anymore. He was becoming someone he didn't like and wasn't sure how to stop it.

"We'll get the cash," Ned said. "We'll meet you after school."

"I can't tonight," Christian said, emotionless. "I gotta go to Nonno's."

"Gotta go to Nonno's," Russ mocked in a high-pitched voice. "Tell your grandpa I loved his mug shot. How much time he spend in the slammer?"

"None," Ned laughed. "Papers said they couldn't convict him."

Christian rolled his eyes and ignored their comments. Even if he had wanted to defend his grandfather, he couldn't. Like everyone else in town, he didn't know the truth from the fiction.

When they pulled back into the school parking lot, Christian climbed out of the truck. "Sell that stuff down in LA."

"Naw, thought we'd sell it down the street," Ned teased.

"See ya tomorrow." Christian leaned into the car. "Don't smoke it all."

Russ nodded then peeled out of the lot.

Christian stood for a moment, turned, and ran smack into a mammoth brick wall. He looked up. The lines on Bruno's face were hard, and his temples pulsated. Taking a step back, Christian swallowed hard and began to regain the confidence he had lost. "What's up?"

Bruno grabbed the lapel of Christian's jacket and forced him to walk to the car. "How many times I gotta tell you—you can't run off like that."

Christian rolled his eyes.

Bruno tightened his grip. "I want it stopped."

"What you gonna do about it? Tell my mommy?"

Bruno's face hardened. The red from his neck ran all the way to the top of his head and showed through his short military-style buzz.

"I just went out for lunch." Christian pushed Bruno's hand away. "You gotta understand what it's like to have you follow me around. It just ain't cool. I look like some spoiled kid actor."

"Where'd you go?"

"Grabbed a burger then stopped by the new store to see Mom. Call Frank if you don't believe me. He'll tell you I was there."

"I'm here to protect you."

"You're here to babysit me." Christian straightened his jacket. His hand brushed against a hard object. *The beaker.* "Look, neither one of us wants to get in trouble. I'll say you were with me if you want."

"Don't do me any favors." Bruno pulled a cell phone from his pocket, dialed a number, then placed it to his ear. He looked down at Christian as he spoke into the phone. "I got him. Says he went out to lunch, then by the new store . . . sure thing." Bruno handed the phone to Christian. "It's your dad."

Christian sighed and placed the phone to his ear. "Yeah?"

"Bruno said you ran off." His dad's voice sounded firm but not harsh.

"Dad, I just can't have the guy hang around me all the time."

"He's there to protect you."

"He's cramping my style."

"You set up a roadblock?" Sonny had a hint of laughter in his voice.

"You should've seen it. It was cool. He was so mad." Christian's smile returned until he looked at Bruno, then it faded. "I went to see Mom at the new store, but she wasn't there."

"Did you need something?"

"Just time away from prison without the warden."

"We agreed you wouldn't pull anything like this again. You've been gone for two hours."

"But Dad—"

"No, Christian. You're grounded. I want you straight home after school for the next week. Bruno will drive you, not your friends."

"Oh, come on."

"Don't argue with me or it'll be longer."

"Okay."

"Christian?"

"Yeah, Dad?"

"I love you."

The right side of Christian's mouth curled into a slight grin. "Yeah, me, too. See you tonight." Christian tossed the phone to Bruno. "Gotta get to class."

***

Across town, Sonny slipped his cell in his pocket, then stared out the window of Antony's office on their father's estate. The sun cascaded through the trees, down the large property that was tucked away in the hills of Ventura.

The office had been a gift to Antony from Lorenzo five years ago. Sonny got the CEO position.

"Everything okay?" Antony raised an eyebrow.

Sonny turned toward him and rubbed the back of his neck. "Christian ditched Bruno again."

Again. A word Sonny was tired of associating with his son. The excuses were getting better. Christian had evolved from gnarly waves to studying at the library, only last night he never went to the library. He went to Ned's.

"Christian's getting good," Antony said.

"He doesn't need to hear any more *when we were your age* stories."

"What?" Antony's grin brought out dimples that were still as deceitful as they had been growing up. "Oh, don't worry, I wouldn't dream of telling him everything."

Sonny undid the top button of his white shirt and loosened his tie. His deep brown eyes cut to his brother who leaned back in his chair and rested his feet on the walnut desk. A toothpick rolled across his tongue.

"He's fifteen. He doesn't need any more ideas." Sonny combed his hand through his hair.

Christian had already been kicked out of one private school, and Sonny's choice of high schools wouldn't even consider him until he proved he could stay out of trouble for one semester. It didn't look like it was a goal Christian was even considering.

"Yeah, yeah," Antony egged him on. "I wouldn't dream of telling him how many times we ripped off Kuehler's store or when we stole the ol' man's car."

Heat made its way up Sonny's neck, and his temples pounded. A hot temper was a trait both brothers were born with, and it only seemed to grow over the years.

Antony winked. "Calm down." He pulled the toothpick from his mouth and tossed it in the trashcan. "Let's get back to this." He opened the folder that lay on his desk. "Renato's is ready to ship that computer equipment to Asia. Just needs your stamp of approval."

"Stole it and wrecked it," Lorenzo grunted from the corner.

"What?" Sonny turned. He'd forgotten his father was there. He sat in his wheelchair, his tall, lean body reduced to shriveled old skin wrapped on useless legs. His once thick black hair was now thin and white, and age spots covered his hands and face. The only love that managed to penetrate his heart was wiped out the day his beloved wife died.

Lorenzo's eyes rose to meet his son's. "You two stole and wrecked my car."

Sonny glanced at Antony who shrugged his shoulders. He looked back at his father. Lorenzo's eyes were cold and distant. "You read these?" Sonny asked out of respect. He'd sign the papers regardless of what his father thought.

Lorenzo nodded.

Sonny flipped to the back page and signed his name on the line below Antony's. He tossed the pen on the desk then looked at his brother. "We doing lunch with Dimitri tomorrow?"

"Yeah."

"Did he ever say what he wanted?"

"He mentioned a possible business deal."

"You think he can be trusted?"

One side of Antony's mouth went up into a grin. His arrogance lingered in the air with every word that fell from his lips. "It's not a matter of trust. It's duty."

Sonny slid his hand into his pocket and clutched his mother's rosary. It didn't hold the same meaning it had to her, but he carried it every day just the same.

"This business deal. Can you keep it legal?" Sonny rolled the beads over his fingers, and a knot formed in his stomach.

"Of course. I always do, don't I?"

Sonny couldn't argue that. Being unethical wasn't a crime. "I want to know about the deal. Before you agree to anything."

"Sure thing. I wouldn't dream of doing anything without your approval." Antony's jaw tightened. "You are in charge."

"He's in charge," Lorenzo bellowed from the corner, "because you killed your mother. Don't you ever forget it."

"How could I?" Antony cut his eyes to his father. "You remind me of it every day."

"Let's not do this." Guilt gnawed at Sonny's stomach and made it churn. The surfacing of Dimitri didn't just revert his father back to the old days, but it brought back painful memories that he'd tried to bury. They made him doubt his very existence.

Antony's face softened. "I'm not worried about Dimitri."

Lorenzo wheeled his chair closer to Antony. His breathing was shallow and fast. "Just see what he wants."

Antony rolled his eyes.

Lorenzo's face grew hard. Red filled it, making his white hair glow. His liver-spotted hand shook as he pointed at Antony. "You will do nothing unless Sonny says so. Understand?"

The blood drained from Antony's face as quickly as the smile did. He paused then grinned at Sonny. "Okay, Papa, but if it turns out he's back for revenge, I'll gladly take care of him."

Lorenzo's eyes narrowed, and his stare intensified. After a long, fierce moment, he wheeled himself out of the office, leaving the brothers alone.

"Stop doing that to him." Sonny combed through his hair with his fingers.

"Doing what?"

"You know what. Talking to him like we're the Corleone's. Quit feeding his fantasy."

"He's old. Let him indulge." Antony walked over to the mini-fridge and pulled out a bottle of water, regaining his composure after being so easily dismissed by his father.

"I meant what I said. I'll keep a close eye on Dimitri. He shows any signs of revenge, I'll take care of him."

Sonny stared into his brother's dark eyes. They reeked of survival. If Dimitri was back for revenge, he couldn't think of a better person to protect him and his family.

Conceding, he gave Antony a single nod.

***

Dimitri's greasy hair was tightly pulled back into a ponytail. His oversized black body fit awkwardly in the small kitchen chair. The gaudy, gold rings cut into his sausage-like fingers, but he refused to have them removed. They had once been his father's. His tan, short-sleeved cotton shirt showed off a knife tattoo.

He stared at his grandmother. Genevra's body, which was once quite large, had disintegrated over the years. Her skin hung from the bones, flapping with every movement. The weight loss was one good thing that came out of her battle with cancer. The distraction of his grandmother's ordeal had stopped the nightmares, but over the last couple of years, they had returned.

Images of his brother lying dead from a single gunshot wound and pictures of the mangled car his parents were killed in invaded his sleep.

A similar scene I once lived, his grandmother used to tell him, in her sick attempt to help a fourteen-year-old in his grief. The stories of how his grandfather was killed and avenged always ended with a hot flood of anger at the Luciano's for killing her only son and oldest grandson. Her rage would persist as she stood in her thin cotton housedress that resembled a cheap nightgown. She'd slave over the hot stove, canning jars of homemade spaghetti sauce.

Now, twenty-five years later, she would open the previous year's sauce and mix them with various Italian recipes, all the time wondering out loud if they were still any good. He had listened to her for years about revenge. Her stories of the old days danced in his dreams before they turned into the nightly tribulation. His plan for the Luciano's was a simple one—walk in as a friend, gain their trust, then destroy them.

They had arrived on the west coast a few months ago. His reason was simple—the weather was better for his grandmother's lungs. Now, she mumbled on about the Rat Pack. That was Las Vegas, Dimitri would tell her, but it was like talking to the TV.

"The artifacts are planted in the Lucianos' store?" Genevra asked.

"Yes."

"When will they be ready to move?" Genevra turned from the stove and placed both hands on her bony hips, the sauce-stained apron wrapped twice around her waist.

"Soon." Dimitri chewed on the butt of the unlit cigar.

"You will vindicate Gino and Carlo?"

"And my mother."

Genevra ignored the comment. It was no secret she had hated Martina. She sprinkled more garlic salt in the sauce. "They'll get what they deserve for killing my boys?"

"Yes, all wrongs must be avenged. Is dinner about ready?"

"Patience." She stirred the thick sauce. "Isn't that what my son always told you?"

"Don't worry, I remember everything Papa taught me."

FIVE

VICTORIA OPENED THE EIGHT-FOOT etched glass doors of the original Francesca's, which stood in the heart of Woodland Hills. She made her way through the three floors of designer clothes and customers as they browsed the elegant store.

She stopped at a stocked clothing rack that had arrived that morning. Taking down the sweater trimmed in faux fur, she held it up to herself and studied it in the full-length mirror. The black contrasted beautifully with her tanned skin and long auburn hair, which she had pulled back in a hair clip. She frowned, unsure about the fur, and returned it to the rack.

"Good choice." Doc came out from behind. "That made you look like you were trying to be eighteen."

Victoria turned to see his crooked smile. "I'm only thirty-seven."

Doc raised his eyebrows and placed his hands in the pockets of his khaki pants. "Did I say you were old?"

She grinned and walked to the service elevator that was quicker and faster than the old rustic one the customers and tourists adored. Doc followed.

"You went over the security at the new store?" she asked.

"Do you doubt my ability to protect you?"

"Never."

It was true. That was why he was not only her bodyguard but head of security. When the doors to the elevator closed, she turned to him. "What about that new guy in accounting?"

"He only accessed the orders for the new store, so I think I believe his story. It must have been a mistake."

Victoria raised an eyebrow.

"Believe me, I'm as suspicious as the next guy, and that's why he was canned. I don't know how he got into those pages, but it won't happen again."

The elevator door opened, and they both stepped off.

"Don't let it."

"Yes, ma'am." Doc clicked the heels of his shoes together and saluted her. "I'll be in my office if you need anything."

Victoria laughed, readjusted her purse, and walked farther down the hall.

Her secretary looked up and smiled.

"What?" Victoria's brows wrinkled.

"Nothing." Stacie picked up the small stack of phone messages and handed them to Victoria's outstretched hand, then handed her a folder. "Here are those invoices you wanted to look at."

"Thanks."

Victoria grinned as she went into her office. The sweet aroma of the two dozen white roses floated in the air. Next to the roses, taking up almost half her desk, was a large but thin art portfolio.

She picked up the tan leather portfolio by its handles and breathed deeply, entranced by the smell of the new leather. She unzipped all three sides and opened it. Inside was twill lining and two large pockets that could easily hold numerous twenty-by-twenty-six sketches.

Stacie walked in with a carafe of coffee. "Beautiful, isn't it? Did you see the inscription?"

"Yes." Victoria ran her fingers over the small gold engraved plate that read Designs by Vic. She had been drawing dress designs for years, and over the last few months, her dream was becoming a reality. The factory was underway, and by this time next year, she would launch her own designer label.

At breakfast, Sonny had assured her he was not upset about the argument they'd had the night before, but she had no idea he'd go to such lengths to prove it. Disagreements about Christian had become a daily routine. Nothing they did got through to him. He skipped school, his grades were bad, and childish mischief had taken over his life.

Last night, Christian had been caught at Ned's house instead of the library. Sonny had given him one more chance, and Victoria didn't approve.

With a shake of her head, the argument was gone. She pulled some papers from her briefcase and handed them to Stacie. "These need to go out."

Stacie nodded and closed the door behind her.

Victoria cupped one of the roses and took in its sweet aroma. She smiled. Sonny. Even when they fought, their love remained strong.

The card sat in the center of the vase, surrounded by the long-stemmed roses. She reached in, and a thorn pricked the top of her hand. She retreated, dabbed away the blood, and reached back in, only this time, her hand emerged triumphantly with the card.

Her heart pounded as she sank into the chair. "Antony?"

A tap on the door startled her.

Before she could say anything, Antony walked in. "Got a minute?"

"Sure." She tossed the card on her desk.

"What do you think?" He pointed to the portfolio. "Is it big enough?"

"Yes, it's beautiful." She caressed the smooth leather. "But you really have to quit doing things like this."

"You're the future of the Lucianos. My attention has a purpose."

"And what purpose is that?"

"You haven't figured it out yet?"

"I've figured it out. In fact, you've told me on numerous occasions." Victoria leaned back in her chair. "I love Sonny."

"I know you do. I also know you love me."

"Okay, I admit it. I love you." When his eyes widened, she added, "Like a brother." She laughed and hoped he'd drop the subject. She couldn't deny that he could spark a yearning deep within her soul.

"Really?" As he walked to her, his killer dimples deepened. His voice was hypnotic. "Like a brother?"

"Yes." Were the gifts sent to entice her or stroke his ego? A mixture of both, she decided. She stood and brushed past him. His woodsy cologne touched her nose and quickened her heart. "You need to stop doing stuff like this." The statement was more for her sake than his.

Antony nodded in agreement, his eyes devious.

"You have no intention of stopping, do you?"

"Nope."

Antony sat on the corner of the desk and clasped his hands together.

She walked to the filing cabinet, pulled out a folder, and handed it to him. "Those figures you asked for yesterday."

"Thanks." Antony tucked the folder under his arm. "Did Sonny tell you Dimitri's in town?"

"Yes." Her face softened. "That must be hard for you."

"Hard for me?"

"It can't be easy to be reminded of what happened."

Antony cocked his head.

"When you accidentally killed his brother?"

"Oh, that." He clicked his tongue against his perfectly straight white teeth that he'd once told her had cost a fortune. "I think it's harder on Sonny."

"Why would it be harder for him?"

Antony walked to the black shelves and stared at the newest framed clipping from the society page. One of the delegates from Ventura had entered the Miss Teen California USA pageant, dressed by Francesca's and Victoria Luciano. "You should ask him."

"Okay." By his passiveness, she knew there must be something he wanted to tell her. "But I asked you first."

He walked toward the door. "You'll be at Papa's tonight?"

"I wouldn't miss dinner with my husband for anything." Dinner at Lorenzo's was a weekly affair. Something she hoped she'd get used to over the years, but tension ran rampant at Lorenzo's. The evilness he once lived in still engulfed him like the smell of a bad cigar.

"With your husband?" Antony laughed. "You're lucky I'm always around to keep you company."

It wasn't luck, and she knew it. It was deliberate. That was the only time Antony took pleasure in being excluded from the family business.

"Until later, my love, I must bid you a sweet adieu." Antony winked and backed out of the office.

Victoria laughed. Despite Antony's ridiculous idea that he could still win her heart, she cherished his friendship.

A sweep of the mouse lit the computer screen. Victoria punched in her password and leafed through the pages of clothes, determined to finalize the orders for the new store.

There were two knocks on the door, then Doc came in with his suit jacket draped over one shoulder, his Glock in plain sight. "You ready?"

"Is it four already? Give me a minute." She loaded the invoices into her briefcase and hung her white blazer on the coat rack, exposing her simple white dress with two-inch banana straps.

"Antony give you a hard time?" Doc asked.

"You know Antony. He's always trying to stir things up." She removed the clip, gently rubbed her fingers along her scalp, and allowed her hair to fall down and hang on her shoulders with a slight curl.

She picked up her briefcase, tucked the large portfolio under her arm, and walked toward the door. "Call Tanya and tell her to have the kids ready."

"Sure thing, boss."

***

The noise from the backseat escalated and made Victoria tighten her grip on the steering wheel. She hit Doc on the shoulder. "Would you stop those two from fighting?"

Doc turned around. "Rachel, leave Christian alone." He tried to be firm, but he couldn't help but smile at her.

Rachel's hair was a soft brown with natural curls. Her huge brown eyes were full of distress. "I want a turn with the headphones. He promised."

"Where are yours?"

"I forgot them."

Victoria glanced in the rearview mirror and recognized the pout on Rachel's face. At fourteen, she already understood how to use her charms to get her way. Victoria glanced at Christian, his headphones in his ears, staring out the window, looking innocent. "Give her a turn."

Christian pulled one earbud out. "What, huh?"

Her eyes narrowed. "You heard me."

Christian nodded then stuck the earpiece back in his ear.

Victoria glanced at Doc. "I'll bet you're so glad you are head of my security. Think of it, you could be back at the house playing cards with the other bodyguards. Instead, you get to break up fights between my two kids."

"Better fights between them than the alternative." Doc opened his jacket, exposing his gun.

"Don't let them see that."

"Yeah, yeah, Mrs. L., I've heard that lecture before."

"See what?" Rachel yelled from the backseat. "His gun?"

Victoria looked in the rearview mirror just in time to see Christian pull the earpiece out of his ear. "Yeah, his gun, stupid."

"I ain't stupid."

"Christian," Victoria said. "Don't call her names."

"Yeah, don't call me names." Rachel stuck out her tongue.

"Sorry, squirt." Christian replaced the earbud, his head bobbing to the music.

Rachel crossed her arms.

Victoria pulled the car between the large iron gates of Lorenzo's estate. Next to the main house sat a smaller guesthouse where Vince and the four other bodyguards lived.

She parked between Sonny's Escalade and Antony's Durango and killed the engine. Rachel jumped out and hurried down the long patio to the front door.

Clay, Sonny's assistant and bodyguard, leaned against the Escalade. His Tony Lamas peeked out from under his suit pants. Doc gave him a single nod then assumed the same position.

Christian walked next to Victoria, the volume so loud on his iPhone she could faintly hear the screeching of what he called music.

Sonny opened the door. He hugged Rachel. "How's my girl doing?"

"Hi, Daddy. Where's Uncle Tony?"

"He's inside."

"See ya." Rachel disappeared down the long hallway.

Sonny reached out to Christian, who jerked his head away from his father's large hands. "Watch the doo, Dad," Christian shouted. The music made him misjudge his volume.

Victoria rested her hand on Christian's shoulder and gently squeezed it.

Christian hit the stop button and looked up at her. "What?"

"Tell your dad who made the junior varsity basketball team."

"What?" Sonny looked at Christian, who stood almost at eye level to him. "You made it?"

"Yeah. That'd be me. The new point guard."

Sonny put his arm around Christian. "Good job."

"Did you doubt my ability to shoot hoops?"

"Never. Now try to be sociable."

Christian nodded and took a couple of steps forward before turning back to them. He grinned, stuck the earbuds back in his ears, and bobbed his head to the music. He spun around and strutted into Lorenzo's.

Sonny took Victoria's hand, pulled her to him, and gave her a kiss. "Man, you look good."

"Thank you." She backed away and did a slow spin. "This is from that new line we got in last week."

"I like it." Sonny raised his eyebrows as he pulled her back into his arms. He nibbled on her ear, gave her a long, passionate kiss, then took her hand and led her into the house.

Lorenzo sat in his wheelchair near the sofa in the den. Rachel was next to him talking about her day. No one would ever guess him to be the same man portrayed in the tabloids as one of the biggest criminals in the Midwest.

"Uncle Tony," Rachel shouted when Antony walked in. She left her Nonno and walked into Antony's outstretched arms.

"My favorite niece."

"I'm your only niece." She giggled.

"You'd be my favorite if I had more."

"When are you going to come ride horses with me?"

"How about tomorrow after school?"

"Promise?" She held out her hand.

"I promise." He shook on it. "I think Consolata made cookies. Bet you could sneak one before dinner."

She disappeared into the kitchen.

Antony pulled one of the earbuds away from Christian's ear. "You ever shut that off?"

Christian looked at his father, who raised an eyebrow at him. Sighing, Christian pulled the earbuds out and let them hang around his neck. The music escaped and echoed softly in the room.

"Guess who will be the next star of the Ventura High School basketball team?" Sonny said.

Antony pointed to Christian. "You?"

"Well, junior varsity. I'll try out for varsity next year. Nonno? Will you come to a game?"

"Sure."

"Maybe we can get a game of horse going after dinner," Sonny said.

"Count me in." Antony poured himself a drink.

"Cool." Christian got up and went out the French doors that led into the garden. Moments later, they heard a basketball pounding on the pavement.

Antony glanced at Victoria. "I looked over those figures, and there are a few things we should talk about."

"I told you to drop it," Sonny sipped his ice tea.

"Drop what?" Victoria asked.

"Nothing."

Victoria placed her hands on her hips.

"Okay. Antony thinks you've been a little overindulgent on some of the artwork you purchased for the new store."

She turned to Antony. "Almost everything I bought was a replica. You just can't envision what I have in mind. Wait until you see the store completely finished. Besides, I never went over the budget."

Antony raised his hands in defense. "I just think a few items are frivolous. Do you sell clothes, or are you an art dealer?"

"I'm selling atmosphere, too, and if you'd just—"

The deep bongs from the antique grandfather clock echoed loudly, as if scolding her, and the argument dissolved. It was one thing to argue with Antony, because Sonny would back her up, but with Lorenzo in the room, neither of them stood a chance. Lorenzo had made it clear on numerous occasions how he felt about Francesca's. He'd close them down in a second if given the chance.

"Thank God," Lorenzo bellowed. "Food."

Sonny yelled for Christian before he took the handles of his father's wheelchair and pushed him into the dining room.

Antony motioned with his hand for Victoria to go ahead then followed behind. She'd been there thousands of times, but her eyes were always drawn to the large crystal chandelier that hung from the ceiling.

Lorenzo pointed up as Sonny pushed him to the table. "My wife picked that out on one of our trips to Paris." He repeated the same words every time they sat down for a meal. "It's beautiful, isn't it?"

"Yes, it is." Victoria admired the way his eyes lit up when he spoke about his wife. It was the only time he looked truly happy.

Lorenzo closed his eyes and sniffed the air. "Smells like homemade gnocci."

Consolata, the housekeeper and cook, walked into the room chattering in Italian. Once a week, she went to her hairdresser and had her black hair shampooed and styled in the helmet hairdo made popular in the fifties.

She set the food on the table and wiped her hands on the stained apron that hung around her large stomach. Lorenzo said something to her in Italian, and they both laughed.

Rachel always sat next to Uncle Tony. When they were together, it was one of the few times Antony's face was free from anger and hatred. Free from envy and jealousy.

Sonny took Victoria's hand in his. She reached over and took Christian's, who took Rachel's.

Antony looked around the table. All eyes were on him as he held the breadbasket over his plate. He conceded, placed a piece of bread on his plate, then set the basket on the table. "I swear . . ."

"Swearing's bad, Uncle Tony." Rachel pounded the back of her hand on the table.

Antony looked down and sighed, then took her hand in his. "Thank you for pointing that out, Rach."

Victoria smiled and gave Sonny's hand a squeeze. He offered a blessing for the food.

Lorenzo grunted, ignored them, and began to eat.

***

Dimitri shuffled through the stack of old black and white photos. Which one should he send today? He smiled and picked up the photo of a young Lorenzo, cuffed, with two detectives on either side of him. Sonny and Antony stood in the background with a look of shock on their faces.

He stared at it for a moment before placing it on top of a typed letter filled with small tidbits of information about Lorenzo Luciano and his life in Kansas City. The tabloids would love it.

SIX

DETECTIVE ZOË STONE HURRIED through the Ventura Police Department, a half-eaten doughnut hung out of her mouth. She juggled two thick files, her oversized purse, and a hot cup of coffee in a *Cops Fear No Evil* mug. Her long, blond hair was pulled back in a failed attempt at a bun.

A bar fight in college had left a bump in the middle of her dainty nose. Months later, she'd been sitting at a restaurant where an average Joe stared at her in a perplexed way.

He'd approached her and politely introduced himself as a plastic surgeon and offered to restore her nose to its original state. She'd not only had the nose job but liposuction and a tummy tuck. Hidden under her masculine, I'm-a-cop attire was a Barbie doll body that had drained most of her savings.

"Stone!" Jackson shouted above the endless ringing phones and chatter of fellow officers.

Zoë turned and ran into him. Coffee splashed out of the mug and landed on the floor. It barely missed Jackson's worn-out penny loafers, minus the pennies. "Crap."

"I'll get it." Jackson took the mug from her hand then grabbed Kleenex from a neighboring desk, bent down, and wiped up the spill. "Captain's in your office."

An office that consisted of a desk and a chair hidden behind three eight-foot partitions. She did count herself lucky because she was one of the few who sat by a window.

She bit through the doughnut and pushed it to the side of her mouth. "I'm late, aren't I?"

"Always." Jackson tossed the wet Kleenex in a trashcan then grabbed the files from her hand. He was a good cop from a long line of cops. Short brown hair with average looks and build, but there was nothing average about Jackson. He was the last of a dying breed. A true gentleman. Not once had he hit on her or blamed her sporadic behavior on PMS.

She took another bite of the doughnut, chewed twice, and swallowed. "You sleep in that suit?"

"All night surveillance." He sipped her coffee.

"Hey, *I* need that caffeine."

"Not as bad as I do."

Zoë tucked the loose strands of hair behind her ears.

"You missed your hair appointment." Jackson pointed.

"My roots tip you off?" She shoved the last of the doughnut in her mouth then licked her fingers. "Thanks for noticing."

"I hadn't noticed." Jackson held up a pink phone message. "The beauty shop called." He eyeballed her hair. "But now that you mention it, I'd reschedule if I were you." He handed her back the files and mug then disappeared.

She tilted the cup and sighed. He'd left her one swallow. Giving it a gulp, she shifted the files in her arm and walked around the partition into her office.

Captain Rollins' silver bifocals sat low on his nose. He looked like he was reading the gold-embossed invitation to the reception for the grand opening of the new Francesca's, but she knew better. He was there to reinforce his belief that through her sister, Victoria, and the Lucianos, she could nail Dimitri.

"You going to this?" he asked.

"Maybe."

"I'll bet Dimitri Romeo will be there. He's already contacted Antony."

"And you expect me to just walk up to Antony and pump him for information? The Interpol case is cold—it's over twenty years old." Zoë leaned over and set the coffee mug down, then allowed the files to fall on her desk. She picked up the Romeo file and leafed through it. "I quote, 'The Boston Field Office has given up hope of ever recovering any of the paintings or artifacts from the 1980 Boston Museum heist.'"

"Until recently." Rollins tossed the invitation on her desk. "When the feds got a tip that led them to Dimitri."

"If the Boston Field Office hasn't been able to track down this artwork, what makes you think we can?"

"They're FBI, we're cops. We know these streets."

"And I know the Lucianos."

"Exactly." Rollins removed his glasses and slid them into his shirt pocket. "My gut tells me Dimitri's into more than some batch of stolen artwork. Those paintings for Interpol would just be a feather in our cap."

Zoë tapped on the Romeo file. "I've read this. Dimitri could teach Crime 101."

"You're not up to the challenge?"

"I'm always up for a challenge."

"Good." Rollins walked to the doorway then turned back to her. "An old friend is in town." He motioned for someone outside the office.

Martin Tucker stepped in the doorway. He hadn't changed a bit. His Wranglers still clung to his body and showed off his toned muscles. His shoulder-length dishwater-blond hair hung free. The white button-down shirt and thin solid blue tie was his office attire. It was the nicest he'd ever looked, even at their wedding. The twenty-four-hour Little Bell Chapel hadn't required much, nor had she.

"Martin?"

His whole face grinned. "How you doing?"

"Wow." She stood. "How long has it been?"

"Over a year." His voice was deep.

"What are you doing back?"

Rollins left, and Martin walked closer. "You going to just stand there?" He opened his arms. "Come here."

Zoë walked around the desk. They hugged.

"It's good to see you." She pulled away. "When did you get back in town?"

"A few months ago. I heard you're going to the reception at Francesca's."

"Everyone sure is interested in my social life. You trying to catch Dimitri, too?"

"Why would you ask that?"

"Because the brass is all over me to spy on my family, and then you show up. Dimitri sure has everybody worked up."

"I always knew you were a good detective."

"I was more than that."

It was true. They had been inseparable since the first day they laid eyes on each other. His quick wit and charm had enticed her, not to mention his tight police-issue navy slacks. She had stood on stage at a memorial for officers killed in action, representing her father. Martin was a new cadet.

She'd always wanted to pursue police work, but Victoria had persuaded her to go after her second dream, interior design. After meeting Martin, she decided she could do both. They became partners both on and off the job. Their marriage was short and ended in an amicable divorce.

Her eyes were drawn to the one dimple on his left cheek. It was deep and sexy when he smiled. "Where you been for the last year?"

"Kansas City. Undercover."

"You're the mole?"

"In the flesh."

"Doing your dream job, huh?" She sat down behind her desk. "Is it all you thought it'd be?"

"Only thing missing is you."

"Someone had to stick around and clean up the mess from our last case."

"We closed that case."

"The only case we closed was the casket, again. Brass didn't appreciate the prime suspect delivered in a body bag."

"You know what I always say . . ."

"A dead killer saves the taxpayers money."

Martin's face turned serious. "You think you can find anything out from the Lucianos?"

"You haven't changed a bit, have you? Catch the bad guy—it always comes first."

"I *am* a cop."

"Me, too."

Their eyes met, and neither broke the stare. Their years of competitiveness shot across the room, and they grinned at each other.

"You got any leads not mentioned in the file?" Zoë asked.

"Not yet, but I've got it covered."

"A woman?"

"Yeah, but this one's different."

"You say that about every chick you stumble on in a case." Zoë put the end of the pencil in her mouth and chewed on it. The small bits of eraser crumbled, and she spit them out on the floor and tossed the pencil on her desk.

"She's different—I promise. She'll give me the information I need."

Zoë rolled her eyes.

"You going to work with me or not?" Martin asked.

"Of course." When he winked at her, she added, "It is my job."

His smile didn't diminish. It only got wider.

"What?" Heat filled her face.

"Nothing." He paused. "You still got your side business?"

"Yes." She reached into her pocket and pulled out her card. *One of A Kind Designs* was inscribed in navy raised letters. "It's doing very well."

"I bought you a present." Martin stood and raised an eyebrow. "I didn't forget."

"You missed it by two weeks. Besides, didn't you hear? I'm not having any more birthdays. I stopped at thirty-four."

"Then call it a necessity for the case." He pulled out a compact gun. "It's a Cobra Derringer. What do you think?"

"Only you would buy me a gun for my birthday."

"I figure since you're going to be surrounded by all those fancy, high society types, you'll need something small to hide. You can't walk around with that Glock tucked in your pantyhose."

Zoë was one step ahead of Martin. She'd already filled out the paperwork to check out a smaller weapon.

She picked up the gun. The stainless steel felt good in the palm of her hand, which almost concealed it. She turned to the window, held her arm up, and pointed it outside, aiming at a scrub jay that was perched in a tree. "It's nice. It's an auto?"

Martin rounded the desk to point to the gun. "Yeah. Five-round magazine and light as a feather." He stroked the two-inch barrel. "It'll fit in a leg strap or in your purse."

"Thanks. Really."

Martin gently kissed her cheek. "Good luck. I'll see you on the inside." He walked to the door then turned to her. "Remember. You don't know me."

She looked at him coolly. "I know how to do my job."

"I know you do." Martin disappeared.

***

Sonny sat across from Antony in the restaurant and drummed his fingers on the table. "He's late."

Antony pulled a toothpick from the breast pocket of the navy suit jacket. "He'll be here."

"You go by DeLuca's?"

They'd chosen their mother's maiden name to call the low-income housing development, which had become a joint venture. It was one of the few times Sonny had to eat his words. He had condemned Antony when he bought the property out from under the developers to build his high-rise condominiums, only Antony had already bought land to relocate the shelter. Sonny read it in the paper when everyone else in town did.

"I went by this morning," Antony said. "It should be open by the end of the month. We're getting good press."

"We need to counteract that last story in the tabloids."

"That bothers you?" Antony gulped his drink. "Look who wrote it. Just ignore them."

Sonny let out a burst of air, rubbing the back of his neck. "Ignore it? They called me an ex-don's son who coached a local soccer team." Sonny grunted. "Ex-don? You'd think Papa sold the story—it'd fit right in there with his fantasy."

"It doesn't matter what people think. We have power and money, and if a few good deeds keep us in the graces of the common folks, then I'll be standing next to you, cutting ribbons with that cute gal from the chamber of commerce. What was her name? Susan?"

"That's why you bought the land and built the apartments? To stay in good graces with the common folks?"

Antony's grin deepened. "That's the difference between you and me. You've got integrity. I do things like that to make me feel important."

Antony pushed Sonny's drink toward him.

Sonny took a sip of the tea then slowly spun the glass around as he talked. "You see the donation check we got from Dimitri?"

"Yeah. It should pay the bills for the whole complex for a solid twelve months." Antony raised his glass at the waitress. "I let the press know. Might give Dimitri an image boost."

"And if he wants revenge?"

Antony patted his side where his gun hung safely in its holster. "If he does, your God can use me to save you. I'm a willing participant." Antony looked toward the door then leaned into Sonny. "Dimitri just walked in."

"Man, he's gotten big."

Sonny stood and offered his hand to Dimitri as he wobbled to the table wearing a navy polyester suit with a tan knit shirt that hung untucked. His thick gold necklace matched the rings that glistened on his fingers.

Dimitri grasped Sonny's hand and gave it a hard shake. He then turned to Antony and took his hand. Antony pulled Dimitri to him, gave him a firm slap on the back. "It's been a long time."

"Too long." Dimitri returned the gesture then backed away and gently wiped his hand along his well-greased black hair that was pulled into a ponytail.

Sonny motioned for Dimitri to sit.

Antony waved the waitress over and ordered Dimitri a drink.

Dimitri nodded at the server as she set the drink down. "How's the family?"

"Good," Sonny said. "And your grandmother?"

"Cancer's been in remission for almost two years now. She loves it here." Dimitri smiled at Antony. "How's that girlfriend of yours?"

"Girlfriend?" Antony laughed.

"The one the tabloids say you're engaged to," Dimitri said.

"Lauren? The tabloids will say anything to sell their paper."

"So you're not engaged?"

"Lauren's not the marrying type." Antony grinned. "But she looks good on my arm, doesn't she?"

Antony and Dimitri bellowed in laughter.

Sonny sipped his tea. He hated the way Antony and Lauren used each other, but he had to admit that whenever Lauren was around, Antony's focus was temporarily removed from *his* wife.

"And you," Antony asked Dimitri. "You married?"

"Divorced twice, but quickies in Vegas don't count."

They both laughed again.

"We got your check for DeLuca's," Sonny said. "Thank you."

"Not a problem." Dimitri winked at Antony. "You know I'm all for helping those less fortunate than myself."

Sonny studied the glances that shot back and forth between the two men. He wondered if he would ever find out what had happened all those years his brother lived on the streets. Maybe he didn't want to know.

"I wondered"—Dimitri leaned into Antony—"if you could help me out?"

"That depends." Sonny drew Dimitri's attention to him. "On what you want help with."

Dimitri raised a questioning brow at Antony. "What's with him?"

"He's the boss." Antony swirled his drink around in his glass.

"Never thought I'd see the day."

One side of Antony's mouth went up into a grin. "That makes two of us."

Dimitri grunted out a laugh then turned to Sonny. "I'm going legit, like your old man did."

"Really?" Sonny raised an eyebrow.

"Yeah."

"Then what do you need us for?"

"I'm the first to admit, I don't have the best reputation. I just need to be connected with someone who'll give the community confidence in me, make me look good. I want respect from decent people. I've got money, so I can invest in anything you say."

The Lucianos might boost Dimitri's image, but with the tabloids digging up the past, being seen with a presumed criminal would only hurt theirs.

"Can you help me out?" Dimitri folded his hands and tapped his thumbs together.

Sonny studied him. He appeared to be telling the truth. If he was, they couldn't turn him down. "We'll do what we can."

Dimitri lifted his glass in gratitude. "Thanks, man."

Sonny's cell phone chirped. He looked down to see Victoria's number. "Excuse me, I've got to get this." He put the phone to his ear. "Yes, all right. I'm on my way." He ended the call and slid the phone into his pocket. "I've got to go." He stood. "I'll send over an invitation to my wife's reception for her new store."

"Thanks."

***

Antony gave his brother a single nod before he left then turned to Dimitri. "This money you want to invest. Does it need cleaning?"

The maroon linen napkin slipped off Dimitri's lap and fell to the floor. Dimitri leaned over with a groan, grabbed the napkin, and spoke as he sat back up. "It's clean, I swear."

Antony snapped his fingers at the waitress. They ordered some food then brushed her away.

Dimitri smiled. "It'll be like old times."

Old times on the street in KC. Times Antony tried to forget. He wasn't proud he'd collected for Vito, but he'd needed cash. More than once, Dimitri had saved him from the lunatic who pursued him with a tire iron. A crazy guy Antony never could collect money from until Dimitri came along.

"Yeah, I owe you, don't I?" Antony moved his drink so the waitress could set the steak in front of him.

"At least one." Dimitri looked down at his steak and licked his lips. "Man, this looks good." He picked up the small white cup and smothered the meat with a wine, garlic, and mushroom sauce. He pointed to the full cup that sat on Antony's plate. "You gonna use that?"

Antony shook his head.

Dimitri grabbed it off Antony's plate and poured it over his steak. He swished his bread around the sauce then shoved it into his mouth. A trail of the garlicky wine sauce ran across the table to the napkin tucked into the top of his shirt. Sauce escaped from his mouth as he chewed. He grabbed the napkin and wiped his chin.

He eats like a pig. A blue-ribbon pig at a state fair. Antony looked away and scanned the restaurant. He stopped on a beautiful woman who sat with a heavyset man. She smiled at Antony. He winked before Dimitri's words drew his attention back to the table.

"You'll set me up on some investments?"

"I'm not Edward D. Jones."

Dimitri grunted. "Which of your many endeavors needs money?"

"Clean money?" Antony asked as he brushed a crumb off the table onto the floor.

"You don't trust me, old friend?"

"I'll trust you until you prove yourself untrustworthy."

"Now, there's the Antony I know and love." Dimitri gave him a hard slap on the arm.

Antony grinned. *Will I soon see the Dimitri I know and despise?*

Dimitri waved his fork at Antony while he spoke. "This reception, should I bring a date?"

"Sure." *If you can get one.* "Only let's not have a repeat of the last party we went to together."

"My conduct was impeccable."

"Yeah, right."

"Hey, I'm not the one who threw the bottle."

Antony stood up. "You were threatening the guy with a steak knife."

"I didn't threaten him. I was gesturing."

Antony laughed and tossed some cash on the table. "Call me at the office."

***

Victoria stared at the opened boxes, her hands on her hips. Could she really believe her own son would steal from her? Christian had been in and out of all kinds of trouble over the past year. Yeah, she could believe it.

Frank shifted. "I just said he was acting kinda weird."

"Weird?"

"Nervous, frightened." Frank slid his hand under the Dodgers cap and scratched his head.

Heavy footsteps echoed on the hardwood. "I got here as soon as I could." Sonny leaned into Victoria and gave her a quick kiss on the lips. "What happened?"

She waved her hands at Frank, giving him permission to repeat his accusation. It was an absurd story. One that Sonny laughed at.

"Did you see Christian with any of the items?" Sonny asked. "You stood right next to him."

Frank shook his head.

"He's your prime suspect?" Sonny's amusement turned to anger. He turned to Victoria. "Call the cops. Any one of these workers could've stolen that stuff. There must be fifty who had the opportunity."

"I'm not saying Christian did this." Victoria touched his arm. "But he hasn't been a saint lately. I called Zoë, and she's offered to help, off the record."

"It wasn't Christian." Sonny shook his head. "It couldn't be. He wouldn't steal from us."

"I hope you're right."

An hour later, Zoë walked into the offices on the fourth floor. She had on her cop face. "I found a pawnshop in South LA. They had three of the four pieces. Said some kid brought it in."

"And?"

"The description didn't fit Christian."

"I knew it." Sonny turned to Victoria. "I told you, didn't I?"

Victoria nodded, but Zoë was still being a cop. She tapped her pencil on her notepad, her face emotionless. "The perp was about seventeen, had shoulder-length black hair, and drove a dark blue Toyota. Does he sound familiar?"

Victoria stiffened.

Zoë looked at her. "You know him?"

"It's a kid Christian hangs out with sometimes." Sonny paced. "Why? I don't understand—Christian's got everything. We told him Russ was trouble."

"Why doesn't it surprise me that he didn't listen?" Victoria said.

"You want me to talk to Christian?" Zoë asked.

"No," Sonny said.

"Then find out what he knows." Zoë tucked the notepad into the front of her pants. "Let me know if you want to file charges."

"Thanks, Zoë," Victoria said. "You coming to the reception?"

"If I can find a date." Zoë laughed. She hugged Victoria. "Christian's going to be okay. All kids his age go through some sort of rebellion."

"Thanks." Victoria turned to Sonny. "I'll go pick him up from school."

Sonny placed his hands on her shoulders and gave her a smile. "I've got to stop by Renato's, then I'll meet you at home. We'll talk to Christian together."

SEVEN

SONNY AND VICTORIA'S GEORGIAN estate sat on a small acreage in Ventura, a few miles from Lorenzo's. The red brick exterior was adorned with multiple gables. A curved portico enhanced the entrance that led into a large foyer.

To the right of the foyer sat Sonny's home office. The afternoon sun peeked through the clouds, filtering into the room through the bay window behind his desk.

Sonny stared out at their five horses that stood at the fence, anticipating the children and the usual afternoon treats of apples or carrots. The newest member, a white foal, pranced around the other horses like he owned the field. It reminded him of Christian—headstrong.

"I've got those papers." Clay came in wearing brown trousers, a white shirt, and a holstered Smith and Wesson. His sandy blond hair was cut short, and his face was soft, expressing his easygoing personality.

Clay handed Sonny the financial report. "Lorenzo called. He wants you to call him. Said it's important."

Lorenzo's idea of important could range anywhere from a big business takeover to the latest masseuse Antony hired for him.

Sonny tossed the report aside without giving it a glance.

"You okay?"

"Christian's in trouble again." Sonny did a quick pace of the room. "Do you think those articles in the tabloids are making him act this way?"

"Yeah. You should tell him about the past."

"Just like that? Tell him about the past?" Sonny was troubled that the suggestion birthed such anger in him. "What part of the past should I tell him?"

"Tell him what Lorenzo used to do." Clay took a step toward him and lowered his voice. "And tell Victoria the truth about who killed Carlo."

"Tell Victoria? Why?"

"How much longer do you think Antony's going to keep it a secret? The way your father rides him, I'm surprised he's kept it this long." Clay slid his hands into his pockets and jiggled the loose change. "Dimitri's stirred up feelings you've all tried to suppress. It's only a matter of time before the truth comes out."

"Antony would never tell Dimitri."

"No, but he'd love to tell Victoria. You know how he still looks at her. He doesn't even hide his flirtation anymore."

Sonny couldn't argue that. Despite Antony's desire, Sonny knew Victoria meant it when she vowed to forsake all others and keep herself only unto him. But if Antony revealed the truth, a seed of doubt would be planted. A seed that Antony would carefully, and purposely, water.

Car doors slammed and drew Sonny's attention back to the window. Victoria's black quarter horse bobbed his head at her, expecting attention. Victoria walked to the fence, gave his nose a quick rub, then followed Christian up the walkway to the house.

"You're right. I need to tell her." Sonny rubbed the back of his neck and turned back to Clay. "Get a hold of my father and tell him I'm in a meeting."

Sonny walked down the hallway that led into the great room. Reflections of the sun off the pool shot shards of light through the double French doors and enhanced the neutral painted walls and vaulted ceiling.

Sonny's eyes met Victoria's as she and Christian walked into the room. He forced a smile, but she didn't respond.

"Hey, Dad." Christian plopped on the couch. "Mom said you needed to talk to me." He picked at one of the many holes in his jeans. "What's up?"

Sonny placed his hand in his pocket and caressed the cross attached to his mother's rosary. "Your mother had some things stolen from the store yesterday. You know anything about it?"

"What?" Silence filled the room, and seconds later Christian sat staunchly. "Why would I know anything about it?"

"Because you were at the store," Sonny said. "Why'd you go there?"

"To talk to Mom."

"And Russ drove you?"

"Yeah." Christian's eyes widened. He flew to his feet. "You think I did it, don't you? You think I stole that stuff?"

"Did you?"

Christian paced the room and cracked his knuckles. "This is unbelievable. You really think I would steal from you?" He stopped and stared out the French doors before he turned and looked at Victoria for a second then averted his eyes. "Mom, I wouldn't steal from you. You gotta believe me."

"I don't know what to believe," Victoria whispered.

"I didn't." Christian clenched his fists. "I didn't do it."

Sonny rubbed his forehead, took a deep breath, and tried to slow his heart. "Sit down."

Christian sat with crossed arms. "I didn't do it."

"We know Russ pawned the stuff down in LA. I don't care about that. What I want to know is if you knew anything about it." Sonny stared deep into his son's eyes. They seemed cold and deceitful. "I want the truth."

"Just 'cause you and Uncle Tony did that kind of stuff doesn't mean I do."

"What?"

"I can read the papers. Nonno, a small-time gangster. You and Uncle Tony got kicked out of school, stole a car, and ran numbers. Man, I ain't stupid."

Sonny could see the damage he'd caused by keeping his father's past a secret. Telling Christian was inevitable, but first he had to deal with the present.

"Why did you go to the store?" Sonny asked.

"I told you, I wanted to talk to Mom."

Victoria touched his arm. "About what?"

"There's this girl . . ." His lips pursed together, and his face flushed. "It's nothing. Okay? I just had some questions. I was sick of school and wanted to talk. That's it. I didn't steal anything."

Victoria looked up at Sonny.

Sonny sighed. "Go to your room."

"You believe me, don't you?"

No, Sonny wanted to shout, but until he had proof, he wouldn't call his son a liar or a thief. "I don't know what to believe."

Christian glared at him then flew up the stairs, taking two at a time.

"You think he did it?" Sonny asked Victoria.

"If he didn't, he knew about it. He couldn't look either one of us in the eye."

Sonny nodded. "I think he's trying to live up to the image the tabloids are portraying of me and my family."

"Maybe, but it doesn't excuse him."

"I hate what they're writing. There are things in my past that I'd rather not have dug up. Things even you don't know." He looked into her eyes. "Things I should've told you about a long time ago."

"About Dimitri?"

Sonny's eyes narrowed. "What?"

"Antony came by my office yesterday. He mentioned Dimitri was back in town."

Sonny paced the room with clenched fists. "What else did my brother say?"

"It was strange. I could tell he wanted to tell me something, but he wouldn't. He told me to ask you."

Relieved it wasn't too late, he gave his hair a quick comb-through with his fingers. "Let's go talk." Sonny led her into his office and closed the door behind them. Standing at the window, he shut his eyes, allowing the silence to blanket the room. Images flooded his head and made it pound.

"What's going on?" Victoria asked.

When he didn't say anything, he felt her hand on his shoulder. "Whatever it is, it's okay."

He turned to her. "You know Carlo was Dimitri's brother."

"Yes."

He looked down at his opened hands. He could still feel the kick of the gun, the warmth of Carlo's blood, the life instantly gone.

"Antony didn't shoot Carlo." He brought his eyes up slowly to meet hers. "I did."

"What?"

"I was the one who accidentally killed him, not Antony. Antony admitted to shooting him to protect me."

Victoria's face was unreadable.

"That's why Antony lived on the streets?" she asked.

"He was ordered out." Sonny lowered his eyes. "Papa disowned him."

"I asked you about this years ago. Why didn't you tell me the truth then?"

"Antony and I have carried the lie for so long that it's just easier to believe he did it."

She took his hand. "It wouldn't have changed my feelings for you."

Pulling her to him, he kissed her and allowed her love to consume him. "Thanks." He breathed deeply and took in the sweet smell of her perfume. Her beauty made his pulse quicken. "I needed to hear that."

"I love you no matter what. You know that."

"I know." He kissed her again.

"What does Dimitri want?" she asked.

"He says he wants to go legit, but he's got a bad reputation. He wants us to make him look good."

"Is he sincere?"

"I don't know. I think so."

"Then you need to help him."

"I'd planned on it. It's the least I can do."

The muffled bass of Christian's music pounded through the ceiling. Each beat made Sonny's head throb harder. "What are we going to do with him?"

"I don't know. I thought we did everything right. We took him to church, got him involved in sports, family dinners." She shook her head. "Where did we go wrong?"

"Maybe Zoë's right." Sonny felt her stiffen, but he didn't care. "All kids go through some sort of rebellion."

"You always give him the benefit of the doubt. But if Christian is trying to live up to an image portrayed in the tabloids, then you have to tell him what's true and what isn't. Tell him who his grandfather was. That you did things when you were his age—things you regret."

Sonny caressed her cheek. He tried to smile, but shame overcame him. He released her and retreated to the security of his desk. Resting his elbows on his legs, he rubbed his hands together, his head low.

"How do I tell him Papa was a small-time gangster?" His eyes met hers. "That his Nonno hurt people?"

Victoria went to him and rubbed his shoulders. "I didn't run out when you told me about Lorenzo's past. Christian's your son. He loves you."

Sonny closed his eyes, allowing her gentle massage to soothe him. "You're right." He turned the chair around and faced her. His frustration waned. He pulled her onto his lap and kissed her. "Are you going back to the store?"

"I'm supposed to meet Antony at the new one, but I can call and cancel."

"No, you go."

"You sure? I'll go up there with you."

"I need to do this alone."

"Okay." She touched his cheek. "Any idea what Antony wants?"

Sonny pulled her close with a smile. Yeah, he knew what Antony wanted. He was holding it, but Antony would never have her, not while Sonny had a breath in his body. "He probably wants to go over the final paperwork. He's a stickler for that."

"I didn't think borrowing money from Renato's would be so much work for you."

"It's no trouble. You know Antony. He takes special care in certain deals. With the reception and the grand opening only a week away, he just wants to make sure everything's going smooth."

"I'd just rather meet with the boss than his brother."

"The boss has family problems. Now go. I've got to talk to Christian."

"I'll see you in an hour or so." She leaned in and kissed him. "Good luck."

Sonny sat for a moment and wondered what he could say to bridge the distance between him and his son. The chasm seemed to grow larger every day.

Christian turned the music louder. He walked into the closet, grabbed the backpack, and unzipped it. He reached in and pulled out the beaker.

What had he done? How did he let Russ and Ned talk him into it?

He rubbed his forehead and shook his head. Had he forgotten everything he'd learned about right and wrong? Falling to his knees, he cupped the beaker between his hands and closed his eyes. "Lord, get me out of this. If you do, I promise I'll change. I'll live how You want me to."

He opened his eyes and rolled the beaker up in a t-shirt, put it back in the backpack, and zipped it up. Chewing on the inside of his cheek, he knew what he had to do. He had to get rid of the beaker, fast.

***

Victoria and Doc stood in the center of the new store. She looked up at the cathedral ceiling where a large crystal teardrop chandelier hung from a backdrop of mirrors. The banisters on the three balconies were adorned with greenery and small lights.

She grinned. "Looks beautiful, doesn't it?"

"Looks like someone had money to burn."

"Always the comedian. Go make yourself useful."

Doc took two steps back and rested his arms on a clothing rack. "How's this?"

Victoria grabbed his arm and made him walk with her. "You know, there was a security breach."

Doc stopped immediately. "What?" He eyed her up and down. "You've been breached? When? Where was I?"

She slapped his arm. "You know what I'm talking about."

"Ah." He winked. "Told you, Mrs. L. The computer problem was taken care of, and our thief, well, Sonny's taking care of that."

"Double-check the security anyway."

"You're a slave driver." He looked down, opened his jacket, and patted the Glock that hung in its holster. Looking back up at her, he grinned. "Security's fine."

"I'm glad, because in a few minutes, I'll be sitting over there with Antony."

"And you don't want to be breached?"

She smacked his arm.

He grinned his crooked grin. "I'll be upstairs checking out the cameras."

"You do that." She turned and walked to the small coffee shop at the east end of the store.

Antony was bent over one of the glass cases where different artifacts and sculptures were displayed. Her heels clicked loudly on the gray marble floor, which brought him around to face her.

His afternoon shadow, deep dimples, and her new insight into his heart made him sexier than ever. Her faithfulness to her husband was unwavering, but there were a few times she feared the feelings Antony stirred in her. It wasn't just his looks that made her feel that way, it was his dedication. She could see that he savored every word, every glance, and every gesture she bestowed on him.

He ran his hand down the front of the black, three-button, Armani suit coat. "You like?"

"It's sharp." Walking around him, she checked the fit. "It looks like the ones we just got in."

"I told the gal to put it on my tab."

He gestured to the walls of the coffee shop that were a mixture of dark greens, accented with high gloss black. "I was worried about this, but it looks good."

"Thanks." She welcomed his approval. He was a shrewd businessman and had made millions for Renato. "What can I do for you?" She grabbed her long hair, spun it around her fingers, and looped it into a knot.

"I heard you had a break-in."

"We had four sculptures stolen. They're not worth much, and we've recovered three of them."

"And the thief?"

"Sonny's taking care of it."

"Having a problem with security?"

"No." She sat on a walnut carved armchair. "Doc is on top of things." She clasped her hands together and said a silent prayer for peace, but from the bedevilment in Antony's eyes, she could feel him sucking it out of her. *How he can entice me one second then throw me into turmoil the next is beyond me.*

"He'd better be, or he'll answer to me."

She narrowed her eyes.

"You're sexy when you're angry."

"I'm not angry."

"You are. You're doing that thing with your eye."

"What thing?"

"Your left eye flutters. It happens every time you get upset." His wide grin made it flutter even more.

She rubbed her forehead in an attempt to conceal her irritation. "Would you quit doubting our ability to run things?"

"Renato's has a lot of money riding on this. I have every right to be concerned. Okay, so you've got it under control." Silence blanketed the room. "You okay?"

Victoria twirled the three-carat wedding ring on her finger. Part of her cherished their friendship, but every time she opened up to him, it gave him an edge. Tiny pieces of her that she wasn't sure she wanted him to have.

"Christian's gotten into some trouble." She brought her eyes up to meet his. "Sonny's telling him about the past."

Antony made a long *whew* sound, and removed the sports coat, exposing a chrome-plated Colt 40 that hung in a black leather holster on his belt. He sat down, his face soft, consumed with her problem. He stared deep into her eyes. Something he always did when he talked to her. "Sonny's doing the right thing."

"Sonny told me the truth."

"The truth?" Antony took a toothpick from his shirt pocket. Leaning back, he crossed his leg and let his ankle rest on his thigh. He tapped his finger on the side of his shoe. "About what?"

"He accidentally killed Carlo, not you. That was very admirable of you to take the blame all these years."

Antony stood and walked to the counter where he rested his hands on the marble countertop. He breathed deeply then turned back to her. His mouth tipped wryly. "I'm not a saint."

"A saint? I'd never think that. I understand Sonny keeping the secret, but why didn't you ever tell me the truth?"

"Believe me, it crossed my mind more than once, but I couldn't. As much as I love you, I'm loyal to him. He's my brother. Would it have made a difference?"

"No, I would've still married Sonny. I'm as devoted to him as you are."

"Devotion. Look where it's gotten me. I answer to him, and I have a father who hates me."

"In Sonny's defense, he has bent over backward to give you everything . . ."

"Except the company I am supposed to run."

"Not yet."

Antony rolled his eyes. "I'll never get it, at least not while Papa's alive."

"Then why continue the charade? Tell Lorenzo the truth."

Antony raised his eyebrows. "And shatter Sonny's life?"

"Shatter his life? Hardly."

"Telling Papa the truth would just cause more problems." He walked back toward the table, pulled a piece of paper out of his pocket, and laid it in front of her. "Chelsea Dover. She's available to work with you on your idea for helping the Women's Center this Christmas."

Victoria took the paper. She knew it was his way of ending the conversation. "Is she good?"

"Yes." Antony tossed the jacket over his shoulder. "She's expecting your call. With the latest tabloids, Sonny needs all the good press he can get."

"That's not why we're doing it."

"I know." He winked and disappeared.

***

"Christian?" Sonny gently tapped on the door before opening it.

"What?" Christian killed the stereo then spun his desk chair around to face his father. His arms were crossed, his expression indifferent and uncaring.

"I want to talk to you about something." Sonny was still unsure how to explain a lifestyle he detested. One he was forced to live.

He remembered how scared he'd been when he told Victoria, but she didn't flinch at his touch after that. His honesty had drawn them closer than ever. Like Victoria, Christian would hear only part of the story. There were some things he'd never tell.

"Ya gotta believe me," Christian said and looked away from his father's eyes. "I didn't steal anything."

"I want to talk to you about this." Sonny tossed the tabloid on the bed and pointed to the article that said Lorenzo had mob connections and that an unfortunate accident had left him paralyzed and out of the ranks. Sonny scoffed. *Everyone knows that if you're in the mob, there's only one way out. Death.*

"I want you to know," Sonny said, "that you can ask me anything, and I'll tell you the truth."

"Really?" Christian's eyebrows wrinkled. "Anything?"

Sonny nodded.

"Was Nonno in the mob?"

"No. He worked the streets as a loan shark. A two-bit criminal."

Christian's eyes widened. "Did he kill people?"

"Not that I know of."

"Did he hurt people when they couldn't pay?"

Sonny breathed deeply. "Sometimes. It's a past I'm ashamed of and always hated. That's why I never talk about it."

Christian's eyes intensified. "Was it true what they said about you and Uncle Tony stealing a car?"

"Yes, but it was your Nonno's car."

"Were you kicked out of three different schools?"

"No. We got suspended a few times but never kicked out."

"What about running numbers?"

"We did a few times, for cash." Sonny sat on the bed and rubbed his hands together. "Why are you acting like a juvenile delinquent? Did you read this and think you have to live up to the image?"

"You a shrink now?"

Sonny resisted the urge to knock some sense into him about respect, but if he gave into that temptation, he'd be no better than his dad. "What's gotten into you?"

Christian tipped his chin. "Do you know what it's like for me at school? I have kids and teachers back away from me, afraid of what my father or my Nonno might do to them. Do you know what that feels like?"

Sonny smiled without humor. "Yes. I do."

"Then you know what I'm up against. Some days I can't fight it anymore. I have to be who they think I am."

"That's a cop-out. You always have a choice. I'm not proud of my past, but that's not who your Nonno is anymore, and it's not who I ever was."

Christian looked down then slowly brought his eyes up to meet his father's. "How can you go to church every week? Don't you feel like a hypocrite?"

"I used to, but I've learned that the past is just that. The past. I'm not proud of it, and the reason I don't discuss it is because people judge me, like they're judging you. You have to decide if you're going to be the bigger man and not let this run your life."

Christian yanked a string free that hung from the hole in his jeans. "How?"

"Walk away when your friends are doing something wrong."

"It's not that easy."

"You're right. It's not going to be easy, but you know what's right and wrong. You can feel it in your gut. Follow that, not your friends."

Christian nodded.

Sonny picked up the tabloid and walked to the door.

"Dad?"

Sonny turned back to him. "Yeah?"

"You gonna tell the cops about Russ?"

"I don't know. Should I?"

Christian looked away from his father. "No."

Sonny knew Christian was involved. To what extent, he didn't know, and at the moment, he didn't care. His heart pounded. "If anything like that ever happens again, you'll have a private tutor, and your classroom will be the office next to mine."

"It won't happen again. I promise." Christian's eyes widened. "I won't let it."

"Make sure of it." Sonny stood for a moment. His face softened as he rubbed the back of his neck. "You want to shoot some hoops?"

A faint smile lit Christian's face. "You're serious?"

"Yeah, come on." Sonny grabbed the basketball off the floor.

They walked out to the court in the backyard. Sonny tossed the ball to Christian.

Christian grabbed it and rested it on his hip. "I'm sorry, Dad."

"I know." Sonny outstretched his arms to defend him. "We play to ten."

Christian smiled. He dribbled the ball, drove to the net, and jumped into a perfect layup.

EIGHT

ZOË GAWKED EVERY TIME she pulled up to Antony's French-style home. Its modern, clean lines and tall square columns gave it a unique look.

Antony's car wasn't in sight, but that didn't mean he wasn't home. He had a five-car garage, and she had never seen one of his three cars parked in front. She killed the engine of her silver PT Cruiser, got out, and walked to the front door.

The floral dress swung high on her thighs. She tugged at the hemline and wished it would miraculously grow in length. Her freshly dyed, blond hair hung straight and fell on her shoulders.

She rang the doorbell then strained to see inside the beveled glass that made up most of the front door. She gave one last tug on her hemline before giving up.

Antony opened the door. His eyes widened. "I can't believe it." He motioned for her to come in. "Super cop, in a dress?" When she stepped into the entryway, he walked around, eyeballing her. "Must be important."

"What?"

"Whatever it is you want from me." He grinned, his dimples deep. "I don't think I've ever seen you look so good."

Heat filled her face. "Thank you . . . I think."

A large wooden arch framed the great room. The walls were painted cream, and the floors were natural wood. Antony walked behind the wet bar. "Can I get you something?"

"No, I'm fine." Zoë's eyes followed the crown molding to a second archway where she could see into the den. She walked toward it, stopped, and leaned against the doorway. Inside was a stone fireplace with numerous trophies of Antony's hunting expeditions. The heads of an antelope, a kudo bull, and a cape buffalo stared down at her. She moved closer and glanced at pictures of Antony that hung on the wall. He stood next to guides and their kills. A shiver ran through her.

"So," Antony said from behind, startling her. "What do you need from me?"

She smiled then turned. "What makes you think I need something?" She walked past him, back into the great room.

The ice in Antony's tumbler clicked against the glass. His cockiness bled through his words. "Because you haven't looked me in the eye since you got here."

She turned to him and tried to act cool, but she did need something from him. That fact gave her a strong desire to slap the grin off his face. "Okay, I need a date for the reception."

"And I came to mind? Don't we love to hate each other?"

Zoë placed both hands on her hips. "You got a date or not?"

Antony sat on the overstuffed black chair and placed the tumbler on the round cherry coffee table. "Why would you ask me?"

"I hate going stag to these big social events." Zoë sat on the gray Bancroft sofa. The taffeta pillows crinkled as she leaned against them. "Besides, I know you're not seeing Lauren anymore."

"Have you been spying on me?"

"No." She crossed her long legs then tugged at the hem of the dress as it crept up her thighs. "We've got a secretary down at the station who is infatuated with one of the richest and most eligible bachelors in the world. Isn't that what people called you? She clips out everything about you then proceeds to fill me in." Zoë flirtatiously flipped her hair over her shoulder. "In fact, she'd die if she knew I was here."

"Maybe I should take her to the reception." The grin never left his face.

"You're going to make me beg?"

"The best of them do."

"Well, you know I won't." She stood, annoyed.

Antony looked up at her. His eyes sparkled. "I could toss around the idea of taking you if you answer a question."

Zoë sat back down. "That will depend on the question."

"What have you heard about Dimitri Romeo?"

"Why are you asking me and not your source at the station?"

"I have." His grin deepened. "But you must know something else because you're trying very hard to impress me, and I'll admit, it's working."

She pursed her lips together as the heat made its way back over her face.

Antony leaned back into the chair. "You and I both know that a man with his past doesn't move into town unnoticed. You got anything on him?"

"If I did, you think I'd tell you?"

"How bad do you want me to go to the reception with you?"

"Not that bad." Zoë hoped it would deflate his ego. She walked to the French doors and stared outside then turned back. He stood and moved closer. She tried to see past his good looks and intrigue and remember he lived only for power, money, and her sister. Her heart pounded harder the closer he got.

He stopped in front of her and stared deep into her eyes. His woodsy cologne was soft, almost unnoticeable, but it was a scent she would never forget.

"I think we're both after the same thing." His voice was alluring.

Zoë licked her lips. Desire flashed in his eyes, and for a second she thought he'd kiss her. Swallowing hard, she finally spoke in a whisper, "And that is?"

One side of his mouth went into a grin as his voice—rough, sexy—said, "Knowing what Dimitri is up to."

"Oh." She brought her hand to her chest in an attempt to hide her pounding heart. She brushed past him and regained her composure. "Yeah. We could help each other out." Flustered at herself for her momentary lapse into his charms, she put on her cop face. "I'm gathering information on him. You know, just checking him out."

"And you thought you could get information from me?"

"You two are friends, aren't you?"

"We knew each other from the old days."

"Do you know why he's in town?"

"The California weather is better for his grandmother. She had cancer you know."

"So I heard." If he knew anything, he wasn't about to share it with her.

"I'll make a deal with you." Antony slid his hand into his pocket. "You go as Zoë Stone. My girlfriend. An interior designer. Not a cop. I'll even recommend you to redecorate Dimitri's house. In return, you fill me in on anything you learn."

Pretending to be Antony Luciano's girlfriend was an assignment any other woman would die for, but she wasn't any other woman. She was Zoë Stone, a cop, and the sister of the woman he loved. "Your girlfriend?"

"Don't trust yourself?"

Heat filled her face. "You're so full of it. Still think every woman is dying to be with you."

"They are."

Zoë shook her head. "Not me."

"Really?" He laughed and sat back down. "Then what's the problem?"

"No problem." Her eyes narrowed. "Okay, I'll pretend to be your girlfriend, but you have to promise to fill me in on anything you learn."

"Deal. I'll pick you up at six-thirty."

Vince, Lorenzo's bodyguard for the past thirty years, sat in a booth in a smoky bar on the south side of LA. His lean face made his high cheekbones prominent. His greasy hair was now speckled with gray. He cracked his knuckles then grimaced in pain. Arthritis. He was getting old.

He had learned long ago that when Lorenzo gave an order, you obeyed. Lorenzo wanted information, and he'd pay well for it. It was Vince's job to find out what he wanted to know.

A large, stocky man walked into the bar. He wore all black, and a cigarette hung from his lips. He glanced around before his eyes settled on Vince.

Vince gave him a single nod, and the man approached.

He sat down, took a long drag on the cigarette, then snubbed it out in the full ashtray. "You got the money?"

"You got the information?"

The man nodded.

Vince reached into his jacket and pulled out an envelope filled with cash. He slid the envelope to the man, leaned in, and listened.

NINE

THE WHITE MULTI-COLUMNED porticoes and entryways gave the Vitale home a Moroccan look. Lavender salvia, yellow Jerusalem sage, and red roses bordered the house. The luscious green grass was so thick it could be mistaken for shag carpet.

Martin pushed the doorbell and waited.

Elisa Vitale, the widow of the late Enrico Vitale, avid art dealer, opened the door. "Hello, Martin." She motioned for him to come in. "My cousin give you some time off?"

She tossed her thick auburn hair highlighted with shades of blond that outlined her face in the style Jennifer Aniston made popular in the nineties. Tall and thin but evenly proportioned, her skin still tan from last summer's sun, she wore tight shorts and a tank top. Small amounts of sweat soaked through her shirt, and she sipped on a bottle of water.

"Sorry to interrupt your workout. Dimitri sent me over."

"What does he want now?" She led him into the house.

"He wanted me to remind you about Friday night."

She stopped and turned to him, arms crossed. Red crept up her slender neck. "Did he send you here to threaten me?"

"No." Martin slid his hands into the pockets of his Wranglers. He leaned into her. "I think he's worried you'll back out. It's great that you're helping him out."

"I'm a saint." They walked into the sunken living room.

The room was stark white, and the undecorated walls gave it a stiff, uncomfortable feel, but it reflected Elisa's innocence. Despite her cousin's criminal record, he knew Elisa was different.

Extracting information from women was easy—he enticed them with his good looks and charm. Elisa, however, never fell for it. She was definitely looking for more than a warm body. She talked of wanting a friend, a companion, someone to love her, and after two months, he felt like he was finally chiseling through her well-guarded heart.

"Do you want a drink?" she asked.

"No."

"I still don't understand why you work for my cousin. You don't seem like the type."

"What type is that?"

"Big and scary like Justice."

Martin nodded at the description of Dimitri's right-hand man. "Justice is one of a kind. You know how he got that scar on his neck?"

"In prison, I heard."

It was courtesy of a fellow inmate at the Missouri Department of Corrections. He'd entered at the age of seventeen and served eight of his fifteen-year sentence.

Elisa walked to the white couch, sat, and curled her legs up under her. "You want to sit, or do you have to get right back?"

"I got a few minutes."

Martin stretched his arms across the back of the couch. His coat flapped open to expose his holstered gun.

She stared at the gun then cut her eyes to his. Stiffening, she stood. "Maybe you should go."

Martin stood. "I'm sorry. Did I do something to—"

"No, no." She set the water down and walked to the front door.

Martin followed her and gently touched her arm, making her turn back to him. He could see her chest pounding. He looked into her eyes and tried to reassure her that he wouldn't hurt her. It didn't work.

He cleared his throat. "Dimitri said he'd pick you up at six."

"Tell him I won't be ready until seven."

Whatever startled her didn't scare her anymore. Now she was angry. Martin mentally rolled his eyes. He'd forgotten. It was all a game.

***

Elisa walked up the stairs to her bedroom. It was white and as cold as the rest of the house. She pulled back the sheers, opened the window, and let the cool breeze wash over her face. She hated being ordered to do anything but feared her cousin's wrath.

She should have turned Dimitri away the day he arrived on her doorstep, but she hadn't been thinking clearly. She'd just buried her husband.

The police had found his body on the beach. It'd been there for weeks, they said. They questioned her, wondering why she hadn't reported him missing. If she hadn't been in shock, she would've laughed. Her husband had been missing their whole marriage.

The sheer flapped in Elisa's face, willing her back to the present. She walked to the dresser and picked up a small wooden jewelry box. When she lifted the lid, it played soft music.

Elisa picked up the faded picture of Antony and brushed her fingers over his image. There was so much unsettled between them. So much love. So much hate. So much unsaid. So much to forgive.

A shudder ran through her. When she'd see him at the reception, he'd either embrace her or loathe her. After what she'd done to him over the years, loathing seemed appropriate.

She replaced the picture and closed the lid—along with any hopes of ever rekindling any kind of friendship with Antony.

Elisa would suffer through the evening because Dimitri was making her. Dimitri. She despised him as much as she had her husband.

***

Sonny tossed the basketball to Christian. "Good game," he said, and they walked into the house.

Rachel's high-pitched voice echoed, "Daddy."

Sonny gave Rachel a hug. "How was cheer?"

"Great, you two been playing basketball?" Rachel asked.

"Yep. You want to go riding?"

"Always," she said, smiling.

"Where's Mom?"

"In your office."

"Go get ready, and we'll go down to the stables."

Rachel ran upstairs as Christian came out of the kitchen and tossed Sonny a bottle of water.

"Thanks. I'm taking Rachel riding. You want to join us?"

"I got homework." Christian walked up a few stairs then turned back. "Thanks, Dad."

Sonny nodded then went into his office. Victoria was sitting behind his desk, staring at the computer screen.

She looked up. "How'd it go with Christian?"

"Good."

"You told him everything?"

"Not everything, but enough."

"Did he steal the artifacts?"

"He didn't confess to it, but I think he did. I can tell he's sorry, and he's promised to stay out of trouble." He took her in his arms and kissed her. "We've been playing basketball. He kicked my butt." He held the back of her neck and pulled her close, savoring the warmth of her beauty. "How'd it go with Antony?"

"He gave me the name of a professional fundraiser. I called her, and she's agreed to help organize our Christmas project. We meet with her next week."

"Tell Clay, and I'll be there."

"It's already on your calendar."

He heard Rachel's faint giggling, a reminder that he'd promised to take her riding. He nibbled on Victoria's neck.

The phone interrupted them.

"Let Clay get it," she whispered.

He glanced over her shoulder. "It's my private line. He won't." He felt her tense up. There were only two people who called on his private line, Antony or Lorenzo.

"I promise, no business tonight. Just you, me, and the kids, and we'll send them to their rooms early." He smiled and raised his eyebrows.

"Promise?"

Sonny nodded and grabbed the phone. "Yeah. Just a minute." Sonny put his brother on hold then looked at Victoria. "It's Antony. Will you take Rachel down to the stables? I told her I'd take her riding before dinner. I'll meet you down there."

"No business. You promised."

"I know." Sonny held her hand as she walked away. When she tried to release it, he pulled her back to him and kissed her again.

"Your phone call," she said in an edgy voice. "Don't want to keep your brother waiting."

Groaning, he buried his face in her neck before finding her lips again. "It'll only take a minute."

"Sure."

His heart pounded as she strolled out of the room. He put the phone to his ear. "Yeah."

"I just got a very interesting visit from Zoë."

"Zoë?" Sonny rounded the desk so he could see out the window. Victoria walked next to Rachel. As if sensing him, she turned to the window and blew him a kiss.

Antony cleared his throat. "You there?"

"I'm here." Sonny stared at his wife. "What'd Zoë want?"

"Information on Dimitri."

That brought him back to the chair. He sat down. "She know something we don't?"

"Nothing she'd tell me. I'm taking her to the reception as my date. Thought I'd recommend her to redecorate Dimitri's new place. Maybe she can find out if he's up to something. Don't let Dimitri know she's a cop."

"Zoë agree to this?"

"Yeah. Tell Vic."

"Anything else?"

After a long pause, Antony spoke. "You told Vic the truth?"

"Yeah. It seemed the right time."

"Just make sure she doesn't say a word to anyone about it." Antony almost shouted, "Did you hear me?"

"Yeah, I heard you."

"If it gets back to Dimitri, he'll come after you. Make sure she understands that."

The realization stung. Guilt washed over Sonny, but he pushed it away. "I'll tell her." Sonny hung up the phone and walked down to the stables. He brought his foot up and rested it on the gate of the corral. Rachel rode her rose-colored Fox Trotter.

Victoria leaned in to him. "What'd Antony want?"

"He's bringing Zoë to the reception."

"How'd that happen?"

"Dad!" Rachel shouted. "Watch this."

Rachel instructed her horse into a perfect foxtrot. The front hoof hit the ground a split second before the opposite rear hoof, then a slight pause before she did it again with the other diagonal hoofs. The hoofs ka-chunk, ka-chunked in a perfect cadence and rhythm.

"That's great." Sonny clapped. "I'm hungry. Let's go eat."

"Good idea," Victoria said.

Rachel led the horse to the gate. Victoria reached up and grabbed the reins. Rachel slid off the saddle. "I'll take her to the barn." Rachel took the reins from her mother, and they walked the horse out of the corral.

Victoria looked at Rachel. "We'll take the saddle off and get Cinnamon in the field. Why don't you head on up to the house and get washed up? You can help me cook dinner."

"Okay." Rachel took off toward the house.

Sonny walked the horse into the stall.

Victoria stared at him. "So?"

"What?"

"Your brother and my sister?"

"Oh, yeah." Sonny poured a scoop of wheat into the metal bucket for Cinnamon to eat while he loosened the girth. He pulled the saddle off and set it on the sawhorse outside the stable.

"It seems your sister asked Antony out." He slid the plaid blanket from Cinnamon's back and tossed it over the saddle, then took a tan block brush and began grooming the horse as she ate.

"On a date? No way."

"Well, sort of. It seems she's interested in Dimitri."

"Why?"

"I guess she wants to make sure he's legit."

"I thought you said he was."

"We think he is." Sonny tossed the brush in the bucket. "Can't be too careful, though." He grabbed the rope and led the horse out of the stall. Cinnamon pushed her nose toward Sonny's side, knowing that was where he usually kept a treat. Sonny patted her neck. "No carrots tonight."

Cinnamon nodded her head up and down as if she thought Sonny was lying.

Sonny opened the palm of his hand and placed it under her mouth, allowing her to nibble on it. "I don't have anything." He rubbed Cinnamon's face then led her to the gate, took off the halter, and gave her a gentle pat on her rear. She trotted out into the open field. Sonny shut the gate, hung the halter on the post, and then wrapped his arms around Victoria.

"Did Zoë know anything about Dimitri?"

"Nope." He moved her hair away from her face. "But Antony wanted us to know she's going to the party as an interior designer, not a cop, at least to Dimitri."

"Interesting."

"Isn't it, though?" He kissed her neck, her ear, then her lips. "Now, don't we have some unfinished business?"

"Mom." Rachel's voice echoed over from the porch.

"And it'll have to wait until after dinner."

Sonny laughed. He kept his arm around her as they walked to the house.

TEN

LIGHTS CASCADED UP THE LARGE fountain that sat in the center courtyard of the new Francesca's just north of Ventura. The evening air was brisk for late September, and the setting sun filled the sky with shards of purple, orange, and red. The brilliant colors bounced off the four stories of semicircular glass that made up the front of Francesca's. On both sides of the circular form were connecting buildings three stories high which held the exquisite clothing store. Corporate offices occupied the fourth floor.

Victoria stood in the center of the store underneath the teardrop chandelier. The small lights that wrapped the banisters reflected off the mirrors that backdropped the ceiling and sent thousands of twinkling stars throughout the atrium.

Victoria brushed away the few curled strands of hair that outlined her face. The rest of her hair was slicked into a tight ponytail with the emerging hair formed into large curls that sat high on her head. The ankle-length black velvet dress had a sweetheart neckline that showed off her new sapphire necklace from the Bahamas.

Three rings adorned her fingers—a three-carat diamond wedding band, the two-carat sapphire and diamond ring, and the simple blue topaz her mother had given her. On her wrist was a black baby Fendi watch, a Christmas present from Antony the year before. Diamonds surrounded the one-inch gold rectangle face.

Sonny stood by her side as they greeted guests in the middle of the large marble foyer near one of three water sculptures. He looked sinful in his double-breasted black Lubiam tuxedo. His thick black hair was combed back, and his stark white shirt made his bronze skin glow.

Victoria was leading one of her favorite clients to a newly displayed dress when her eyes were drawn to the etched glass doors through which she saw Antony getting out of his limo. His entire black tux, shirt, and tie fit his devious demeanor. She smiled when Zoë stepped out and slid her arm through his.

Victoria excused herself and went outside to the red carpet to meet them. She hugged Zoë. "You look beautiful. That color is good with your skin tone."

Zoë straightened the three-layer plum dress. "Thanks. I'm a designer, you know." Zoë grinned and clutched the small handbag that hung off her shoulder.

Reporters pushed their way toward Victoria. One yelled, "Is it true about your husband's past?"

Antony turned and held his hands out. "Back up. She's not answering any questions."

Before Victoria knew it, Doc's arms were around her, pushing her through the crowd. "Come on," Doc shouted over the flying questions. Flash bulbs went off so fast they momentarily blinded her.

"Was your store financed with mob money?" someone yelled.

Victoria raised her hand, shielding her eyes. "Of course not," she shouted. "We have no connections with the mob."

"Inside." Doc forced her into the store while security pushed back the paparazzi and closed the doors.

"You okay?" Antony touched her arm.

"Yeah," Victoria said and scanned the room until she spotted Sonny talking with a client.

As if sensing her turmoil, Sonny looked over and smiled. Doc made his way to him and whispered in his ear. The smile left his face. He nodded, excused himself, and walked toward her.

"Doc told me what happened." Sonny wrapped his arms around her and pulled her close.

"They asked if my store was financed with mob money. Mob money. Can you believe that?"

He continued to hold her. "Don't let them ruin your evening."

She basked in his strength. She took a deep breath, held it momentarily, then let it out and relaxed. "I won't."

"If you'd let me send over some of my guys," Antony said, "They'd take care of the paparazzi."

"I'm sure they would, but our guys will take care of it." Victoria looked over at Zoë. "I'm so glad you came. Let me give you a tour."

"Vic," Sonny said, pointing at a tall man in the corner. "There's a gentleman who has been waiting to meet you. Says he's from Versace."

"Okay. Sorry, Zoë. Antony will have to show you around. He knows the store like the back of his hand."

"Now why doesn't that surprise me?" Zoë took Antony's extended arm.

***

Dimitri walked around the store. He pretended to admire the clothes all the while looking around at the different artifacts. Victoria had a keen sense of art, and he was thankful. Her store was the perfect front for his stolen artwork.

He slowly moved down to the tall blonde who stood admiring a bronze Chinese pitcher. The beaker should've been with it.

He chewed on the unlit cigar. "That's a replica from the Shang Dynasty. 1200 BC."

"Really?" Zoë's head tilted. "Are you an admirer of the Chinese art?"

"Not really. I read it on the card." He grinned before holding out his large hand. "Dimitri Romeo."

"Zoë Stone." They shook. She reached into her satin purse and pulled out a business card. "Interior Designs."

"You help with all of this?"

"I wish." She flipped her hair off her shoulders. "I'm here with Antony Luciano."

"Antony is a good friend of mine. Where is he?" Dimitri looked around.

"He's getting me a drink." Zoë pointed to the corner where Antony stood. He held two glasses of wine. A man talked to him. She walked to the next artifact. "What do you know about this one?"

"The Chinese horse?" Dimitri leaned over and read off the card. "It symbolizes flight and immortality, also from the Shang Dynasty." He looked up at her before he stood straight. "You think that says something about Mrs. Luciano?"

She shrugged her shoulders. "They're interesting, though."

Dimitri looked around. His eyes fell upon the Rembrandt. Everyone believed it to be a replica, but in reality, it was deemed priceless. He had already sold it for fifty million. Then there was the Vermeer that hung safely on the second floor, estimated value, seventy-five million. The only thing he couldn't find was the beaker worth millions.

Zoë touched his arm. "If you need any decorating done, please call."

"I'll let you know." As she walked away, he stared back at the bronze pitcher, wondering where the beaker could be.

Lorenzo's voice came from behind him. "Dimitri?"

Dimitri turned, looked down, and extended his hand. "Lorenzo. How have you been?"

"Fine. How's Genevra?"

"Doing well, thank you."

Lorenzo motioned for Dimitri to come closer. When Dimitri leaned in, Lorenzo whispered, "You cross my family, I'll have you killed."

Dimitri bellowed out a laugh. "Still feisty in your old age." He placed his hand on Lorenzo's shoulder and squeezed it tightly. Revenge for his parents would come, but he'd play along with Lorenzo. No harm done. "I'm here as a friend."

Lorenzo's eyes narrowed. He stared at Dimitri for a long moment before he gave him a single nod then motioned for Vince to wheel him away.

Dimitri scanned the room. He had to find that ten-inch high, two-pound beaker.

***

Antony stared at Victoria. The lights glistened on her auburn hair and showed off the red highlights. A few strands of hair fell softly on her face, accentuating her high cheekbones. The black velvet dress deepened her already tan skin. The watch he'd bought her sparkled on her wrist. He grinned, pleased that a part of him was with her. He could still smell the sweet floral scent of her perfume.

His obsession with her grew daily. He tried to push her out of his thoughts, but it was impossible. Loving his brother's wife was not something he was proud of. Guilt plagued him. He grunted. Guilt? Was it possible he was growing a conscience after all these years?

He shook his head and sipped the wine. He wished he could have something harder, something that would momentarily numb him. After all, it was all he had.

***

Victoria could sense Antony's eyes. She looked at him, and heat filled her face. He had a way of making her feel excited and sinful in the same moment.

Sonny leaned into her. "I'll be right back." He disappeared.

She looked back where Antony had been, but he was gone. She scanned the crowd when her eyes stopped on a large man. His long black hair fell past his shoulders and laid awkwardly on the black tuxedo jacket.

Victoria walked toward him. She outstretched her hand and was about to speak when Antony locked his arm through hers.

"Dimitri," Antony smiled. "Glad you could make it."

He gave Antony a nod then looked at her. "You must be Victoria, Sonny's wife." Dimitri's voice was gruff. He took her hand and shook it. "Dimitri Romeo. It's so nice to finally meet you. Where's Sonny?"

"He's around here somewhere." Victoria turned to Antony. "Would you go find him?"

Antony hesitated. She reprimanded him with her eyes, and he walked to Doc, leaned in, and whispered something before he disappeared to find his brother.

Victoria looked back at Dimitri. "Have you been upstairs to the men's department?"

"Not yet. I'm intrigued by your taste in art." He motioned to the Chinese display. "How did you discover the Chinese culture?"

"My aunt used to be a missionary in China. She couldn't openly share Christ, so she taught English at one of the universities, which allowed her to teach American culture, including religion. She used to send us artifacts when I was a young girl. These are some of my favorites." She touched the tops of the cases where the wine pitcher and the horse sat.

Dimitri stepped closer and pointed to the case with the wine pitcher in it. "A beaker would look good in there. Have you seen pictures of them? They're similar to wine goblets."

"I'm impressed. Not very many people are that familiar with the Shang Dynasty. I think you're right. I should add to it." *Or find the beaker I already paid for.*

A tall, slender woman dressed in a straight black dress walked up to them.

"Victoria," Dimitri said. "I'd like you to meet my cousin, Elisa Vitale."

Victoria outstretched her hand and shook Elisa's. "Nice to meet you. Vitale. Are you the same Vitale that owns Speranza Art Gallery in Monterey?"

"My husband did. I sold it after he was killed."

"I was sorry to hear he died. I never met him, but I bought a few prints from the gallery." The rumors that surrounded his death had made for one heck of a clearance sale.

Sonny extended his hand to Dimitri. "I'm glad you could make it. I see you met . . ." His eyes widened as he grinned. "Elisa? It's been years. Come here." Sonny hugged her. "Have you seen Antony? Does he know you're here?"

"No."

Sonny leaned into Victoria. "Elisa was the love of Antony's life."

"Sonny." Elisa's gaze flickered uncomfortably. She turned to Victoria. "That was years ago."

"I'm glad you're here. We'll give you a tour, and it'll give us a chance to catch up." Sonny motioned toward the stairs. Dimitri followed.

Elisa turned to Victoria. "You guys go ahead."

"Are you sure?"

"Really, you'd be doing me a favor. Tell Sonny I'll talk to him later."

"Okay."

Victoria walked to Sonny and slid her hand through his arm. They climbed up the stairs to the second floor.

***

Antony sipped his wine and scanned the room. His eyes narrowed. Elisa. He couldn't believe it. It would be just like her to come with Dimitri.

It had been almost a year since he'd ridden in to rescue her, like he had so many times, only to have her do what she always did — slam the door in his face. What did she think? Could he let her walk back into his life now that her husband was dead? No. Never again.

He set the wine down and walked straight to her. "Elisa, what a surprise." His fists clenched. "I read you're finally free of your husband."

"I never wanted him dead." She said almost in a whisper. "I'm sorry for the way I spoke to you the last time I saw you. It's just, I couldn't go with you. I couldn't leave him."

"Yeah. It was much better staying with a man who had *accidentally* thrown you down the stairs, again. How long did you take his abuse? Twelve, fifteen years? I'm sure you were happy some of the time."

"As a matter of fact, we were."

Antony shot her a dark look.

"Can we just forget the past and start over? Maybe we could go out for dinner and talk. I'd like to explain."

Antony was about to be Antony, say something cold and uncaring, when Zoë gently touched his arm. A welcomed relief. He would refuse to let Elisa suck him into any of her games. He put his arm around Zoë. "Where'd you run off to?"

"I was around." Zoë wrapped her arm around his waist, playing the part of a girlfriend perfectly. "Did you miss me?"

"Always." He grinned. "I want you to meet an old friend. This is Elisa. Elisa, Zoë."

Zoë reached out her hand. "Nice to meet you."

"And you." Elisa tucked her hair behind her ears. "Nice to see you again, Antony." She turned and disappeared into the crowd.

Antony brushed past Zoë.

Zoë followed. "Whoa, talk about tension. Who was that?"

Antony's eyes cut to her in anger.

"Sorry." Zoë walked around him. "You need a drink?"

"I need a life."

"I thought your life revolved around my sister."

He wasn't about to respond to that.

"Don't look now, but Elisa is staring at you."

Antony grabbed Zoë's neck, pulled her to him, and kissed her, long and hard.

"Wow."

He looked down at her, his left hand still around her waist, his right hand holding her neck. "She still staring?" he asked, his voice deep.

Zoë looked past him. "Nope. That did it."

"Good."

He took Zoë's hand. As they went up to the second floor, he passed Elisa. She turned quickly from him but not before he saw the tears in her eyes.

Leave it alone.

He forced his heart to harden.

***

"Come here." Sonny held Victoria's hand and led her between the racks of Armani suits.

"What?" She giggled like a high school girl.

He stopped and pulled her close. "You look so beautiful tonight." He kissed her.

She pulled away from him. Forgetting about the guests, she became entranced by his eyes. "You look pretty good yourself." She wiped the traces of her lipstick off his lips with her thumb.

"The store's going to be a huge success," he said.

"I think so, too."

He pulled her closer and kissed her more passionately.

"Um . . ." Doc cleared his throat. "Excuse me."

"Perfect timing." Sonny sighed and turned to him. "Did my brother send you?"

"I'm sure Doc has a very good reason for interrupting us." She turned to him. "Don't you Doc?"

"Yes. Francesca Muse just arrived."

"Oh, yes." Victoria smiled. "Thank you."

Sonny scanned the store. "There." He pointed.

They went to greet the original creator of Francesca's.

***

Francesca's was empty of guests. He'd waited two hours for the cleaners to get the store ready for the first day of business. It was three a.m. He had plenty of time.

Replaying the layout of the store in his head, he remembered what he was told about the security system. He'd seen most of it earlier while he mingled with the guests.

He looked around and eased the black suburban into the loading dock. The all-black turtleneck, pants, and leather gloves gave him the assurance that he wouldn't be detected. He adjusted the stocking cap then double checked to see if his Colt, handcuffs, and key were still there.

Slipping around to the side door, he slid the key into the lock. The door opened, and he punched the code into the alarm system and turned it off.

He slid along the wall, pulled the cap over his face, and gave his hands a rub. He ducked under the camera, slipped up the stairwell to the main offices, and waited for the security guard to emerge. Even though the alarm was shut off, a flashing light would acknowledge that someone had entered the store.

He ducked into a doorway and waited. The guard emerged and stood in the hallway. After the guard looked both ways, he pulled the long flashlight out of his belt, flipped it on, and chose a direction to walk. Unknowingly, the security guard walked toward him.

As the guard came to the doorway, the man raised his gun and pounded it full force against the guard's head. He fell to the floor like a limp doll. The man reached under the guard's arms and slowly pulled him into the men's restroom and handcuffed his arms behind his back. He then ran to the security room, shut off all the cameras, and ran back down to the main floor.

He scanned the first floor. His eyes stopped on the beautifully framed picture. *The Storm of Galilee*. He walked closer and looked at the rudder where, if it were the original, it would have an inscription by Rembrandt himself.

"Bingo," he whispered.

He scooted a chair over, climbed up, and took the picture from the wall. He carried it to the second floor where the second picture was. Leaning the Rembrandt against the wall, he reached up and grabbed *The Concert* painted by Vermeer.

With both paintings in hand, he made his way to the back of the store, his heart pounding. He opened the door and looked around before slipping out on the dock and down the stairs to his suburban.

He slipped the paintings in the back, ran to the driver's side, climbed in, and took off. Once out of the lot and along the road, he turned on his lights.

He clutched the steering wheel, his heart steadying. *Piece of cake.*

ELEVEN

HEAT CREPT UP ANTONY'S NECK as he loosened his silk tie and unbuttoned the top button of his white shirt. He clenched his fists at the single nail and empty wall where a picture had hung the night before.

Sonny, holding Victoria's hand, spoke to the police. They stood in the same spot Elisa had been the night before. The only two ladies he'd ever given his heart to. Both had rejected him. Antony rolled his eyes as he turned back to the wall. "Women."

"Sonny'll be a few more minutes," Doc said.

Antony turned, and the lines on his forehead deepened. "What kind of security are you running here?"

"I've already been through this with Victoria and Sonny. I don't need it from you."

Antony grabbed Doc and shoved him against the wall. "I asked you a question."

"We've got a top-notch security system."

"Really?" Antony pushed Doc harder against the wall. "Then how'd someone get in and rob the store again?"

"I don't know." Doc's jaw was tight.

The loud clicking of Victoria's boots drew Antony's attention away from Doc.

She grabbed Antony's arm. "Let go of him."

He released Doc and turned to her. "He's head of your security, and you've been robbed twice." Antony glared at Doc. "Find out who and why."

Doc stood tall, his face hard. "I plan on it."

Victoria tugged at Antony's arm, which brought him around to face her. "He answers to me and Sonny. What's wrong with you?"

"Nothing."

Victoria looked at the empty space where the picture had hung. "Doc." She unbuttoned her long, rust-colored tweed jacket and placed her hands on her hips. "Have someone go buy pictures to cover the empty spots. We can't open like this."

Doc's eyes cut back to Antony's as he readjusted the navy suit jacket then smoothed down his yellow silk tie. "Sure thing."

***

Sonny glanced from the officer to Antony. He gave the policeman a cordial nod then came up behind Victoria and Antony. He touched Victoria's elbow, which made her turn.

"What'd the police say?" she asked.

"They're still checking for prints. They should be out of here within the hour."

"Any idea who would do this?"

"No." Sonny leaned into Victoria. "I need to talk to my brother."

"Okay. I've got a hundred things to do before the store opens."

He waited until she was out of earshot before turning to Antony, who pulled a toothpick from inside his jacket.

"I got on to Doc." Antony rolled the toothpick around in his mouth.

"I saw."

"You can't have a break-in and not get angry at the head of your security. The computer, the artifacts, now this?"

"I know. I'm just as angry as you are."

"It doesn't seem like it. We've got three million dollars invested in this store. If Doc was doing his job, he'd have already caught the punks from the last robbery. It was probably them."

Sonny hated the reminder of what his son had done, but he knew Christian had nothing to do with this. He turned to the empty spot on the wall. "Who would take two paintings? They're not worth more than a few hundred dollars."

"Unless you tighten up security, they'll take a lot more next time."

"You don't have to constantly remind me of what I need to do."

"You've gotten soft, and if you don't put Doc in his place, I will." Antony threw the toothpick on the floor. "I'll keep doing the dirty work, and you can live in your sinless, spotless, imaginary life. My shoulders are broad."

Sonny reached out and grabbed Antony's arm. "You'll do nothing."

Antony ripped his arm from his brother's hand, turned, and brushed past Zoë as she walked toward them.

"Hey," Zoë said. Antony didn't give her a first look, let alone a second one. "And I thought we had fun last night," she yelled, but Antony ignored her.

Zoë turned to Sonny. "What's with him?"

"I don't know." He looked at his watch. "I've got to get to a meeting."

"You can be late. I need to ask you a few things." Zoë led him to one of the corners of the store and pulled out her notepad and pen. "You think this robbery is connected to the last one?"

"You think Christian did this?" Sonny raked his fingers through his hair. "You seriously think he knocked out the security guard and cuffed him?"

"I'm just asking. It's got to be someone who had access to a key and the security code."

"Christian was home all night. If he snuck out, believe me, I'd know."

"I'm trying to figure this out, and this is an angle the uniforms don't know about. Could Christian have gotten access to the security code then told that other kid . . ." She looked at her notepad. "Russ?"

"I suppose anything is possible, but explain this . . . with everything in here, they'd decide to steal two large pictures? Russ is seventeen. What's he want with two pictures that Victoria only paid a few hundred dollars for? Heck, the frames were worth more than the prints."

"Some kids do it for the thrill of stealing."

"I won't accuse my son. He wasn't involved."

"I'm not asking you to accuse him. Just find out if he knows anything. In the meantime, I'll check the pawnshop where they hawked the other stuff. If it was them, we might get lucky and they'll go back to the same place."

"Get lucky?" Sonny snapped. "Do me a favor. Don't mention your suspicions to Victoria."

"All right." Zoë tapped her pen on the pad. "The uniforms told me what the pictures were called. What'd they look like?"

"*The Storm of Galilee* is a picture of Jesus and his disciples on a boat in a storm. *The Concert* is of a woman playing a piano. You want more details, you'll have to ask Vic." Sonny looked back down at his watch. "I really need to go."

Zoë chewed on the inside of her cheek. "Sure thing. I'll call you if I find out anything."

***

Zoë threw her keys on the kitchen table of her small rented house on the beach. It was nothing to brag about except the beach part, but it suited her. Two bedrooms, one for her bed and one for everything else.

She had struck out at the pawnshops. Opening the fridge, she knew she'd strike out there, too. Stale bread, moldy carrots from her momentary attempt to eat healthy, and soured milk. She slammed the fridge door, her stomach growling.

She pushed the speaker button on the phone then hit speed dial. She kicked her shoes off and flipped through the mail. When her favorite pizza restaurant answered, she ordered the usual—supreme minus onions, thick crust, extra cheese.

Landlines were old fashioned, but it worked perfectly for her design company. Zoë turned the speaker on and played her messages. One hang-up and one computerized telemarketer. She fell on the couch, lay her head back, and closed her eyes.

She shot up, her eyes wide. *The Storm of Galilee*? She grabbed her briefcase and pulled out the file on Dimitri Romeo. Dabbing the tips of her fingers on her tongue, she began to leaf through the papers in the file until she got to the list of artifacts stolen in the Boston Museum heist.

The Degas were listed first: *La Sortie Du Pelage*, *Cortege Aux Environs De Florence*, *Three Mounted Jockeys*, and two *Program for an Artistic Soiree*. There was Monet's *Chez Tortoni* . . . and then she saw it—Vermeer's *The Concert*. Her heart pounded. Next were the Rembrandt's—*A Lady and A Gentleman in Black*, *Self Portrait* and *The Storm of Galilee*.

She gasped as she tossed the folder on the coffee table.

Was Francesca's the drop? Had Dimitri planted the originals and the buyer stolen them? But whoever stole the paintings had access to a key and the security code.

She rubbed her bottom lip and frowned. Antony? He might be a lot of things, but an art thief? A small pounding began on the left side of her head.

The landline rang, startling her. She reached across the couch and grabbed it. "Yeah, hello?"

"Ms. Stone?"

"Yes."

"Dimitri Romeo. How are you?"

Zoë's heart pounded. "I'm doing all right."

She jumped up, did a quick pace of the room, then sat at the kitchen table and drew imaginary circles on top, taking long, deep breaths. She loved being undercover.

"I bought a house for my grandmother a few months back. She's pretty eccentric, but I think you could liven the place up. Antony says you do good work. You interested?"

"Sure. I could meet you tomorrow. You live here in Ventura?" She jotted down the address even though she already knew it because it was in the file.

"How about ten?" Dimitri asked.

"I'll be there." She hung up the phone and grinned. This was just the break she needed.

***

Dimitri sat back in the chair of the overpriced, outdated Southern Colonial on the other side of town. He wasn't particularly fond of the house, but redecorating it would keep his grandmother off his back.

Biting down hard on the cigar, he lit it. The room filled with smoke.

"Put that out," his grandmother ordered as she walked around the corner. She waved her finger at him. "I just got rid of one cancer. You think I need another?"

"Cigar smoke is the least of your worries."

"My worries?" Genevra heckled. "My only worry is whether you will get the job done."

"Don't start on me."

"You can't get anything right." She waved her arms in the air, her overstretched skin flapping around as she shouted. "Killing Enrico wasn't the smartest thing you've ever done. He did hook you up with the art buyer."

"One bullet saved us ten million. How stupid was that?"

"You left your cousin a widow."

"I did Elisa a favor."

"Stupid, I tell you." She walked into the kitchen then returned. "When will you finish this brilliant plan of yours?"

"Soon."

"Soon? Means you got nothing." She stormed out.

Old biddy. He could hear her slamming pots and pans and cursing.

He puffed on his cigar and flipped on the TV. He'd settled in the chair when a local news brief flashed on the screen.

Victoria Luciano came on, a microphone shoved in her face. "Yes, we had two pictures stolen. No merchandise, no cash, and no damage."

The reporter went on to mention the two replicas that were stolen, *The Storm of Galilee* and *The Concert*.

The cigar fell from Dimitri's mouth. The burning tobacco made him jump. He grabbed the cigar and brushed the hot ashes from his stomach.

Genevra scurried from the kitchen, a stained wooden spoon in her hands. "Did he just say what I thought he said?"

"Shut up, Grandma." Dimitri's heart pounded as sweat beaded on his forehead.

Genevra cackled. "I knew you'd mess this up."

He pushed himself up from the chair, turned to her, and pointed the cigar at her. "I don't need this from you, old woman."

"Now I'm an old woman. If you'd have listened to me in the first place—"

"Be quiet." His voice raised an octave. "I'm sick of you telling me what I should've done."

She smacked her wooden spoon hard against his arm.

"Ouch."

"Respect, boy." Her eyes grew hard. "No games. Get the paintings, get the money, and kill the Lucianos. Those are not tough orders. If you can't do it, I'll find someone who can."

She swung herself around and walked back into the kitchen.

Dimitri's chest pounded so hard it was beginning to hurt. He walked to the window, taking deep breaths. Who would steal the paintings?

***

The small Italian restaurant was colorful and fancy. Elegant pictures of Italy hung on the walls. Sinatra tunes piped through the dining room.

Dimitri wiped his mouth with the white linen napkin and pushed away his almost empty plate. He leaned into Antony. "I've got a problem."

Antony got out a toothpick and bit down on it. "I figured this wasn't a social call."

"I gotta tell you something, and you . . ." Dimitri pointed a finger at him. "You gotta remember you owe me."

"What?"

Dimitri leaned in and motioned for Antony to come closer. He cracked his knuckles. "Those two paintings stolen from Francesca's. They were originals I'd gotten my hands on."

"Originals?" Antony raised an eyebrow but kept the rest of his face emotionless. One thing he'd learned from years on the street, never act surprised.

"Yeah, worth a couple million."

"I knew you going legit was too good to be true."

"This was my last deal. I swear."

Antony nodded in disbelief. "How'd you get them in the store?"

"One of my men hacked into the computers and saw what Victoria was ordering. It gave us a feel for her taste in art. Then when she came up to Enrico's gallery, we just happened to have a couple of paintings on sale."

"You hacked into the computers then sold Victoria stolen artwork?"

"Pretty smooth, huh?"

"Did you kill Enrico?"

"No, I hooked up with an art broker, Ferdinand. Enrico tried to double-cross him, and Ferdinand killed him."

Antony's heart pounded, but he kept his breathing steady. "What do you need from me?"

"The paintings. I've got to get them back." Dimitri leaned into him. "Ferdinand has already sold them. I'm supposed to deliver 'em."

Antony leaned back in the chair. He wouldn't be sucked back into Dimitri's world. Not again. "You'll have to wait and see if the police turn them up. If they're returned to the store, they're all yours."

"Ferdinand wants them now."

"Tell him there's been a delay."

"I can't. He's already paid me some of the money." Dimitri pulled a handkerchief from the inside of his pocket and wiped the sweat from his forehead. "Okay, a lot of the money. If I don't produce those paintings, the cops will find me with a bullet in my head."

Antony studied Dimitri. Not only were his hands shaking, but his chest was pounding, and sweat was already reappearing on his forehead. Could his old friend actually be scared of someone?

"Did Ferdinand know where the paintings were?"

"No. He wanted to keep his hands clean."

Dimitri looked up as the waitress approached. He sat back in the chair. When she was gone, he leaned back in. "There's one other thing."

"It just keeps getting better."

"There was a small beaker. It looked like a wine glass. A goblet. The one Victoria bought in the Bahamas."

Antony's stomach tightened. "You followed her to the Bahamas?"

"Enrico suggested the shop in the Bahamas, and when she bought it, we switched the fake for the original."

"I don't think the beaker ever arrived from the Bahamas. I haven't seen it at the store."

"Can you check?"

"You said the paintings were worth a couple million? I don't buy it. You could wire Ferdinand that kind of money out of your Swiss account." Antony raised an eyebrow, presuming Dimitri hadn't squandered all of his millions.

Dimitri looked around the restaurant then back at Antony. "Okay, they're worth a lot more. He's already sold one for fifty mill. Just find them, and I'll cut you in."

"I don't want in."

"You owe me."

Heat instantly inflamed Antony's neck. "You'd use that?"

"I took care of that lunatic for you and paid your debt to Vito. Vito would've killed you if I hadn't paid him off."

"I wouldn't have owed Vito the money if you hadn't strangled the guy I was collecting from."

Antony could still see the dead man in the dumpster. It was bad enough Dimitri killed the guy, but it was Antony they tried to pin the murder on. After six months in jail, Dimitri's hired lawyer and missing evidence freed him. Dimitri claimed it was the least he could do for taking the rap, but Antony knew better. Dimitri liked the idea of having Antony indebted to him.

"Antony, I need the beaker and those paintings, or I'm dead."

"You're serious."

"You think I'd share this money if I didn't have to?"

"No, I don't." It was true. Dimitri wouldn't share a penny with his closest relative if it didn't serve his purpose.

"And it's not just me I'm worried about, it's my grandmother, Elisa, and you guys."

"Why us?"

"Because if the missing items don't turn up soon, I'll have to explain why there's a delay. Ferdinand may just think you and Sonny were involved."

Antony's jaw tightened. "Don't threaten me."

"I ain't threatening. I'm just telling you how it is."

Antony did a mental eye roll. Dimitri had done it again. He'd sucked him into his sordid world. By killing Enrico, Ferdinand proved his intentions. Antony sipped on his drink. No matter how he played it, Ferdinand would think he and Sonny were involved. He'd have to find the paintings and get Ferdinand and Dimitri out of his life forever.

Only one question bothered him. Was this Dimitri's way of getting revenge? If carried out properly, it was a perfect plan. Tell Ferdinand that he and Sonny took the paintings, Ferdinand would kill them, and Dimitri's hands were clean.

He'd have to play this very carefully. Antony gave Dimitri a reassuring nod. "I'll see what I can find out."

Dimitri's shoulders began to relax. "Thank you."

"This will make us even."

"Yes, yes, anything. Just find the paintings and that beaker."

***

Dimitri got into the car. Justice slammed the door and trotted to the driver's side. His entire outfit was black, including the driving gloves.

Dimitri pulled a Cuban cigar from his pocket and bit down on it. "He bought it."

"And?"

"Torch my place in three days as planned."

"Will your grandmother be gone?"

"Who cares?" Dimitri flicked the lighter and puffed deeply on the cigar, a grin painted on his face.

TWELVE

NED THREW THE BOOKS inside his locker then slammed the metal door shut. "Come on. You gotta go with us."

"Surfing? Now?" Christian chewed on the inside of his cheek. Muted voices from fellow classmates tried to drown out the words of warning that danced in his head. "Man, I get caught, I'm dead. They're still not over us stealing that stuff."

"They ever come out and say you did it?"

"No."

"They ask you about that wine glass looking thing?"

"No."

"Then they don't really think you did it."

Christian leaned against the lockers. "I don't know."

"Oh, come on, how long you been outta trouble?"

"A week."

"That's a record. It's just a couple of classes. Russ will pick us up at the side door. Tex will never be the wiser." Ned put his arm around Christian. "Picture those glassy emerald peaks and us doing an awesome aerial or stylish layback."

"You couldn't do a layback if your life depended on it."

"You in?"

"I don't have my wet suit."

"Russ has an extra."

Christian hesitated, but he wasn't stupid. He knew fall delivered the best waves. "Okay. I'm in."

"Yeah." Ned pulled out his cell phone. "I'll text Russ. Meet me at the south door after class."

***

Russ and Ned straddled their surfboards. Christian lay face down and paddled fiercely, chasing the incoming wave. He heard Russ yell, "You'll never get her done. That wave's weak."

Weak? He'd show them. As it rose, Christian got to his feet, his adrenaline rushing. Just as he got his balance, the wave crested, jumped over his back, and smacked him down.

Christian dove into the water and heard the muffled laughter of Russ and Ned. He swam up to the surface and treaded water. "That wave was mush!" Christian swam toward his surfboard. He pulled himself up on the board and straddled it.

Russ and Ned laughed.

"Yeah, well at least I tried it. Where were you?"

"That wave was deteriorating fast," Russ shouted. "Only a kook would've tried to hit it."

Christian jammed his palm into the ocean and shot a strong stream of water at Russ's face.

Ned jerked his head at the shore. "Looks like we got company."

"Oh, no." Christian's heart pounded. His dad and Bruno leaned against the black Escalade. Both men wore dark sunglasses. His father's arms were crossed. "That's totally my luck. I get busted skipping when the surf starts really pumping." Christian leaned over and paddled to shore.

"Stay cool, man," Russ yelled.

Christian jumped off the board and dragged it along the sand. He looked up at his father, tucked the surfboard under his arm, and walked to the car.

Sonny threw a towel at him.

Christian brushed the towel across his hair then draped it around his neck. "Look, I'm—"

"I don't want to hear it." Sonny's face reddened. "Get changed."

Christian reached into the bed of Ned's truck and pulled out his clothes. He peeled the wetsuit off his arms then pushed it down around his waist. He looked over at his father's hard, angry face. There was no way to talk his way out of this one. Russ and Ned's screaming made him turn toward the ocean. *Now the waves are punching.*

Christian pulled his shirt on then ran his hand through his hair. He scoped the area for cops before wrapping the towel around his waist and peeling off the rest of the wetsuit. To get busted for indecent exposure was not something he needed right now.

He struggled to put his jeans on his still damp legs. *It's like putting on pantyhose,* Ned's sister had said once. He finally got the jeans up to his waist, yanked the towel off, and buttoned the fly.

"Woo-hoo. Getting her done now," Ned screamed while doing an off-the-lip. Christian stopped and stared. Now he'd tried an aerial but wiped out. Christian laughed. "You stink, man." He grabbed his shoes with his socks tucked deep inside and carried them to the car.

"Dad . . ."

"Just get in the car."

***

Pictures of remodeling ideas for the kitchen lay scattered on Genevra's table. Zoë wanted to completely overhaul it, beginning with the 1980s white cabinets and replacing them with all-natural wood. She'd almost sold Genevra on the idea, but without Dimitri's approval, the old lady wouldn't make a move.

When Zoë asked about Dimitri's whereabouts, Genevra chattered on about how Victor Newman on *The Young and the Restless* was cheating on Nicky again while endlessly looking over tile and wood samples, never deciding on anything.

The worst part of the case was the five pounds Zoë had gained from Genevra's authentic Italian cooking. She pitied Dimitri. No way could anyone grow up with her cooking and not end up overweight.

"Mrs. Romeo, that was about the best chicken parmesan I've ever tasted." Zoë set her fork down and brought the napkin to her face. "Where's Dimitri again?"

"A business meeting. He'll be here. You eat some dessert. Put some meat on those bones." Genevra wiped her hands on the sauce-stained apron before pulling out a pie from the oven. She returned with two small dishes.

Zoë learned to never get up and help. Genevra Romeo was an old biddy, set in her ways. The kitchen was hers.

"That pie smells good." Zoë breathed deeply and took in the aroma.

Genevra slid the knife into the center and made large, even slices. Zoë reached over to steal a taste, but Genevra smacked her hand with a wooden spoon.

"Ouch."

"Patience, girl. That's the problem with this generation. Patience, you remember that."

"Yes, Mrs. Romeo."

Zoë placed a warm bite in her mouth. The dessert was deceiving. It was wrapped in a dry, flaky crust but filled with the taste of cheesecake and a snippet of orange. It made her want to melt. She closed her eyes and moaned. "This is wonderful. What is it?"

"Torta di Ricotta."

"It's scrumptious." She scraped the last bits off the small plate and wanted to ask for more but waited. Genevra would insist soon enough, and Zoë would pretend to be full then happily oblige.

The sound of breaking glass came from the living room.

Zoë's eyebrows wrinkled. "What was that?"

"I'll check. Probably some lousy kid. Kids today, I'll tell you. No good, that's what they are." Genevra scurried into the other room.

The explosion sent Zoë to the ground. When she looked up, heat engulfed her. Flames shot from the living room. There was no way to see if Genevra was even alive. A smaller explosion shook the house as she scrambled to get out. Pain shot up her back instantaneously and made her dive out the back door.

She rolled on the ground to extinguish her clothes. Breathless and in excruciating pain, she lay face down. The smell of burnt hair and flesh made her queasy. She turned her head and lost consciousness.

***

Doc burst into Victoria's office. He grabbed her jacket off the rack. "Come on."

"What?"

"Zoë's been in an accident."

Victoria's dad flashed into her memory. Two bullet holes in the chest. He'd died two days later. "She's been shot, hasn't she? I told her not to be a cop."

"She wasn't shot."

"Then what happened?"

"I'll tell you on the way. Come on." He rushed her through the store, out the side door, and into the car.

Doc weaved in and out of traffic. "Zoë was doing some interior design work for Dimitri Romeo when the whole place went up."

"A fire?"

"Explosion first, I guess."

"The house exploded?" Her chin quivered. "How bad?"

"She's alive. I don't know anything else. Sonny just said to get you to the hospital."

Doc slammed on the brakes at the hospital entrance.

Sonny flung the car door open. "Zoë's in the burn unit. Come on." He led her inside.

Victoria walked quickly and held tightly to his hand. Christian stood by the elevator, his eyes bloodshot, his hair damp. "What're you doing here, and why're you wet?"

"I caught him skipping school. Surfing."

"I'm sorry." Christian sniffed. "I just want to see if Aunt Zoë's okay."

Victoria hugged him. For the moment, she didn't care that he'd skipped school again. "Let's go see how she is."

Victoria walked between Sonny and Christian. She held both their hands, trying to draw strength from them. Two men stood outside Zoë's room.

"Who are they?" Victoria asked.

"Plainclothes police officers. Rollins, Zoë's boss, said to say they're Antony's men. Stay here," Sonny said to Christian. "Vic, we can go in."

Victoria gasped and brought her hand to her mouth. The scent of sterile alcohol pervaded the room, but it couldn't hide the foul smell of burnt flesh and hair.

Zoë lay on her stomach on what looked more like a massage table than a hospital bed. The headrest was in an upside-down U shape and appeared to support her face comfortably.

Patches of short burnt hair peeked through the cracks in the gauze that wrapped her head. Her arms were outstretched as if she were sunbathing, and large white squares of gauze had been placed on her back. A mirror lay on the floor.

"Zoë?" Victoria whispered, her eyes filling with tears.

Zoë slowly opened her eyes. "Vic?"

Victoria walked toward her, unsure of what she should do. Sit down, stand up, touch her, don't touch her. She finally squatted for a moment, but her legs instantly went numb. She sat in the chair and leaned forward to see Zoë's reflection in the mirror. "I just heard. What did the doctors say?"

"My back is burned." Her eyes closed then opened again. "I'm on some pretty heavy painkillers, so if I doze off on you . . ."

Sonny knelt down. "What happened?"

"I was doing a design job for Dimitri." Zoë took short, shallow breaths. "Someone threw something in the window. A bomb, I guess." Zoë closed her eyes momentarily then opened them. "Genevra is dead."

"Thank God you're all right," Victoria whispered.

"Doctor says I should be fine. He said the burns would heal, and I won't need skin grafts."

"That's good then." Victoria sighed.

Zoë dozed off.

Sonny ran his hand through his hair. "She'll probably sleep for a while. You want me to get you some coffee?"

"Yes, thank you. I want to be here when she wakes up."

***

Sonny went into the hallway.

"How's Aunt Zoë?" Christian asked.

"She's going to be okay."

"Can I see her?"

"In a little bit, I've got to make a quick phone call, and then we'll get your mom some coffee." Sonny pulled his cell phone from the clip on his belt and dialed Antony's number. The explosion at Dimitri's house wasn't an accident. Something was going on. If Antony didn't already know what it was, he knew his brother could find out.

***

Elisa sat numbly in the oversized white chair at her home in Ventura, thinking about Genevra. Grandmothers were known for cookies and happy stories of the past. Hers had always preferred to cook up memories of hate with a sprinkle of murder and a good dosing of revenge. Despite that fact, the news of the explosion and her death hurt just the same.

The doorbell startled her. She wiped her eyes and looked through the peephole to see Dimitri. She took a deep breath and slowly exhaled then opened the door. "What?"

"That's how you greet me? Our grandmother was just killed." He shoved the cigar in his mouth and puffed on it.

Elisa stared at Dimitri for a moment but quickly looked away. His eyes always scared her. They were hollow and full of evil. "I'm sorry about Nanna."

"Yeah, me too." He pushed by her and walked into the house. "I need a place to stay."

"Why not get a hotel?"

He turned to her, patted her cheek, then grabbed her face and squeezed her cheeks. "Why would I do that when I have my loving cousin in town?"

She trembled under his large hands and waited for him to release her. When he did, she backed away. "How long will you be staying?"

"Oh . . ." He walked along the room and ran his hands on the back of the couch. "I don't know. Weeks. Months." He turned to her. "Does it matter?"

"No. You can have any one of the guest rooms."

Dimitri nodded, his face emotionless. He clicked his fingers at Justice, who stood in the doorway. "Bring in my things."

Justice walked into the house with two large suitcases. She stared at them. Her heart began to pound, and she clutched her hands to stop them from shaking. "Upstairs, first door on the right."

"I'll need a key," Dimitri said. "I've got business tonight and don't know how late I'll be."

"Yeah, sure." She went into the kitchen, opened a drawer, and grabbed an extra key. She stood and tried to think of a way to get him to leave, but there wasn't one. She'd have to let him stay.

Dimitri's voice echoed from the front room. "Write down the security code. Wouldn't want to bring the cops out here." He bellowed a distasteful, haunting laugh.

"No." She handed him the key and the code. "We wouldn't want that."

THIRTEEN

FEW THINGS MADE ZOË STOP and reflect on life. Her father's murder. 9/11. Killing her first perp. And now this. Darkness consumed the sky and her. Since her accident, she'd seen pairs of shoes and the reflections of four concerned faces—Sonny, Victoria, Christian, and Rachel. Cops taking statements and nurses doing their job didn't count.

Staring at the floor was as depressing as having only four visitors. The crumpled-up Kleenex that had missed the trash can hadn't moved, and she doubted that any more black dots had reappeared on the square tiled floor, but she recounted them anyway.

Most days, she was satisfied with her life, but there were times being single stunk. This was one of them. Was it so wrong to want a man to worship the ground she walked on? Okay, she'd settle for a man who merely enjoyed her company enough to bring her a pizza.

Last year, she'd tried to fill the man void with a wire-haired mutt from the pound. Brillo lasted two weeks before he decided he was better off on his own. Probably ran off with the stuck-up white poodle down the street.

Zoë was the first to admit she'd neglected him. He may have lacked attention, but he never went hungry. He ate her Birkenstocks, Adidas, and her favorite, well, only, pair of Manolo Blahnik's.

Brillo was lucky he ran when he did. The Blahnik's had cost her a fortune, and she was serious when she'd threatened to use him for target practice.

When the door opened, Zoë rolled her eyes. "I thought you weren't going to bother me again. My vitals haven't changed over the last thirty minutes." She didn't see white nurse's loafers but a pair of men's shoes. "Who's up there?" She tried to see a reflection in the mirror.

The left foot began to tap.

"Not funny. You'd make me guess?" She sighed and stared at the shoes. "Men's. Black. Clean as a whistle. That narrows it down."

"Super cop can't work under such duress?"

"Antony." A slow smile spread across her face. "You wouldn't happen to have a pizza, would you?"

He leaned over and set a vase of yellow tulips next to the mirror. "Sorry, just flowers." He tossed a pillow on the ground and sat on it, leaning against the wall. "You were almost killed."

"Sorry to ruin your day."

Antony slid the mirror over, scooted away from the wall, and lay flat on his back directly under her. "That's so unfair." He slipped the pillow under his head. "We've had our differences, but I'd never wish you dead."

"Yeah, that would break my sister's heart, and you wouldn't want that. You come here to order me to live?"

His eyes softened, and the left side of his mouth went up into a grin. "Would it help?"

"Don't worry. I wasn't hurt that bad." Her eyes bounced from the floor to him. Her chin quivered, and tears flooded her eyes.

"Super cop crying?"

"The stress of the day, I guess." She lied. She wasn't about to confess to him she wanted a man to love her. A man devoted to her as much as he was to her sister. A love that ran so deep nothing could diminish it.

"This is more than stress." Antony grabbed a tissue and dabbed the tears. "You in pain? I can get the doctor."

"No. I've just been thinking."

"About what?"

"Life." Her eyes were drawn to his, and she was unable to stop herself from asking the next question. "Why do you love her so much?"

"Victoria?"

"Yeah."

"I just do."

"She'll never leave Sonny."

"I know, but I can't help the way I feel."

"You think you'll ever get over her?"

"What exactly are you asking?" He raised his eyebrows at her.

"You're so conceited."

"Are you interested?"

"Interested in you?" Zoë gave a grunting laugh. "Never."

"One kiss gets them every time." He grinned.

"You're chasing a dream that will never be a reality." Zoë could see the love he could give. Love when it wasn't masqueraded behind his cold, uncaring attitude. "What about Lauren or that girl from the reception, Elisa?"

That erased the grin. "What happened at Dimitri's?"

"It was a bomb. Fire marshall confirmed it."

"You find anything out before the place went up in flames?" Antony crossed his hands on his chest and tapped his fingers.

"Ah, the real reason for the flowers and the visit."

"You promised to fill me in. Is there anything I should know?"

"I read that Lauren has a kid. They say he's fifteen. You think he's yours?"

He smiled. "If she had my kid, she'd have her hand so deep in my pocket I'd never get rid of her. What'd you find out about Dimitri?"

"I'm thirsty. Could you get me a drink?"

Antony reached up, grabbed a cup of water and held the straw to Zoë's mouth. When she released it, he returned the cup to the table. "Dimitri?"

"He's dealing in stolen art. You know anything about it?"

"Why would I?"

"We had a deal. We'd share information."

"If I knew anything important, you'd be the first to know."

"You don't think it's strange that Dimitri's dealing in artwork and Francesca's had pictures stolen?" Zoë stared into Antony's eyes. If he knew anything, he wasn't going to tell her, at least not while she lay immobilized. He hated cops and tolerated her badge only because she was Victoria's sister. "You going to Genevra's funeral?"

"Yeah."

"Then you need to know that Martin's working undercover. You might run into him."

"Great." Antony rolled his eyes. "Your ex-husband undercover at Dimitri's. How do I explain that to Vic and Sonny without any suspicion?"

"You don't. Hopefully, they won't run into each other. He's been undercover for over a year."

"And I'll bet he hasn't found out anything, has he? You police are worthless."

"Ha, ha. Be nice, for me?"

"Okay. Only because you're my girlfriend." He winked.

"Thank you. Will you stay a while? We could watch TV. Well, you could watch TV."

"Sure." His eyes were soft. "I'll be right back."

She heard him come back into the room. "What are you doing?"

"You'll see." On the floor, he laid a small TV on its back. Tilting it up, he positioned a pillow under one end, plugged it in, then flipped it on. Instant fuzz.

"What do you think?" he asked.

"A station would be nice."

"You're so demanding."

"Where'd you get the TV?"

"Nurse's station."

"Couldn't rip the one off the wall?"

"I could've but figured the cable wouldn't reach." Antony moved around the antenna and flipped the channels until he found a local station. "There. A TV."

"You're a genius."

"I've been called a lot of things but never that."

***

Lights shot from the Vitale house and shattered the darkness. Martin's temples pounded. He breathed deeply and hoped to flush the heat from his face. The explosion didn't just ignite the Romeo house but his anger and urgency to close this case. Zoë wasn't just his ex-partner and his ex-wife, she was his friend.

Despite his deep feelings for Elisa, maybe even love, he had to get information out of her. With her grandmother killed, she was vulnerable, and vulnerable women always gave the best info.

Combing his hand through his hair, he pushed the doorbell and waited. The door opened a crack. Elisa peered out.

"Can I talk to you?" Martin asked.

"Is Dimitri with you?"

"No. He's at the club."

Elisa opened the door and shivered in the night air. The blue tank sweater and slacks made her skin appear tanner than the last time he'd seen her. She bolted the door behind him, breezed by, and went into the living room.

Martin followed then pointed to a chair. "Can I sit down?"

Eyes bloodshot, Elisa nodded and sat on the couch. She grabbed a pillow, pulled it onto her lap, and wrapped her fingers in the tassels that hung from it.

Martin stared at her. She looked away but not before her chin quivered. "You all right?"

"Why do you care?"

"Your grandmother was just killed. I thought maybe you needed a friend."

A single tear rolled down her cheek. She wiped it away. "You know Dimitri has moved in."

"Yes." He knew she had no friends, no one to talk to, but trust wouldn't come easy. He had to get her to open up, prove to her he was on her side. "Do you think Dimitri was the target?"

Her eyes met his. "Why would you ask that?"

"I hear things." His stare intensified. "You think this house may be next?" He paused and waited for an answer. When none came, he added, "You can talk to me."

She stood and walked to the French doors. "I couldn't talk to you even if I wanted to. You work for my cousin."

"What I do for Dimitri is just a job."

"To you, maybe, but not to him. Dimitri owns his employees." She went out on the patio.

He followed. "Dimitri doesn't own me."

Chilly air swirled. Elisa hugged her bare arms and shivered. Since his gun was strapped to his ankle, he took off his jacket and rested it on her shoulders. He walked around the patio, admiring the garden that surrounded a long Olympic-sized pool. It was filled with red roses, violet hibiscus, and yellow daisies. "This is nice. Did you do all of this?"

"Yes." She pulled the coat tight. "My husband liked everything white. The garden was the only place he let me add color."

"You could paint the inside. He's been dead for months."

She nodded and tucked her hair behind her ears. "It doesn't matter anymore."

"Why do you say that?"

"You don't recognize self-pity?"

He turned to her. His heart quickened. *She's part of the job.* She had most likely married for money, but there was an innocence about her that made her beauty enthralling. "I don't see self-pity. I see a beautiful woman wasting away behind these colorless walls."

Her face flushed as she sat with downcast eyes. "Thank you."

"Why do you do that?"

"What?"

"Never look at me? You know they say the eyes are the windows to the soul." He knelt down in front of her and tipped her chin up with his finger. "You can trust me."

She pushed his hand away and stood. "I can't trust anyone."

Martin placed his hands deep in his jean pockets. "What can I do to earn your trust? I'll do anything."

"You should leave before my cousin comes home."

"Are you afraid of him?"

She handed him back his coat and walked inside. "You should go."

Martin followed her and laid the coat on the back of the couch. "I don't think I will. Why is he staying here when you obviously don't like him?"

She paced. "I don't have a choice. Okay? Now go."

The lock on the front door wiggled, and Dimitri stood in the doorway. Elisa's eyes widened, and her face paled.

Dimitri staggered into the room and glared at Martin. "What are you doing here?"

Martin gave Elisa a reassuring smile before looking at Dimitri. "I finished those deliveries and wondered if there was anything else you needed before I took off. One of the guys told me you moved in here." He glanced back at Elisa then at Dimitri. "I was sorry to hear about your grandmother."

"I don't need you the rest of the night. You can go."

The smell of booze and stale cigars rolled off Dimitri. Feet glued to the floor, his body made small circles, and Martin expected him to fall over in a matter of minutes. Once on the ground, nothing short of a crane would get him up.

"Maybe I'll just help you up the stairs." Martin took Dimitri's arm. When Dimitri didn't argue, Elisa looked relieved. Martin smiled. He was making progress.

Elisa led them up the stairs to Dimitri's room. "In there." She pointed.

Martin helped Dimitri onto the bed and stood with his hands on his hips. "We did it." He turned and ran into Justice, who stood like a statue. "Whoa." Martin looked into Justice's cold, hollow eyes. "You snuck up on me there."

Justice's lips pursed, and the scar on his neck pulsated.

"I guess you can take it from here." Martin patted Justice's chest. "You're welcome." Martin looked back at Dimitri, who was now passed out. "See ya later, boss."

He backed out of the room, shut the door, and followed Elisa down the stairs. He grabbed his coat and walked to the door. "You'll be okay if I leave you with Justice? The guy never shuts up. He'll talk your ear off."

She laughed. "I'll be fine."

He grinned and felt silly. Like a high school boy on his first date. "Well, I'll be going."

"Okay."

Her eyes smiled for the first time. He took a step then turned back. He fumbled in his coat pocket, pulled out a piece of paper and a pen. "Here." He jotted down a phone number. "My cell. If you need anything, call me."

"Thank you." She tucked the paper in the front pocket of her pants. "Good night."

"Night." Martin whistled as he walked to his car then turned back. Elisa still stood at the door. He waved, got in his car, and took off.

As he drove, he constantly glanced in the rearview mirror to make sure none of Dimitri's men were tailing him. Elisa's face danced in his mind as he pulled into the hospital's parking ramp.

He walked down the hallway, quietly whistling. Elisa's sweet perfume clung to his jacket. He nodded at the plainclothes officers, walked into Zoë's room, then stopped. His eyes widened as he studied Zoë lying face down on the hospital bed. "Holy cow." He took a step closer.

Zoë's long, beautiful blond hair was gone. Short pieces of burnt hair poked sporadically through the gauze. Bandages lay across her shoulders and back.

Her eyes cracked open. "Who's up there?" Her words were slurred from the medication, he suspected.

"It's Martin."

"Martin?" She squinted at him in the mirror on the floor. He stood in silent shock. She spoke softly, "It looks worse than it is."

"I hope so 'cause it looks pretty bad."

"Rollins fill you in?"

"Yeah. He said you were hurt but . . ." Martin sat in the chair. "Man, Zoë, what do the doctors say?"

"I'll be fine. I just have to stay like this for a week or so. Mostly first and second-degree burns."

"You gonna need surgery? Skin grafts?"

"Doctors think I won't. Maybe for cosmetic reasons if anything. Nothing I need right away."

Martin pointed to the TV. "Looks like they're taking care of you."

"Antony got that for me."

"And the flowers? They from Antony, too?"

"He wanted information."

"And he wooed it out of you?"

"I am on heavy medication." She smiled, closed her eyes momentarily, and then opened them. "I asked him if he knew anything about Dimitri and any stolen artwork."

"And did he?"

"Not that he'd say. He knows you're working undercover."

"I figured I might run into him at the funeral."

"Avoid Sonny and Vic. I don't want to have to explain all this to them, at least not yet. You got anything on Dimitri?"

"We could put him away for a few years on minor offenses." Martin rubbed his forehead. "But I want to nail him."

"You heard anything about the paintings?"

"Not yet."

"You better get outta here before he misses you."

"I can stay for a bit."

"You can, but . . ." Her eyes slowly closed. "I may fall asleep."

"I'll go then." Martin kissed his fingers and placed it on her lips. "Love you girl. Hang in there."

"Martin?"

"Yeah?"

"Be careful."

"Always."

FOURTEEN

THE SUN WAS BRIGHT AND WARM for October. The small chapel looked pathetic. The brown paneling was outdated. Heavy red curtains hung over the windows, and sad music played softly in the background. There were more flowers than mourners, and those who were there showed no sign of grief.

A large spray of red and white carnations draped the closed silver casket. Tucked proudly within the flowers was an eight-by-ten, gold-embossed frame that held a picture of Genevra standing by the ocean.

Dimitri and Elisa stood at the head of the casket, dressed in black.

Antony shook Dimitri's hand and pulled the big guy into a hug. "Sorry, man."

"Thanks."

"Where you staying?"

"Elisa is letting me crash at her place."

Antony glanced over at Elisa. He felt a sting of desire but quickly squashed it. He wouldn't let her into his heart. Not again. He leaned into Dimitri and whispered, "This the work of your art broker?"

Dimitri nodded. "You gotta help me."

Heels clicked loudly on the wooden floor and drew Antony's attention away. Victoria's long black cardigan hung to her ankle boots. Sonny, in a navy suit, held tightly to her hand.

Antony turned back to Dimitri, leaned in, and whispered, "I'll help you, but I don't care how much money you got riding on this. He hurts anyone in my family, he's dead."

"I know. I've beefed up security at Elisa's."

"Good." Antony studied Dimitri. He appeared apathetic, but he never mentioned retaliation for the killing of his grandmother. It was strange and unsettling.

Antony moved toward Elisa. "I'm sorry about your grandmother."

"Thank you." Elisa smiled. "I'm sorry your girlfriend was hurt. Is she doing okay?"

"She is. Thank you for asking."

"I sent flowers this morning," Dimitri said. "Maybe I should stop by and tell her how bad I feel."

The last thing Antony wanted was to have Dimitri anywhere near Zoë, aka super cop. "She can't have visitors, but I'll tell her for you. Do you mind if I talk to Elisa?" Antony took Elisa's arm.

"Sure, go ahead." Dimitri turned to shake Sonny's outstretched hand.

Antony led Elisa out a side door and down a cement path to a garden area where the chrysanthemums and roses were in full bloom. They sat on a concrete bench.

"I need to ask you something." He loosened his tie. "And I need an honest answer."

Elisa nodded, her eyes downcast.

"Have you heard about any stolen paintings?"

She rested her arms on her legs, dropped her head, and covered her eyes.

Antony frowned. "Are you crying?"

Her dry eyes cut to him, and he mentally kicked himself. Of course, she wasn't crying. Dimitri's men were everywhere. He reached his arm around her and pretended to comfort her.

The sweet and innocent scent of her perfume danced in the air around him, jolting his memory. Her brown eyes were soft, soothing. She stirred things inside of him. Things he'd thought he'd buried.

Part of him wanted to take her away, to protect her, but he wouldn't. She had made her choices—let her live with them.

"Do you know anything?" Antony asked.

"I found out Dimitri and Enrico had a big deal going down before Enrico was killed."

"About paintings?"

"I guess. I don't know." Her eyes darted around like she was looking for someone. "You think I'm lying, don't you?" She pulled away.

Lying? He wasn't so sure, but he wasn't stupid. Enrico owned an art gallery, and if he and Dimitri were doing business together, it was safe to assume it was about paintings.

"It wouldn't be the first time you lied to me."

Her body jerked at his cold words, but her voice was soft and loving. "Be careful. I don't trust Dimitri, and I don't want you getting hurt."

His heart hardened. "All of sudden you care?"

"I always have."

"Only when it's convenient."

"And you only care when you need answers."

Antony grabbed her arm, anger exploding inside of him. "Don't accuse me of using you. If anyone did the using—"

A hand gripped Antony's shoulder. He turned to see Martin standing over them. He looked out of character in the black suit. His face was hard, his eyes serious. "Leave her alone."

Antony released Elisa and stood. He glared at Martin. He knew he'd run into him, but not as Elisa's protector. He was, no doubt, playing her for information. Antony's eyes narrowed. "Martin?" A slight grin spread across Antony's face. "I can't believe I'm running into you."

"You two know each other?"

"Yeah, we've met." Martin's hazel eyes narrowed, red crept up his neck. He moved his suit coat back and rested his hand on the gun that was holstered on his belt. "We met in Kansas City years ago."

The blood pounded through Antony's body. It wasn't Kansas City, it was in Ventura, and they had hated each other the minute they laid eyes on each other.

"You working for Dimitri?" Antony raised an eyebrow.

"Yeah." Martin leaned into Elisa. "Are you okay?"

Antony's eyes narrowed. This was more than an undercover cop doing his job. Martin seemed genuinely concerned about Elisa.

"I'm fine. I need to get back inside."

Antony pursed his lips as they walked away. All the pain she had caused him sat in the pit of his stomach like undigested food. What was he supposed to do, believe she really cared all of a sudden? No, he wouldn't play that game with her. Elisa had Romeo blood in her, and Romeos only looked out for themselves.

Sonny and Victoria came out of the chapel as Martin and Elisa walked toward it. Martin whispered something in Elisa's ear then ducked behind a shrub and disappeared from sight. Victoria said something to Elisa and gave her a hug, then she and Sonny walked toward him.

Sonny reached into his pocket and pulled out his sunglasses. "You ready to go?"

Antony glanced back at the chapel. Elisa opened the door then stopped and turned to him. Antony stared at her for a moment before she turned away and the door closed. It was what she did every time he got close, shut him out. He wouldn't fall for her again.

"Yeah." Antony put his sunglasses on. "Let's go."

***

Antony sat in his office at Lorenzo's estate, staring at the TV, the remote in his hand. In the late afternoons, he usually welcomed the rays of sunlight, but today he had pulled the shades. The recording of the burglary at Francesca's played over and over. He had to give Doc credit for making copies of it before the cops took them.

He pushed play on the five-second reel. The thief's motions never changed. There was something familiar, but he couldn't put his finger on it. He knew it had to be an inside job. Someone who could get the security code.

Pushing rewind then play, he gulped the last of the drink. Nothing. He rubbed his eyes.

Think, man, think.

The man's back was to the camera. He pulled the cap over his face, rubbed his hands, and then moved out of the camera's sight.

Antony stood and paced the room. He grabbed the remote, pointed it at the DVD and hit play. The man made the same motions.

A knock on the door distracted him. He pushed the power button off, tossed the remote on his desk. "What?"

Vince opened the door and pushed some papers at him. "Your father wanted me to give you these."

Antony snatched them. "What is it?"

Vince rubbed the back of his hand. "The invoices on the shipment of computers. He said he read them, and it looks like everything's in order."

Antony tossed the papers on his desk. Like he cared what his father thought. The shipment had already gone out. Antony glanced back up at Vince. "Anything else?"

"No."

Vince left.

Antony sat back in the chair, propped his feet on the corner of the desk, grabbed the remote, and pushed the power button on the DVD. Hitting play, he rubbed his forehead.

He jerked up, wide-eyed. His heart pounded as he leaned forward and stared at the screen. Antony hit pause at the spot where the man rubbed his hands. "Arthritis," he said aloud. "Vince took the paintings?" He laughed. "Lorenzo's still got some kick in him, the old fart, but how did he know?"

Antony walked into the hallway. "Vince. Where's Lorenzo?"

"A couple of the guys took him to the pond to fish. You need me to get him?"

"No. I won't need you the rest of the day. Why don't you join him?"

"You sure?"

Antony squeezed Vince's shoulder. "Yes, go. Try out that new rod he bought you. They just restocked the pond. There's some good-sized catfish in there."

Vince looked down and opened and closed his hands then rubbed them. "Danged arthritis. Medicine is worthless. None of it works."

Antony waited until Vince disappeared over the hill before going down the wooden stairs to the basement to look for the paintings. It wouldn't take long to search. It was unfinished, but it was a reasonable place to start.

A few boxes in one corner labeled *Living Room, KC* had an abundant amount of dust on them. They held trinkets from the house in Kansas City—things that were too good to throw out yet unimportant enough to unpack. The floor was a big slab of concrete, and there were three partially completed rooms.

He looked behind the boxes and in the corners but found nothing. At the electrical box, he paused for a moment then decided against it. The box held the keypad to the safe rooms that were secretly tucked behind the brick wall. Lorenzo was adamant it was never accessed unless it was a life or death emergency. He'd search them last.

Back in the den, Antony glanced out the window to make sure no one was returning to the house, then went to Lorenzo's room. Designed for Lorenzo's handicap, the clothes in the closet hung at a level Lorenzo could reach, and a short dresser and a desk in the corner were both the perfect height for a wheelchair.

Antony searched the closet first then pulled the top dresser drawer open and felt around the clothes when he came across something hard and square. He pulled the object from under the t-shirts and stared at a picture of his mother. She reminded him of a young Jackie Kennedy. Her short brown hair was styled perfectly, and her short-sleeved, pink angora sweater brought out her ivory skin.

He smiled, brushing his fingers across her image. Antony remembered sneaking into the funeral home and seeing her in the casket, touching her cold hand and kissing her cheek. He had gone to the gravesite despite his father's orders, crouched behind a headstone, and had watched his father cry for the first and last time. Sonny stood tall even though the tears ran down his face. His hand rested on their father's shoulder.

It should have been me standing there, comforting Papa.

"Stop," Antony said aloud. "It won't change anything."

"Mr. Antony?" Consolata's voice came from behind. "You looking for something? Let Consolata help."

Antony dropped the picture back in the drawer and slammed it shut. "I was just looking . . ." He stood tall. "I don't need any help." He brushed past the live-in housekeeper and went into the game room.

He ran his fingers across the green felt on the pool table then took the seven ball and flung it across the table, knocking it into a group of balls. He looked around before walking behind the bar. He scanned the area with his eyes and felt the places he couldn't see. Nothing.

He tapped his fingers on the gray marble bar top. "Where would Papa hide them?"

The shed.

Antony placed both hands in his pockets as he walked across the backyard. The shed was where his father stored a large collection of fishing tackle.

He squeezed the metal handle and opened the door to the barn-shaped building. He walked in and shut the door behind him. It was dark except for faint glimpses of sun that peeked through random cracks in the walls.

Something brushed past his face. He waved his hands in the air, grabbed and pulled the thin rope that hung. The light turned on.

There were rods and reels for all kinds of fishing. Salt water to fresh water, swordfish to bass. Lorenzo's new sport was endless, and he owned just about everything you needed to do it properly, even down to the Chris Craft Commander Cruiser parked in the marina.

Antony looked around at numerous black tubes that held more fishing poles. One, he was sure, held the rolled-up paintings. He walked around the workbench, stood in the corner, and began his search. His frustration built with each tube he opened. He threw down the ones that contained rods and continued looking.

He finally picked up a tube that he noticed didn't rattle. His heart pounded. It had to be the paintings. He pulled the cap off, looked inside, and saw canvas clinging to the outer walls. "Finally." He capped it closed and began to step over the mess when he heard the door open.

Antony crouched behind the workbench. The sunlight bounced off a metal object, momentarily blinding him at the same time he heard the gunshot.

The force of the bullet ripped through his thigh. Instinctively, Antony dropped the paintings and pulled out his gun. When his eyes adjusted to the light, he saw the outline of a wheelchair. With his gun held high and finger on the trigger, he saw his father's face. "You shot me!"

"What?" Lorenzo's gun was still aimed at Antony.

Antony groaned and clutched his bleeding leg, trying to move to a standing position, the gun still in his hand. Tubes rolled across the floor. Antony fell down on the other knee, and the warmth of the blood ran down his leg. "Put your gun down."

"What are you doing out here?" Lorenzo bellowed, his eyes dark and sinister.

Vince ran in behind Lorenzo. "I thought I heard a . . ." His eyes darted from the two men, both still held their guns on each other.

"Get the ol' man's gun."

Vince raised an eyebrow at Antony then looked down at Lorenzo who slid the gun between his thigh and the side of the chair. Vince shrugged.

Antony rolled his eyes, replaced his in its holster, then unbuckled his belt and pulled it out of his pants. He wrapped it around his upper thigh and cinched it tight, cringing. He looked up at Vince. "Get me a rag or something to tie around this."

Antony, his leg throbbing, stared at his father. "Are you crazy?"

"I thought you were stealing—"

"The paintings?"

"Where are they?" Lorenzo bent over his lifeless legs and grabbed at the endless identical black tubes that lay scattered on the floor.

Antony brought in his lower lip and bit down on it as he tried to ignore the pain.

Vince ran back into the shed with a rag.

"Tie it up." Antony gasped as Vince wrapped the rag around his leg and pulled it as tight as he could. He grabbed Vince's arm and pulled himself up to a standing position. "Get me to the house."

Vince helped Antony into his office.

He fell on the couch and closed his eyes. His leg burned.

"I'm sorry, man," Vince said.

"Call my doctor. See if he can see me."

"He'll tell the cops. You can't."

"He won't. Make the call, now."

Vince hung up the phone. "Answering service says he's out of town until tomorrow."

"Check and see if the bullet went through."

Vince peeled back the rag. "Looks like it grazed the outside, pretty good chunk of skin gone, though."

"Is it gushing or oozing?" Antony gritted his teeth.

"Oozing."

"Tie it back up."

Vince stared down at him. "You know he didn't mean to. He was just protecting—"

"Paintings that you stole. Get them."

"I can't do that, not unless Lorenzo says so."

"Get out."

Vince left.

Antony lay on the couch. His leg throbbed, and the pain was almost unbearable. He began to feel lightheaded. *God, Mama always said You loved me, show it by helping me.*

He grunted. What was he doing? Was he actually praying?

***

Elisa knocked on the front door of Lorenzo's estate then nervously shook her car keys and looked around. Was she crazy? She wasn't sure what she had overheard, or if Antony would even listen, but she knew she had to try.

Consolata opened the door. "Yes?"

"I need to see Antony."

"Mr. Antony is resting."

"It's important."

Consolata nodded and led Elisa to the door of Antony's office. Consolata reached up to knock when Elisa touched her arm and said, "Thank you."

Elisa waited until she left then knocked and waited. When there was no response, she opened the door. "Antony?"

When her eyes adjusted to the dark room, she gasped. "Oh, God, no."

***

Victoria rolled a head of lettuce under the water faucet. The phone rang. Dropping the lettuce in the sink, she shut off the water, grabbed a dishtowel, and half-heartedly dried off her hands before picking up the phone. "Hello."

"Mrs. Luciano?"

"Yes?"

"It's Elisa. We met at the reception and my grandmother's funeral. I think Antony's been shot."

"What? Where are you?"

"At Lorenzo's."

"I'll be right there."

Victoria slid the phone into her pocket and ran into the great room. "Rachel, Doc."

Rachel skipped down the stairs. "Yeah?"

"I've got to run an errand. Will you tell Christian?"

Rachel nodded. Victoria tossed the keys to Doc. "Come on." She grabbed her purse and hurried out the front door.

On the porch, she glanced over at Bruno, who was sitting next to Max. "Bruno, I need you to come with us. Max, make sure Christian and Rachel don't go anywhere."

Bruno jumped to his feet and followed.

She climbed into the car. "Lorenzo's. Hurry." Victoria dialed Sonny, but it went to voicemail. "Why isn't Sonny answering? What good is a cell phone if you never answer it?"

"What's going on?" Doc asked.

"I got a strange phone call from Elisa. She said she thinks Antony's been shot."

"What?" Doc gunned the car, swerved in and out of traffic, laid on the horn, and shouted at people who couldn't hear him.

"I don't know what's going on," Victoria said. "But I want your guns out."

Doc gripped the steering wheel. "You didn't just say that, did you?"

Victoria narrowed her eyes.

"It was a joke." Doc glanced at her then back at the road. "Relax, we know what to do."

Victoria pulled out her cell phone again.

Doc glanced over at her. "Who you calling?"

"Nine-one-one."

He grabbed the phone. "If the cops aren't already there, there's a reason Antony didn't call them."

"Don't lecture me about family loyalty."

"Wouldn't dream of lecturing you, Mrs. L." He was apparently unscathed by her anger because he grinned his crooked grin while his eyes bounced from the road to her.

Victoria glared at him, her hand outstretched. "Give me my phone."

He placed the phone on her hand. She slid it into the pocket of her brown leather jacket.

They pulled into the estate. No cops in sight.

They jumped out of the car and ran to the house. Victoria turned the doorknob. It was unlocked.

Doc and Bruno pushed past her and searched each room with drawn guns. She walked only when they motioned that it was safe. She bent down, touched a drop of liquid, and rubbed it between her fingers. She looked up at Doc and Bruno. "It's blood."

Victoria followed them farther down the hall. A sudden noise sent them against the wall. Doc moved closer to the corner before he jumped around it and aimed his gun at whoever might be coming toward them.

Consolata screamed at the barrel shoved in her face. She tossed the laundry in the air and cursed in Italian.

Doc pushed her against the wall and motioned for her to be quiet. He slowly opened the door to Antony's office.

Antony was lying on the couch. Elisa sat next to him.

Victoria pushed past Doc and knelt down. "Antony?"

"I don't know what happened," Elisa said, "or how long he's been like this, but by the looks of the bandage, he's lost a lot of blood."

"Did you call nine-one-one?" Victoria laid her hand on his forehead to see if it was warm. It wasn't.

"The cops?" Elisa asked. "Of course not."

Victoria looked at the makeshift bandage. The blood had soaked through it, his pants now absorbing the overflow. "Antony?" She shook his arm. "It's me, Vic."

He opened his eyes. "My guardian angel."

"What happened?"

"Lorenzo accidentally shot me." Antony pushed himself up. "The bullet grazed my leg."

Victoria glanced up at Doc. "Find Lorenzo." She turned back to Antony. "We're taking you to the hospital."

"No."

"Why not?"

"Gunshot wounds are always reported."

"Your doctor, can I call him?"

"Already tried. He's out of town until tomorrow."

"Then you have to go to the hospital. If it was an accident—"

"No. He's my father."

"And loyalty always comes first?" Victoria snapped.

"Spoken like a true Luciano."

"Help him up." Victoria motioned to Bruno, who nodded and wrapped Antony's arm around his shoulder. He pulled Antony up and grabbed him around his waist, taking as much of his weight as he could.

Doc jogged back into the office and got on the other side of Antony. "Lorenzo says he accidentally shot Antony. Said he thought he was a robber."

"Put him in the car." Victoria turned to Doc. "Where's Lorenzo?"

"On the patio."

"I'll be right back." She walked outside to where her father-in-law tossed birdseed next to a beautiful sculptured rock waterfall.

"Lorenzo?"

He ignored her. Normal. Lorenzo said and did what he wanted, and only when it served his purpose. "Antony is coming with us. Do you know what you did?"

Lorenzo turned, his neck red and his eyes hollow. "He shouldn't be sneaking around stealing my things," he bellowed.

Victoria stiffened.

Vince grabbed her forearm and led her back inside. "He's getting senile."

"Senile? Hardly."

Vince gave a presumptuous laugh.

Victoria peered over Vince's shoulder at Lorenzo. She had never known him to truly love anything. It appeared his years in a wheelchair had only hardened an already cold heart. Sighing heavily, she stared back at Vince for a long uncomfortable moment. His face appeared friendly, but his eyes were dark and uncaring.

Doc's voice came from behind and startled her. "We need to go."

"Okay." She turned to him.

Vince's voice echoed through the room. "Take care of Antony."

Doc's hand pressed against her lower back, forcing her to ignore the comment and walk to the car. She slid into the backseat next to Antony.

Doc gunned the engine, tearing out of the estate. Bruno sat in front, and Elisa followed in her car.

Antony leaned against Victoria, his head on her shoulder, his eyes closed.

"I don't care what he says," Victoria said. "Take him to the hospital."

"Doc," Antony's voice was soft and weak. "I said no."

"I heard what you said." Doc glanced in the rearview mirror.

Victoria glared at him.

Antony reached over and took Victoria's hand and gave it a squeeze. "Thank you for coming."

Victoria reached her arm around him as he laid his head on her lap. "No problem." His eyes closed. She looked down at the blood-soaked bandage, and a chill coursed through her.

She pulled out her cell phone and tried Sonny again. Nothing. She slid it back into her pocket.

Doc pulled into the emergency entrance. He jumped out and opened the back door. Bruno disappeared then returned with a wheelchair and Elisa close behind.

"Why are we here?" Antony asked with a quiet firmness.

"I don't work for you." Doc scooted the wheelchair closer to the car and helped Antony into it. "I work for Mrs. L." He turned to Bruno and Elisa. "Stay out here."

They whisked Antony through the emergency room doors. Doc glanced at Victoria. "Let me do the talking." He pounded on the counter at the nurse's station. "We need some help. Now. He was cleaning his gun, and it accidentally went off."

A nurse came around the counter, grabbed the wheelchair, and pushed Antony into a trauma room. Nurses flew in and out as a young intern barked orders.

When the bandage was slowly peeled away, Victoria saw a three-inch chunk of thigh missing. It exposed hamburger-like flesh or muscle — she couldn't tell which, maybe both. Her stomach churned, but she couldn't look away.

A nurse pushed her toward the door. "You'll need to step outside."

Victoria nodded, backed out of the room, and turned to see two police officers walking toward them. She leaned into Doc. "I'm telling them the truth."

"I may work by your side every day, but I'm loyal to all the Lucianos, including your father-in-law." Doc's face hardened. "I'll do the talking."

One of the police officers pulled out his notepad. "The nurse said there was a shooting?"

"He was cleaning his gun and didn't realize it was loaded," Doc said. "It went off."

"Do you have the gun with you?"

"No, it's still at the house."

Victoria took a step closer to the officers. "My name is Victoria Luciano, and my sister is Detective Zoë Stone."

One officer nodded. "I was sorry to hear of her accident."

"Thank you." Victoria hesitated. She looked at Doc's scolding eyes then back at the officer. "You can only imagine what the press will do with this story. Is there any way we can keep this quiet? Maybe I can talk to Zoë's partner or something."

"Let me make a call." The officer stepped away, made a quick phone call, then walked back to them. "I'll just need to get the gun and a statement from . . . who was it that shot himself?"

"Antony Luciano," Doc said.

FIFTEEN

TWO HOURS LATER, ANTONY SIGNED himself out of the ER against the doctor's wishes. Doc and Bruno carried most of Antony's weight and helped him into Sonny and Victoria's house.

"Put him in here." Victoria opened the door to one of their spare rooms. "Gently."

They laid Antony on the bed. Doc backed away. "I'm heading over to Lorenzo's to meet the detectives, then I'll get these prescriptions filled. Antony?" He gave Antony's shoulder a gentle nudge. "Where'd you get shot?"

"In the shed." Antony barely opened his eyes.

"You should've just told the police the truth." Victoria pulled the comforter over him. "There's no reason to lie."

"Keep the police away from Lorenzo," Antony ordered in an almost whisper.

"If he doesn't give me the gun, he'll have to confess." Doc walked to the window and separated the mini-blinds to look outside. "Sonny's home. You want to tell him?"

"Yeah." Victoria felt Antony's forehead to make sure there was no fever. "I'll be down in a minute."

Antony's breathing deepened, and she turned to Elisa, who was sitting in a chair next to the bed. "I'll be right back."

Victoria descended the stairs, clutching her stomach. She felt sick. How could a father shoot his own son and act like nothing had happened? She had always felt an evilness lingering around Lorenzo no matter how much Sonny insisted his father had changed. Today, Lorenzo proved he was still the insensitive, coldhearted man painted in the tabloids.

Sonny met her on the landing. "Doc said you needed to talk to me. Is that blood? What's happened? Are the kids okay?" He pushed her aside and started up the stairs.

She grabbed his arm, making him turn back. "The kids are fine. Max took them riding." She waited until the color returned to his face. "It's Antony." She took his hand and led him up the stairs. "Your father shot him in the leg."

"What?" Sonny's forehead wrinkled, and he grunted a laugh. "Is this some kind of joke?"

"No, it seems your father thought Antony was a burglar. Elisa found him and called me."

Sonny pushed past her and went into the spare bedroom where Elisa sat over Antony as he slept.

"How is he?" he asked.

"He lost a lot of blood," Elisa said.

Sonny reached for Antony, but Elisa grabbed his wrist. "He really needs to sleep. He should've stayed in the hospital, but you know Antony."

Victoria took Sonny's arm, led him into the hallway, and shut the door.

Sonny shook his head. "There's no way. Papa would've never shot him." The lines on his face hardened. "Did Papa or Antony tell you this?"

"Both. Antony didn't want to go to the hospital because he insisted your father not take the blame, but we took him anyway. Doc told the police Antony was cleaning his gun and it went off. I've been trying to call you all afternoon."

"I was on one of the ships. You know I can't get service on them. You should've had someone track me down."

Nodding, she walked into their bedroom. Sonny followed.

"Doc's over at Lorenzo's meeting with two policemen." She pulled the bloody shirt over her head, tossed it on the floor, then yanked a clean shirt off a hanger and put it on. "Antony's on some pretty heavy pain medication, so he could be out for a while."

Sonny tossed his suit jacket on the bed then leaned against the dresser. "I'm going to go talk to Papa."

"No." Her eyes widened. "It didn't faze him that he had shot Antony. He left him there in the office. Alone. If Elisa hadn't gone over when she did, he could've bled to death, and your father wouldn't have cared."

"I don't believe that."

She bent over, grabbed her bloodied shirt, and walked past him. In the bathroom, she pulled the plug in the sink, turned on the cold water, and dropped the shirt in. She looked at Sonny's reflection in the mirror. "Your father sat in the garden feeding the birds like nothing had happened."

"This doesn't make sense."

Victoria sighed. Antony always claimed Sonny was blind to his father's abuse, but this was the first time she had witnessed it. As she looked down, the sink turned red.

Sonny reached around her and shut the water off. She turned to him. He cupped the back of her neck and pulled her close. "I have to talk to Papa and find out what really happened."

"He's crazy, Sonny. I don't want you anywhere near him."

"If it'll make you feel better, I'll have Clay frisk him."

"This is no joke. Your brother was shot by his own father. That man clearly despises him."

Sonny released her, his face inflamed. "Papa doesn't despise Antony. He loves him."

"No, he doesn't."

"And it's all my fault, isn't it?"

"I didn't say that."

"But you're thinking it, aren't you? If Antony hadn't taken the blame for killing Carlo, Papa wouldn't hate him for killing my mom, and he wouldn't have shot him." Sonny shook his head and grabbed his jacket. "My brother has finally sucked you into his fantasy world. Papa shooting Antony was an accident. It had to be. And if by some insane chance it wasn't, Papa would never hurt me. I'll be back."

She couldn't argue that one. Sonny was definitely the beloved son.

***

"Doc's lucky those cops took my gun or I'd have shot him, too," Lorenzo bellowed, wide-eyed and red-faced. "Barking orders at me, telling me what to say." He pointed at Sonny. "He needs to be put in his place."

Sonny paced the den. It still didn't make sense. "You shot Antony because you thought he was stealing a fishing rod?"

"Don't you start in on me. Your brother got what he deserved. He's got no business sneaking around my property. He's lucky I only hit him in the leg. I could've really made him pay for killing your mother. I still owe him for that."

Sonny stopped and stared at his father. This wasn't Papa just protecting a fishing rod. This was his way of justifying Antony's latest punishment. Over the years, he'd overlooked his father pulling the plug on many of Antony's business acquisitions and passing his brother over for CEO when he was clearly the better man for the job, but he couldn't look away from this.

The guilt was overwhelming. He could end his father's hatred toward Antony by simply telling him the truth. Maybe it was time. He owed it to Antony. He raked his fingers through his hair. "Papa . . ."

"Don't defend him. You know I ask two things from both of you, loyalty and respect. Your brother has tested me since the day he was born. Thank God Rachel gave me another son. One I could count on. One I could be proud of."

Pride birthed from deceit.

"Your brother is lucky." Lorenzo wheeled himself to the wet bar and made himself a drink. "I only let him work at Renato's because you wanted it so badly. I'd have gladly let him stay on the streets."

"He's made more money than I ever would've."

"All that money is useless without loyalty and respect. Gino was like a brother to me, and if Antony respected me, he'd have never been fighting with Carlo in the first place."

"But Carlo was the one who pulled a gun on Antony."

"And I'm sure Antony did nothing to deserve it, did he?" Lorenzo waved his hand in the air. "Enough of you defending him."

"But—"

"I said enough. His actions killed your mother. Nothing can change that. Life's been hard enough with one son I can't trust. You keep on, and I'll begin to doubt your loyalty." He glared at Sonny with empty, hollow eyes. "Then I'd have to deal with you, too."

Sonny stood stunned. Antony had warned him countless times over the years about what confessing to Papa would do. Antony was right. It would only lead to the destruction of them both.

"You can say what you want, but you have to be proud of Antony. He survived the streets you forced him to live on and then came back and made your company richer and more powerful than ever."

"You don't know anything, do you?" Lorenzo slammed the tumbler on the coffee table and wheeled himself out of the room.

Sonny sighed heavily and left.

***

Darkness engulfed the estate. Victoria shut off the late news and walked to the picture window. Sonny's car was pulling in. She opened the front door and waited.

"I was beginning to worry."

He gave her a quick kiss. "I'm sorry. Clay and I stopped by Renato's."

The lines on Sonny's forehead were deep. "You okay?" she asked.

"Yeah. How's Antony?"

"Still sleeping."

"I'm sorry for getting angry earlier. I didn't want to believe what you said about my father."

"It's okay. Come on." She took his hand and led him into the house. "I've got a couple hours before I'm scheduled to relieve Elisa. Did you eat dinner?"

"No."

"I'll make you a plate."

They went into the kitchen where she reheated homemade ravioli and set it in front of him. "Did Lorenzo tell you he shot Antony?"

"Yeah. He said he thought Antony was stealing a fishing rod, but there's more to it."

"You think he meant to shoot him?"

"No. I believe it was an accident, but he's justifying it by saying Antony deserved it. He was protecting more than a fishing rod." Sonny stabbed the last of the cheese ravioli with his fork, ate it, and pushed the plate away. "Are you planning on sitting with him all night?"

"Just until he wakes up. The doctors said the first twenty-four hours are the most critical. If he spikes a fever, we have to get him back to the hospital."

"Well," he grabbed her hand, giving it a squeeze. "I'm going up to bed."

"I'll come with you."

***

Antony was seven. He held tightly to his mother's hands. They danced around the open field of wildflowers, her white dress flowing in the breeze. Her voice was angelic as she sang, *Jesus loves me, this I know. For the Bible tells me so. Little ones to him belong. They are weak, but He is strong.*

Lorenzo walked over the hill, his face hard and his voice bellowing. Mama gathered Antony in her arms, whispering, *You are weak, but God is strong.* She kissed him on the cheek as Lorenzo ripped him from her arms. The back of Papa's hand caught the side of his face. When he cried, his father laughed. The clouds rolled in, darkening the sky. A bolt of lightning shot down, and the thunder shook the hillside.

Antony's body jerked. His eyes shot open. A hint of moonlight sliced into the room. Victoria was sleeping. Her head was resting on his hand. He moved his leg, but pain shot through it. "Oh, man, that hurts."

Victoria sat up and rubbed her eyes. "You're awake?"

"Yeah. What time is it?"

She stood, stretched, then turned on the small light. "It's about four a.m. How you feeling?" She grabbed the medicine bottles, opened them, took two pills, and handed them to him. "Antibiotic and for pain."

Antony took the pills and placed them on his tongue before taking the glass of water she pushed toward him. He swallowed the pills and handed back the glass. "You've been here the whole time? My hand doesn't make a very comfortable pillow. I think you slobbered on it."

"I did?" Victoria wiped her cheek. "I must've fallen asleep."

He smiled and took her hand. He had wondered if anyone would miss him. She would've, and he knew why. Despite her love for Sonny, she still had feelings for him. A ray of sunshine in his otherwise dark world.

"Where's Sonny?"

"Asleep." She squeezed his hand. "What really happened?"

"I told you, I tried to take something of Papa's. It was something that meant a lot to him." Antony held her hand, his lifeline. She was the one person he could count on.

"This *thing* must've been important. What was it?"

"Nothing." He stared at the ceiling. "I reacted like he did. I pulled my gun so fast." He took a deep breath and slowly let it out. "I could've shot him, Vic."

"But you didn't."

"I wanted to. I wanted him to pay for all the pain he's caused me." He turned to her, wondering what reaction his confession would bring. When her face continued to appear loving and nonjudgmental, he continued. "I stared into his eyes, and there was nothing there, just an empty, heartless man. It was like looking in the mirror."

"You're not like him."

He looked away, not wanting to see her innocence. "Yes, I am." He knew she only saw what he allowed her to, but the furthest depths of his heart would always hold contempt and bitterness for the life he had been dealt. "Thank you for coming. How'd you know?"

"Elisa found you."

"Elisa? What was she doing at Lorenzo's?"

"I don't know, but she's the one who called me."

"Where is she now?"

"Asleep in the other room. You can thank her in the morning." Victoria smiled. "It looks like you're going to be okay."

"Did you doubt?" He grinned and fought the heaviness in his eyelids. He loved talking to her, having her all to himself. "I prayed you would come." He raised his eyebrows. "Yeah, I prayed." His words began to slur. "I'm glad you came . . ." He fell asleep.

SIXTEEN

THERE WAS A TAP ON THE DOOR. "Yeah?" Antony leaned against the headboard and readjusted his leg.

Elisa came in and set down the breakfast tray. "I brought you something to eat."

"Thanks." Before a spark of excitement could ignite inside of him, it was quickly extinguished by the anger that had smoldered for years.

"I could change that bandage."

"That's okay." Antony picked up the two bottles of pills, ignoring her soft, caring eyes.

Elisa pointed. "One is an antibiotic, and the other is for pain." She handed him a glass of orange juice.

"I know." He popped the two pills in his mouth and washed them down with the juice. "Victoria said you're the one who found me. Thank you." He reached for the plate of food, grabbed a piece of toast, and took a bite. "What'd you stop by for?"

Elisa walked to the window, opened the blinds, and allowed the sun to infiltrate the room. "I overheard something I think you should know about."

"And?" Antony crossed his arms.

She sighed and turned to him. "Are you ever going to stop hating me?" The roll of his eyes drew her back to the chair where she sat. "I'm sorry I professed my love to you over and over again only to go back to Enrico."

"Did you mean any of it?"

"I loved you very much."

"Then why did you keep going back to him?"

"I was afraid. You don't understand the hold Enrico had on me." Her eyes met his. "Do you think you can ever forgive me?"

Rachel's voice shrieked in the hallway.

"Christian," he heard Victoria say. "Leave her alone. Uncle Tony is trying to sleep."

"Uncle Tony's here?" Rachel shouted then burst into the room.

"Oh, boy." Antony wrapped his arms around her. "What a way to wake up."

"What are you doing here?" Rachel nestled into his chest. "You spend the night?"

"Yes. Is that all right?"

She nodded. "Mom said we had to be quiet because you were sleeping."

Victoria walked into the room and grabbed Rachel's hand. "Sorry."

"See, Mom, Uncle Tony isn't sleeping."

"I see. Now, you need to eat so you can leave for school."

Rachel ran to the door then stopped abruptly. She walked back to Antony and threw her arms around him. "I love you." She kissed his cheek.

"Me, too, babe." He held her hand. "Have fun at school."

"Okay." She gave him a quick wave then left.

"Let me know if you need anything," Victoria said. "I'll be downstairs."

"Thanks."

When Victoria left, Elisa looked back at Antony. "So?"

"Forgiveness, huh?"

"I don't expect you to care about me or even be my friend. I'm only asking you to forgive me."

Her eyes pleaded with him, but he stayed silent. How could he believe her? What made this time different? "Why were you afraid of Enrico? What was the hold he had on you?"

"Enrico said he'd kill you if I ever left him."

"And you believed him?"

"He knew some powerful men."

"I could've handled Enrico. He was a low life punk."

"I was scared."

Antony tried to figure out if she was telling the truth or if this was one of her lies. He pulled the covers off his legs, spun them around, and sat on the edge of the bed wearing a pair of shorts. He vaguely remembered Doc helping him change into them the night before.

"What are you doing?" she asked.

"I'm getting out of this bed."

"It's too soon. You should give it a day or two."

Antony closed his eyes and held his breath as he pushed himself into a standing position. "Man, that hurts."

Elisa reached out to help, but he batted her hands away.

"What'd you overhear Dimitri say?" He hobbled to the windowsill, turned, and leaned against it.

"Dimitri said that once he had the paintings, he could get rid of him for good. I think he meant you."

"He meant the art broker who's selling the paintings."

"I don't think so. He's never mentioned an art broker."

"You think he's out to avenge Carlo?"

"Yes."

"Why?" He limped back to the bed then sat down and let out a sigh.

"The day the bomb blew up Dimitri's house and killed my grandmother, he showed up at my doorstep with two suitcases."

"So he stopped and bought new clothes."

Her brows lifted. "And packed them in suitcases?"

"Maybe he was going out of town on business. Did you ask him?"

"Just forget about the paintings, Antony. Don't look for them."

Seeing the love in her eyes, his heart softened. "Lorenzo has the paintings. As soon as my hands are on them, I'll give them to Dimitri, and he'll be out of my life—forever."

"And you'll be safe. Good."

Realizing what he had just told her, he grabbed her wrist. "That's between us."

"I know. I won't betray you."

"Make sure you don't."

A sharp knock on the door eased the tension. His eyes held steady to hers as he released her and yelled, "Yes?"

Sonny walked in. "Can I talk to you?"

"Sure. Elisa was just leaving."

Elisa gave Sonny a nod then left.

"What are you mad at her for?" Sonny asked.

"I'm not mad. It's nothing."

"I talked to Papa. He said he thought you were trying to steal one of his fishing rods."

"Yep."

"Must have been one heck of a rod."

Antony's eyes cut to him.

"You going to tell me the same story?"

Antony grabbed the bottle of painkillers, popped another in his mouth, jerked his head back, and swallowed.

Sonny leaned against the windowsill and crossed his arms. "I don't believe either one of you."

"Believe what you want."

"I can't help you if I don't know what's going on."

"Help me?" Antony almost laughed. "I don't need your help." He grabbed his shirt and pulled it over his head. "I've got everything under control."

"Yeah, I can tell." Sonny pointed to his bandaged leg. He picked up a pair of navy sweats and tossed them at Antony. "They're mine, but they should fit."

Antony sat on the bed and struggled to stick his foot in them. Sonny knelt down and slid the pants over Antony's foot and up his bandaged leg. "You know, despite the way Papa acts, I don't think he meant to shoot you."

"Papa never means it, does he?" Antony stood and pulled the sweats over the shorts.

"Don't you ever want to just get over it?"

"Get over it? How can I do that when I'm reminded of it every day? The man tolerates me. He doesn't love me. He never has, and he never will."

"Because of me? And the lie you carry?"

"I don't blame you, Sonny. I did what I did because I love you, but I'll never love Lorenzo the same way you do."

"Your heart is cold, brother."

Antony gave a derogatory laugh. Cold wasn't the right word. More like frozen, and he liked it that way. The less love he gave, the less pain he felt. He had accepted that as his lot in life. Maybe it was punishment for his father's sins. He didn't know, but he had learned to live with it, and in some strange way, he had accepted it.

"I need someone to take me home," Antony said.

"Max is downstairs."

Antony limped toward the door.

Sonny grabbed his arm, forcing Antony to turn back. "Why do you feel the need to protect me?"

"What?"

"You're keeping something from me, something I should know about. What is it?"

Antony's mouth tipped arrogantly. "It's between me and Papa."

"Sure it is." Sonny moved out of the way.

***

Elisa sat on the couch at her house and sipped on a hot cup of tea. She was exhausted and thankful to be alone. Classical music played softly on the stereo, and it soothed her as she stared out the window. The tree branches swayed in the wind.

She closed her eyes and allowed the music to take her away to another place and time, to the only time in her life she had truly been happy. Before Antony disappeared, before Carlo's death. She had been babysitting for a neighbor when Antony came over with a single rose, stolen from the cooler at Kuehler's store he had later confessed.

The twins were two and a half. Elisa had welcomed Antony's help. Antony wrestled with the boys and even changed their diapers. After tucking them into bed, she overheard the boys asking Antony to say prayers with them. He appeased them, even got on his knees.

He didn't ask to stay after that, claiming he didn't want her to get in trouble, but as they stood at the door, his eyes looked deep within her. It was then he said he loved her.

Hearing a sound, she opened her eyes. Startled, she turned to see Dimitri, his long black hair tied back in a ponytail. A coldness in his eyes shook her to her inner core.

"Where were you all night?"

Elisa took deep breaths, praying he would not see the fear that ran through her body. She set down the tea, hoping the minor change would ease the blood that pounded through her veins.

He took off his jacket, which exposed two guns, walked toward her, and laughed. "Don't look so worried. I'm not going to hurt you.

I just want answers." He rubbed his hands together. His voice thundered through the room. "Tell me."

Terror consumed her. She couldn't move. "I was helping a friend."

"A friend? Your car was parked at Sonny's all night. I'm assuming you saw Antony." Dimitri cracked his knuckles.

Elisa stood and walked toward the back door. Her entire body shook.

Dimitri took a step toward her. "I want to know what you told them."

"I don't know what you're talking about."

"You don't think you overheard me by accident, do you?"

"I didn't tell them anything."

His hand came across her face, hard. The force of the blow split her lip. Crying out in pain, she covered her mouth.

"You're lying!" he yelled.

In one motion, he grabbed her. His large hand clenched her narrow neck, and his hot breath was on her face. "Always the faithful friend even when he can't stand to look at you. I know you told him what I said." A glazed look overcame him, and his grip tightened around her neck. "What did he tell you?"

Panic engulfed her. She hit and grabbed at his hands. Her head began to spin with each shortened breath. "Lorenzo." She gasped for breath. "Lorenzo has the paintings."

He released her. She fell to the floor and held her neck, trying to catch her breath.

"You're pathetic." The maliciousness ran thick in his voice. Revenge radiated from his eyes. "I hope you kissed him goodbye," he bellowed. "Justice, she goes nowhere and calls no one."

Justice nodded.

Dimitri left.

Elisa laid on the floor, sobbing.

After a quick stop at the doctors, where Antony had the gunshot wound rechecked and rewrapped, Max pulled into Antony's estate.

"Wait here." Antony climbed out of the black Hummer, limped inside using the cane the doctor had given him, and felt his phone vibrate. A message. He pushed play. Lorenzo's voice said, "We need to talk. Get over here."

Antony went into his room, slipped off Sonny's sweats and shorts, grabbed a pair of loose-fitting black slacks, and slid them on. He pulled on a gray knit shirt, went into the bathroom, ran a comb through his hair, and brushed his teeth.

Exhausted, he sat on the couch in the living room. His leg throbbed. The phone rang. He looked at the caller ID and rolled his eyes. Lorenzo again.

Antony reached down and grabbed the cane. He pulled himself up and went back out to the Hummer where Max was still waiting.

"Take me to Lorenzo's." Antony laid his head on the seat and closed his eyes.

What seemed like seconds later, Max nudged Antony. "Hey, we're here."

Antony lifted his head and rubbed his eyes. "Thanks."

"You need me to stick around?"

"No, my car's here."

"You think you should be driving?"

Antony climbed out of the Hummer. "I shouldn't be walking." He slammed the door and went into the den where he thought Lorenzo would be waiting.

Relieved to find it empty, he stretched out on the couch and let the pain medication drift him back to sleep.

"It's about time," Lorenzo bellowed and pushed against Antony's legs.

Indescribable pain shot through Antony's body. "Watch it." He sat up, slowly swung his leg around, and rested his head on the back of the couch. With clenched fists, he grimaced. "What are you doing?" He squeezed his leg. "Man, that hurt."

"You go to the doctor?"

"Yeah, I'll live." Antony stared at his father. He looked so old and fragile, but he was far from it. He was still sharp and keen even if he was a bit trigger-happy. "Where are the paintings?"

"They're safe." Lorenzo snapped his fingers at Antony then pointed to the bar.

"You're unbelievable. I'm not making you a drink. Roll over there and make it yourself." Heat crept up Antony's neck. "How did you know Dimitri had those paintings at Francesca's?"

Lorenzo laughed while he rolled himself to the bar. "You didn't think your old man still had it in him, did you?" He raised his glass triumphantly.

"No, I didn't." Antony picked up the cane and pulled himself up. He hobbled to the French doors and looked out at the garden. "But why?"

"If Dimitri's back for revenge, we have leverage."

"I gotta have those paintings to get Dimitri out of our lives." Antony turned. "Give them to me."

The ice clinked against the glass as Lorenzo brought the drink to his mouth.

"Lorenzo?"

Lorenzo glared at him.

"Papa?"

"Don't call me that."

Antony pulled a toothpick from his pocket, bit down hard hoping to dull the pain in his leg. "Oh, I get it. You don't trust me?" His eyes narrowed. "If I were Sonny, you would hand them over without a second thought. What do you think your spotless son would do if he knew that you stole those paintings?"

"You're not getting them." Lorenzo sipped on his drink. "And I won't explain myself to you."

Antony clenched his fists. "Man, I could just—"

Sonny's voice shot from the doorway of the den. "What are you two fighting about?"

Antony turned to Sonny. "We were just talking." Antony's eyes cut to his father.

"About what?"

"Trust me," Antony said, "you don't want to know."

Sonny glared at him. "I don't need your protection."

"Oh, really?" Antony raised an eyebrow, sick of being looked down upon. "Okay, the paintings stolen from Francesca's were originals worth millions."

"What?" Sonny's eyes widened.

Antony grinned sardonically, nodding his head. "It gets better. They're here, in this house."

"You?" Sonny glared at Antony. "You used Francesca's to front stolen artwork?"

Antony's neck burned. "You would think that." He turned to walk away.

Sonny grabbed Antony's shoulder. "You broke into the store and had the nerve to lecture me about security? This is just great. Drag our whole family into the world you always wanted. A world I've spent half my life digging us out of."

Antony glared at his brother. "I didn't do it."

"Sure."

Antony nodded in disgust. "Of course, you don't believe me. Once a liar, always a liar?"

"Your words, not mine."

"Oh, man." Antony backed away from him, his hands in fists that he kept tightening and releasing. "There's only one lie I've carried, and this is not it."

Sonny stood staunchly. "Give me the paintings so I can give them to the police."

Antony's dark eyes flashed, a cynical grin on his face. "I don't know where they are."

"You're lying."

Antony dropped the cane and lunged at Sonny. Sonny dodged the punch and brought his fist up full force, hitting Antony in the nose. Pain shot through his face, and he jumped back. Losing his balance, he fell to the floor. A spider web of pain shot through his leg.

He grabbed the cane and pulled himself up. He touched the blood that seeped out of his nose. Nodding, he had to grin. "Good hit," he said then drew back and punched Sonny in the stomach.

"Vince," Lorenzo barked. "Get Antony off him."

Vince grabbed the back of Antony's shirt and pulled him from Sonny who was now doubled over in pain. Antony fell onto the couch. His leg throbbed, and his nose bled.

Lorenzo glared at Antony. "Let Sonny be."

"Let Sonny be," Antony mocked, his head tilted back, holding his fingers to his nose to stop the bleeding. "Sonny, your beloved son." Antony grabbed the towel Vince pushed toward him and held it to his nose. "I'm so sick of your disowning looks."

"After what you did, you deserved to be disowned," Lorenzo barked, his eyes hard and cold. "Killing your mother—"

"I didn't kill Carlo," Antony gritted his teeth. "Sonny did."

"What?" Lorenzo yelled so loud the windows rattled.

Anger seeped from Antony's pores. "Your precious son, the one you love so much. He did it, not me. I've covered for him for years, and I'm sick of your looks. The only thing I did was stand up for Sonny so you wouldn't kill him."

"Is it true?" Lorenzo glared at Sonny. "You killed Carlo, not Antony? You've lied to me all these years?"

Sonny gave a single nod, his face white.

Lorenzo shook his head as a stream of cuss words poured from his mouth, both in English and Italian. He raised the tumbler and threw it at Sonny, who dodged it only to have it shatter against the wall, spraying him with glass and whiskey.

"How's it feel to have him look at you in disgust?" Antony snapped. Sonny looked over at Antony, who quickly looked away from the hurt in his brother's eyes. He'd hoped he'd be relieved when the burden was lifted, but all he felt was remorse.

Sonny glared at Antony. "The paintings?"

"I took the paintings. I am Lorenzo Luciano, and I will not sit back and let Dimitri set us up."

"Set us up?" Sonny glanced between the two men. "Are you saying Dimitri planted the paintings at the store?"

"Ah," Antony said sarcastically and grinned, "you're finally catching on."

Lorenzo pointed his finger at Sonny. His hands shook. "You killed Carlo. You killed your mother. You ruined my life. I should . . . I should . . ." he pursed his lips, rolled the wheelchair to the French doors, opened them, and wheeled himself out.

Sonny stared at Antony for a moment and then followed Lorenzo to the garden.

***

Sonny had always wanted to tell the truth, to know that his father loved him regardless of what had happened years ago, but his fears had held him back—fear of rejection, of being blamed, of having his father turn his back on him. Now those fears were all coming true.

"Papa."

"Stay away from me or I'll kill you." Lorenzo pushed the wheels and went further into the garden.

"Let me explain."

Lorenzo spun the chair around and glared at him. "I have only asked two things of you boys—respect and loyalty. You have both shown me nothing but disrespect over the last twenty years."

"I didn't mean to kill Carlo. I was trying to save Antony's life. Carlo was going to kill him."

Lorenzo took deep breaths and looked like he was calming down. He motioned for Sonny to come closer. As Sonny leaned in, Lorenzo grabbed him by the neck. His grip tightened with each word. "You killed my wife, your own mother."

Sonny's heart quickened. He grabbed his father's hands, trying to pry them off. When he looked up, he saw Antony's outstretched arm with the nose of his pistol pressing into Lorenzo's temple.

"Let him go." Antony's face was hard.

"You wouldn't dare." Lorenzo clutched tighter to Sonny's throat.

Antony pulled the action back and pressed the gun harder into Lorenzo's temple. "Try me."

Lorenzo released Sonny with a shove. Sonny fell back and slid across the cement, holding his neck and trying to catch his breath. He pushed himself to a standing position. His eyes shot from Antony to Lorenzo then back to Antony. He shook his head. "I didn't kill Mama. I didn't."

Sonny walked into Antony's office, holding his neck. Fear gripped him. His father had tried to kill him, and if Antony hadn't stepped in, he believed he would've. Antony had saved him—again. How would he ever be able to repay him for taking the blame, for living the life he had been forced to live?

***

"You okay?" Antony's voice made Sonny jump. "I never meant to tell him, but you kept accusing me."

"I know. Thanks."

"No problem. I'm glad you told him you didn't kill Mama." Antony leaned on the cane. "You didn't, you know. He did. Him and his drinking."

"I don't know how to thank you for—"

"Don't get mushy on me now." Antony hobbled behind the desk and sat down. "We've got bigger problems."

"Dimitri and the paintings? You going to fill me in?"

"Yesterday, I figured out Lorenzo had Vince rob the store."

"And you found the paintings?"

"And he shot me. Those paintings are worth millions. Dimitri's hooked up with a broker, a guy named Ferdinand. When Dimitri didn't show up with the paintings, Ferdinand thought Dimitri had double-crossed him, so he blew up his house as a warning."

"You believe Dimitri?"

"I have no reason not to." Antony's cell phone rang. Grabbing it, he looked at the caller ID. It was Dimitri. "Yeah?"

"He got to Elisa," Dimitri's voice sounded shaky. "I came home and found her. He almost choked her to death. He must've tailed her or something."

Antony mentally kicked himself. "Is she okay?"

"Yes, she's pretty shook up, though. So Lorenzo has the paintings?"

Antony rubbed his forehead. He shouldn't have told her, but he had thought . . . It didn't matter. "I'll call you when they're in my hands."

"I gotta have those paintings, Antony. The sooner I get them, the sooner I can get Ferdinand out of my life."

"I know." Antony slammed down the phone and sighed heavily.

"What's going on now?" Sonny asked.

"Man, I'm so stupid." Antony leaned back in his chair. "I let it slip to Elisa that Lorenzo had the paintings. Dimitri said Ferdinand got it out of her."

"Is she okay?"

"Yeah." Antony picked up the Chinese health balls he'd purchased on one of his trips to China and began rubbing them together. "If what Dimitri says about Ferdinand is true, he'll kill Lorenzo next."

"They can't get through the security here."

"Security?" Antony shook his head. "He's become too relaxed. I've told him that."

"Then what do you think we should do?"

"Get the paintings, give them to Dimitri, and get this guy out of our lives."

Sonny shook his head. "No. We get the paintings and turn them over to the police."

"By the time the police find Ferdinand, someone will get hurt or killed. No. No police."

"We do this legally. Just get Papa to tell you where the paintings are."

"You think he'll tell me?" Antony shook his head.

"Well, he sure won't tell me."

"I find them, I give them to Dimitri." Antony returned the Chinese balls into the red velvet-lined box. "You want to give them to the police, then find them yourself."

Sonny's face reddened. "Just get them."

"If I get them, we'll discuss this."

Sonny conceded.

Antony pulled himself up and limped to the garden. He stared at his father and wondered if he was sorry for sending him away. What would he think if he knew Antony had slept on the streets and ate food out of dumpsters? Would he even care? He shook his head and the thoughts from his mind. "Where are the paintings?"

Lorenzo's age-spotted face glowed red. "Why did you lie to me?"

"Because Sonny couldn't have survived the streets." Antony threw off his anger. "The paintings."

Lorenzo stared at the birds that danced around the bird feeders. "Why would I tell you where they are?"

"Papa, come on."

Lorenzo's eyes cut to him. "I told you, don't ever call me that."

Antony knew his father's anger all too well. He'd have to find the paintings himself. He'd found them once, he could find them again.

He limped back to his office.

SEVENTEEN

THE HITMAN PEEKED THROUGH THE BUSHES. With the earlier commotion, he thought Antony might do the job for him. Lorenzo was getting old and had sent away his bodyguard, but the man wasn't stupid. Someone would still be close.

The sun was beginning to set, and his legs were cramping under his weight. The only other annoyance was his growling stomach. He was afraid someone would hear it. He was going to have to hurry or he'd be late for dinner. His wife's wrath was worse than Dimitri's.

He made sure the silencer was secure on the forty-five caliber Smith and Wesson then aimed it at Lorenzo as he wheeled his chair toward the rose bushes. "Come on," he whispered. "Just a little bit closer."

The man squeezed the trigger and fired one shot in the chest.

Lorenzo's body jerked, and his head fell. The man looked around before he jumped out of the bushes and put the gun in Lorenzo's hand. He placed Lorenzo's finger on the trigger, put his finger over Lorenzo's, aimed the gun high in the air, and fired another shot. He removed the silencer and tucked it in his pocket.

With a second gun in his hand, he headed to the eight-foot brick wall and looked for bodyguards. When there were none in sight, he threw the rope over. The hook caught on the other side. After testing it, he pulled himself up and over.

A few jerks, and it released itself from the wall. Tucking the rope in his pocket, he ran down the street to his car and took off. He grabbed the cell and called Dimitri. "It's done."

***

Antony limped back into the office.

Sonny stood. "You find out where the paintings are?"

Antony shook his head, his mind still focused on his father's words. The confession hadn't changed a thing.

Sonny raked his hands through his hair. "I guess I'll try."

Consolata's scream filled the house. Her words sent a chill down Antony's spine. "Lorenzo, Dio Onnipotentent . . . he's dead."

"What?" Sonny's forehead wrinkled. "Did she just say—" He ran from the office.

Antony limped close behind.

Sonny fell to the ground by the wheelchair, his hand resting on Lorenzo's arm. "I'm sorry, Papa. I'm so sorry."

The great Lorenzo Luciano's life had ended with a gun in his hand and a bullet hole in his chest. His head hung motionless, and blood dripped from his mouth onto his pants.

Vince ran out onto the patio, his gun clutched tightly in his hand. His eyes widened, and a stream of cuss words shot out of his mouth.

"Suicide?" Antony crouched down and looked closer. "Check the grounds. He'd never kill himself."

Vince ran off, shouting orders at other bodyguards.

Antony turned to Consolata. "Call nine-one-one."

He avoided Sonny's eyes, walked into the den, and sat down. He should be sad or angry, screaming at bodyguards and at Vince, but instead, he found himself disappointed. Despite the apparent disgust his father had for him, Antony always believed he'd earn back his father's favor. It never came, and now, it never would.

He glanced back at his father's dead body. If only he hadn't told Elisa. If only she hadn't opened her mouth. He shook his head and pursed his lips. It wasn't his fault or Elisa's. It was Dimitri's. He always swam in a pit of filth, and he had pulled Antony back into it.

"Grounds are secure," Vince said, interrupting his thoughts.

Antony nodded. Another bodyguard led the initial police officers through the den and out to the patio where they immediately roped off the garden with yellow crime tape.

Guys with Evidence Tech written on the backs of their jackets soon invaded the house and began dusting everything outside with powder, checking for prints, while other officers searched the flower beds, the grass, and the shrubs.

Sonny walked through a couple of times, but Antony ignored him. He had to keep his emotions in control, his heart hard, and his head clear. If this wasn't a suicide, then someone had killed their father without even attempting to get the paintings first. It meant any one of them could be next.

Two detectives arrived. One outstretched his hand. "I'm Jackson Cole, and this is my partner Samuel Garcia."

Sonny shook their hands and led them onto the patio.

Antony stood and walked to the doorway, leaned against it, and listened to Sonny talk. "We haven't touched anything."

"Looks like a suicide," Jackson said.

"My father wouldn't commit suicide," Sonny snapped. "He was murdered."

"Any idea who would want him dead?" Jackson asked.

"No," Antony said. He glared at Sonny.

Garcia glanced between the two brothers then squatted next to the body. He looked up at them. "Had he received any threatening letters or phone calls?"

Sonny shook his head.

Garcia stood. Jackson looked over at Garcia. "Have 'em bag the hands, check for powder residue."

Garcia motioned to the officers then followed Antony as he limped into the den and sat on the couch. Garcia pointed to Antony's leg. "What happened to you?"

"An accident."

Garcia raised an eyebrow. "Any idea who would want your father dead?" He paced, his hands deep in his pockets. "Any acquaintances from the past that may have come to collect on an old vendetta?"

Antony shook his head.

"Can you get me a list of people who might be angry at your father, companies he took over?"

"Sure."

Jackson and Sonny came into the den.

"When they're through gathering evidence," Jackson jotted something down in the notepad. "The guys from the morgue will move the body. They'll have to do an autopsy."

"How long will that take?" Sonny asked.

Jackson slipped the notepad into the pocket of his suit jacket. "You should have the body by the end of the week."

Antony looked through the French doors at his father, who was surrounded by roses and gardenias. The garden that his mother had planted when they lived in Kansas City. The flowers Lorenzo had dug up and brought to California. His father had turned back into the man she hated, then died in one of the many things she loved. The irony brought a smile to his face.

Victoria came in like a breath of fresh air. Antony's heart ached as Sonny pulled her into his arms. He narrowed his eyes and hardened his heart. There wasn't time to get soft. Antony would force himself back into his cold existence. Victoria brought a sense of urgency to the situation. This man could strike again, and she could be next. If it cost him his life, he would stop it.

Victoria walked to the couch and looked down at him. "I'm sorry."

"I'm not." Antony glanced up at her then away.

His spiteful words made her turn back to Sonny. She motioned to the men searching through the bushes. "What are they doing?"

"Looking for evidence." Sonny stared outside. "Shell casings, footprints, fibers, anything the murderer might have dropped."

"Murderer?"

"Papa wouldn't commit suicide."

"But who would kill him? Dimitri?"

Sonny glanced at Antony who shook his head.

"I'm not sure." Sonny ran his fingers through his hair. "We'll have to see what the police turn up."

***

Hours later, the coroner loaded Lorenzo's body onto the stretcher and wheeled it past them. Jackson followed. "If we have any more questions, we'll call."

The room cleared out, and the only sound was Consolata's constant crying from the kitchen.

Sonny tapped Antony's arm. "You want to come over?"

"No." He had to find the paintings.

"How did someone get in here to do this?" Sonny asked.

Antony shrugged.

"You going to find out?"

Antony nodded. He already knew Ferdinand had Lorenzo killed. Figuring out how was something he'd worry about later. All he wanted to do now was to find the paintings and the beaker and get this madman out of their lives.

"You going to say anything?" Sonny's eyes filled with tears. "Papa was just killed."

Antony pursed his lips. He knew whatever he said about their father would start a fight, and he wasn't in the mood.

Sonny whispered something to Victoria, kissed her, then left.

Victoria tucked her hair behind her ears. "You okay?"

Antony pulled himself up with the cane and limped to the French doors. He stared at the blood-stained patio. Yellow police tape swayed in the wind.

"Do you remember that beaker you bought in the Bahamas?" He turned toward her, resting against the cane. "Do you have it?"

"No, it was one of the sculptures stolen before the store opened. They pawned the stuff down in LA, but there was no beaker."

"Did you ever find out who stole the stuff?"

"Why?"

"No reason." He looked back at the patio. "What a mess."

"Why don't you come over? You shouldn't be alone."

Antony let out a deep, bellowing laugh. "I have more important things to do than to sit around and listen to my brother cry about a man who despised me."

"Like who killed him?"

"For starters."

"Why do you care so much? I thought you hated him as much as he hated you."

"Because any one of us could be next."

Her face paled. "You really think . . ."

"I don't know." He was sorry he mentioned it. "But I won't wait around and give him the chance."

"Don't do anything stupid. Let the police handle this."

Antony rolled his eyes. "Have you ever known me to do anything stupid?"

She shook her head. "Can I do anything for you?"

"You can leave."

"We love you, Antony. You're not alone."

Antony gave a frustrated laugh then turned back to the patio where Consolata knelt down, scrubbing the blood, tears falling from her face. She chanted in both English and Italian. He didn't turn back around until he heard Victoria leave.

Sighing, he pulled the bottle of pain pills from his pocket, put one in his mouth, jerked his head back, and swallowed it.

***

Sonny lay on the bed and stared up at the ceiling. The door opened. He looked over as Victoria came in.

"Doc told me you left." She smiled. It looked forced. "I thought you were going to wait for me."

"I wanted to be alone before the kids got home from school." He patted the spot next to him. "Is Antony coming over?"

"No."

Sonny drew her closer, and she relaxed in his arms. He kissed the top of her head and pulled her close. "Papa found out the truth today."

"Truth?" She raised up on one elbow. "About Carlo?"

"Yep. We were all arguing. I pushed Antony too far, and he told." Sonny ran his hand through his hair. "Papa was furious." His father's last words echoed in his mind. *You killed your mother.* Sonny knew it wasn't true, but his father went to his grave believing it.

"Anyway, thank you for trying to get through to my brother."

Victoria rested her head on his chest. "What were you guys arguing about?"

"Nothing."

"Antony said the killer might come after us. Do you think Dimitri is behind this?"

"I don't know." As much as he'd like to tell her about Ferdinand and Dimitri's involvement, he wouldn't. Elisa had known too much and already paid the price. He wasn't about to put his wife in the same danger.

"Seems Dimitri would blame Lorenzo for killing his parents," she said. "If he's after revenge—"

"Dimitri didn't do this." He snapped, ending the conversation.

He closed his eyes and tried to hold the tears back, but they came anyway.

EIGHTEEN

ANTONY HELD RACHEL'S HAND. They stood next to Sonny, Victoria, and Christian in front of Lorenzo's casket as it sat over the green indoor-outdoor carpet that hid the open grave. The smell of rain in late October taunted them as the clouds rumbled and rolled over the sky, sending a chill through the air.

Flowers by the dozens surrounded the casket. Business associates, employees of Renato's, and friends formed a large group of mourners. Consolata's sobbing played like background music over the crowd.

The priest spoke a prayer as he swung the gold-plated censer. The three chains clinked together as puffs of incense escaped and floated down onto the casket. The final prayer finished as holy water was released from a sprinkler in the form of a cross over the casket.

A single tear escaped Antony's eye and rolled down his cheek. He brushed it away, bent over, and kissed his mother's tombstone. At the time, he had hated the idea of disturbing her grave, but he was now thankful his father had her remains moved to California.

He touched his father's casket then pulled his hand away. It was like touching a fire that never went out. Rachel touched his arm. Antony moved her golden brown curls behind her ears. "Yeah?"

"Why did Nonno die?"

"I don't know." It wasn't entirely true, but he wasn't about to shatter her innocence if he didn't have to.

"I miss him." Tears rolled down her cheeks.

Antony brushed them away with his finger. "I know you do." He pulled her close and kissed her forehead. She clutched a single rose in her hand. Antony pointed to it. "You want to put that on his casket?"

She nodded then leaned over the casket and laid the rose in front of the large spray of flowers. Sonny placed his hand on Christian's shoulder. Christian took a step forward and placed his rose on the casket next to Rachel's.

They stood silent for a long time before people approached them, offered condolences, and left. The cemetery was soon quiet. Bodyguards were in strategic positions. Dimitri and Elisa stood by their car. Neither had approached them.

Antony glanced at Elisa then turned his attention back to Rachel. Her childish love was pure and unwavering, not muddled by lies and deceit.

He turned to Sonny. "Let's go."

Sonny stared blankly at the casket. "Take Vic and the kids to the car. I'll be there in a minute."

"No. We need to go now." Antony knew what his brother wanted to do. He wanted to make his peace, but now wasn't the time. Despite the bodyguards and the assurance from Dimitri that Ferdinand would give them time to find the paintings, they were too vulnerable.

"Give me a minute."

Antony hesitated. He motioned with his head to Clay. "Take the kids to the car."

Clay stood next to Rachel. Christian walked behind them.

Antony reached out for Victoria's arm.

***

The gunman crouched behind the large tombstone. His orders were clear. Kill Sonny Luciano. He glanced at the picture one last time, memorizing the face, then slipped it back into his front pocket. He opened and closed his hand, taking special care to stretch his trigger finger. He brought the Remington 700 up to his shoulder and looked through the scope. He saw Dimitri then moved the scope to the Luciano brothers, carefully choosing his target. Just a few more seconds. He watched one man take the children and another the woman's arm. He'd wait until he led her away.

He breathed deeply and exhaled, slowing down his pounding heart. He raised his head one last time to check where the other men were positioned. He was confident he could get a shot off before being seen. One shot was all he'd need.

Looking through the scope, he aimed for Sonny's chest and took a deep breath.

***

Antony took Victoria's arm, but she turned back to Sonny. She couldn't leave him, not yet.

A shot rang through the air as heat burst through her shoulder.

Antony dove, knocking both her and Sonny to the ground. "Get down!" He pulled his gun and ran off. Clay dove on top of Rachel and Christian, who were almost to the car.

Half of Sonny's body lay over her. He whispered a short prayer then began yelling orders. Her body jerked when another gunshot went off. She clenched her eyes closed, and her ears rang.

Victoria's eyes shot open at Rachel's screams. She saw Max double over and fall to the ground, clutching his stomach.

"Stay down," Sonny yelled.

Two more shots zinged through the air. Victoria felt Sonny's breath on her face and the beating of his heart against her chest.

"He's down!" Antony shouted. "We got him."

"Call an ambulance. Antony, get over here." Sonny touched Victoria's face. Her body trembled.

"The kids?" Victoria tried to forget the pain that shot through her body.

"They're in the car. They're safe." Sonny applied pressure to her shoulder and kissed her forehead. "I'm so sorry."

Victoria reached up and touched his face. "It's okay." She dropped her hand to the ground. Her body shook again.

When Sonny pushed harder, she cried out.

"I know it hurts."

"It burns." Tears rolled down her cheeks and pooled in her ears.

"You're going to be okay." Tears filled his eyes.

She coughed then cringed from the pain. She looked up into the dark clouds as the sprinkles of rain fell on her face.

The sirens were getting louder. "Vic, the ambulance is almost here. Hang in there."

"Sonny?"

"Yeah?"

"I love you."

She closed her eyes, and everything went black.

***

Sonny yelled at Antony. "Here." The blood oozed between his fingers. "Push here."

"What? No, the ambulance is almost here."

"Do it." Sonny released the pressure on Victoria's shoulder, forcing his brother to react.

Antony dropped his gun and fell next to her, pushing hard on her bleeding shoulder. "What are you doing?" he yelled at Sonny.

Sonny had a mission, and nothing would stop him, not even the yelling of his brother or the pleas of Clay who had shoved the kids in the limo and was now trying to keep up.

Sonny looked down at Doc, who was leaning over Max. He clenched his hands into fists. "How is he?"

"Dead." Doc stood.

"The kids are in the car," Clay said. "You should let them know you're all right."

Sonny nodded. As he walked to the limo, he wiped his bloody hands on his pants. He opened the door. Rachel stared wide-eyed, and tears streaked her face. "Is Mom okay?"

Sonny held her tight and stared into Christian's eyes. "Mom's fine. She's hurt, but she's fine." Sonny kissed her. "Bruno will take you two home, and I'll be there later." He peeled Rachel off, wiped her tears, and gave her a kiss on the cheek.

Christian put his arm around Rachel, pulling her close. "Dad?" Christian's chin quivered.

"Yes?"

"Will you have Mom call as soon as she can?"

Sonny nodded and squeezed Christian's shoulder. "I need you to take care of your sister. I'll be home later."

Sonny slammed the door shut and gave the hood of the limousine a single pound. Bruno floored it. Christian and Rachel both turned around and stared out the back window. He gave them a wave then turned to Dimitri who stood next to the car. Elisa sat inside.

Heat radiated from Sonny's neck, and he knew of only one other time he'd felt such anger. It was the day Carlo had held a gun to his brother's chest. Sonny pursed his lips as he walked to Dimitri.

Elisa rolled down the window, and her voice shook as she asked, "Is she okay?"

"She will be. I need to talk to your cousin."

Elisa nodded and rolled the window back up.

Sonny's face hardened. "I want Ferdinand's number, now."

"Not a good idea Sonny." Dimitri cracked his knuckles.

"You said we were safe."

"He said he'd give you time to find his things. I swear." Dimitri wiped the sweat from his forehead.

"We haven't found the paintings. Give me the number, and I'll talk to him myself."

"I don't have it on me, but I'll get it." Dimitri stared past him and looked at Victoria. "Man, I'm sorry."

Sonny glared. "I want that number."

"Sure thing."

Sonny jogged back to Victoria as they lifted her into the ambulance. He jumped in behind them while Antony backed away. The cops had invaded the scene.

"Meet me at the hospital!" Sonny yelled as the doors closed.

***

Sonny paced the small waiting room. His prayers were persistent but went unanswered. He wanted news about his wife's condition, but nobody came. The only thing he knew was that when they arrived at the hospital, Victoria was unconscious. The bullet looked like it had hit her in the shoulder, but there was so much blood he now doubted what he had seen.

Antony limped into the room, his face hard. "Any word?" He sat down and momentarily closed his eyes and positioned his still-sore leg.

"No." Sonny sat next to him and rested his elbows on his knees. He dropped his head. "She's gotta be okay."

"She will be."

"I told Dimitri I want Ferdinand's number. I'm going to meet with him."

"*We're* going to meet with him."

Sonny looked over at Antony and nodded then silence blanketed the room.

Both brothers stood when they heard footsteps in the waiting area. Sonny folded his arms across his chest. The doctor approached them, removed his surgical hat, and ripped off the mask that hung from his neck.

"Your wife is going to be fine," he said. "She was lucky. The bullet went straight through. It broke through the skin on the shoulder below the acromion, here," the doctor placed his hand on Sonny's shoulder and pointed just below his clavicle. "The x-rays showed no fractures."

"We sutured the wound, and I've got a call into a therapist who will stop by and show her some exercises. She lost a lot of blood, so we'll keep her overnight for observation, just as a precaution."

Sonny extended his hand. "Thank you. Can I see her now?"

"The nurse will take you to her."

***

Antony stood against the wall, staring at Victoria who slept peacefully on the hospital bed. Thanking and cursing God was becoming a daily routine, and he wasn't sure if he liked it. When she began to stir, he walked to the door where Sonny stood talking on his cell phone.

"She's coming around," Antony whispered.

Sonny nodded then spoke into the phone. "Mom's waking up . . . yes . . . I'll call you back so you can talk to her. Tell Rachel she's okay. I love you. Bye."

Sonny slid the phone into his pocket and went to Victoria.

Antony watched from the corner of the room. Sonny stood, her hand in his. She opened her eyes.

"Hey, beautiful." Sonny gave her a kiss. "You're going to be fine. Doctor said the bullet went straight through."

"Are the kids all right?" she asked, almost too faint to hear.

"They're at home. We'll call them in a minute. They're anxious to talk to you."

"Max. Is he alive?"

"No. The shooter's dead, too." He cupped both his hands over hers and brought them up to his forehead in a praying position. "The cops found a picture of me in the shooter's pocket." His eyes met hers. "If you hadn't turned back when you did, he could've killed me."

"Why was someone trying to kill you? Was it Dimitri?"

"We'll talk about this later." Sonny kissed her forehead. "You need to rest."

Victoria nodded, her eyes closed.

Sonny went over to Antony. "Get Ferdinand's number and set up a meeting."

"We should find the paintings first."

"Lean harder on Vince. He's got to know where they are."

Antony walked into the hallway where Vince and Doc stood. "I want guys everywhere. Cover the doors, the elevators, and the stairs. Doc, I want you to wait until they take Vic to a room then stay with her."

"I know how to do my job." Doc's eyes narrowed.

"Not very well or Victoria wouldn't be here, would she?" Antony snapped back.

"You're so conceited." The redness on Doc's face made his hair look blonder than it really was. "You stood right next to her. You profess to love her so much, but not enough to throw yourself in front of a bullet."

Antony shoved Doc up against the wall. "You little punk. Don't you ever . . ."

Vince pried Antony off Doc. "This will get us nowhere."

"You," Antony pointed at Vince. "Get me the paintings."

"I told you, I don't know where Lorenzo put 'em."

Antony's eyes narrowed. "Find them."

Vince left.

Antony walked slowly toward the elevator. It wasn't until he was inside and the door closed that he leaned against the wall and swallowed the guilt. The shooting replayed in his mind. Doc was right. He had failed her. He should've kept her safe. Why hadn't he reacted faster? Why hadn't he known?

The bell to the elevator sounded, and the doors opened. A short, bald man walked in carrying flowers. They rode in silence. Antony's leg throbbed. It had been six days since he was shot and he'd given up the cane. Now he wished he had it. He reached into his pocket, pulled out the pain pills, threw one in his mouth, jerked his head back and swallowed.

The doors opened onto the fifth floor. He limped down the hall and nodded at the two plainclothes police officers. He knocked on the door then walked into the hospital room.

Zoë sat on the edge of the chair in the corner, her arms crossed. The burnt strands of her hair had been razor cut in the latest style. She stood, wearing a loose-fitting shirt and sweat pants. "It's about time." She grabbed her small overnight bag. "You said the funeral would end by eleven. They released me over three hours ago."

"You got no other friends?" Antony spouted then regretted the words after he said them.

"I could've had a cop take me home, but I could just see the morning paper, 'Antony Luciano's girlfriend taken home by the Ventura Police Department.' What would that do for your image?"

Antony swallowed hard. "You haven't been watching TV?"

"No," her eyes searched his. "Why?"

"There was a shooting at the funeral. Vic got shot in the shoulder."

"What?" Zoë's eyes widened.

"She's okay. Lost a lot of blood, so they're keeping her overnight. They're taking her to a room now."

"Why?" she asked, her tone forceful. "You know why, I can see it in your eyes."

Antony walked to the window and stared out at the parking garage. "I'll tell you everything, but you have to promise to do things my way."

There was silence as Zoë contemplated the idea, not that he'd give her a choice. If she told him no, he'd do things his way regardless. Find and return the paintings and kill anyone who tried to hurt his family. It was an easy decision.

"You gonna get me in trouble with the brass?" Zoë finally said.

A satisfying grin spread across his face. "Always." He turned to her and leaned against the windowsill. "But I guarantee you'll get the bad guy."

"Spill it."

He told Zoë about Dimitri, Ferdinand, and the paintings, then asked, "You'll help without the entire police force?"

"I am a super cop."

"What are you going to tell the brass?"

"Very little, for now." She picked up her bag and shoved it to him. "Let's go see my sister."

Antony held the door open and rested his hand on her back, but she jerked away. He cringed at his thoughtlessness. "I'm sorry. I forgot."

"It's still sore." She took his hand, reached it over her head, and placed it on her shoulder. "There. That will be fine."

Zoë tapped on Victoria's door and walked in first. Sonny sat next to the hospital bed. Victoria turned her head and smiled. Zoë took her sister's hand. "I just heard. Are you okay?"

"Yes." Victoria pushed herself farther up in the bed. "I was just trying to get my husband to tell me what's going on. My store was robbed, there was a fire at Dimitri's, Lorenzo was killed, and then this?" Victoria looked around the room. "Is someone going to tell me why?"

Antony pulled out a chair and offered it to Zoë, who sat. Sonny immediately stood and scooted his chair toward Antony. "You should sit, too."

Antony nodded and was thankful to have his weight off his aching leg.

"Have the police been here to take a statement?" Zoë asked.

"Yes, two detectives."

"I told Zoë everything," Antony said. "She's agreed to help without the entire force."

"You told Zoë?" Sonny's eyes widened. "You said no cops."

"I never get a break, do I?" Antony gave his brother a deep eye roll.

"How about someone telling me?" Victoria asked.

Antony gave Sonny a nod of approval. Sonny filled Victoria in.

Victoria looked over at Zoë. "This is why you were pretending to be Antony's girlfriend?"

"Yes. Antony and I had agreed to help each other, only neither of us did, until now."

Victoria looked over at Antony. "And how long have you known about this Ferdinand?"

"Since Genevra's funeral."

Victoria's eyes widened. "You've known for over two weeks, and you didn't tell us that our lives might be in danger?"

"Sonny knew."

Victoria looked at Sonny. "This man has threatened us, and you said nothing? Our kids have been going to school when either one of them could've been next?"

"Nobody in this family ever leaves the house without a bodyguard," Sonny stated. "The family has been safe."

"Yeah," she pointed to her shoulder. "Real safe." She laid her head back and stared at the ceiling, tears flooding her eyes.

Zoë put on her cop face. "Arguing about this will get us nowhere. You guys need to find the paintings."

"Vince is looking now," Antony said. "And I'm staying at Lorenzo's until the paintings are found."

"Get the number for the broker." Zoë glanced between the brothers. "And meet with him."

"Sonny's not meeting with him," Antony snapped. "I go alone."

Sonny rolled his eyes. "Would you stop protecting me?"

"I don't care who goes," Zoë said. "But you'll be wired."

"No way." Antony stood.

Zoë looked at Sonny, questioning him with her eyes. Antony raised his voice. "Don't look at him. I said no."

Zoë sighed. "We'll discuss it."

"No discussion," Antony almost shouted. "No wires."

"Wait a minute." Victoria's forehead wrinkled. "You two are meeting with the man you think had Lorenzo killed and just shot me? You just said he wanted to kill you."

"We have to, Vic," Sonny said. "There's no other way."

Victoria's eyes filled with tears.

"Sonny?" Zoë asked. "I want to stay with you and Victoria."

"Done."

Antony playfully raised an eyebrow. "Maybe you should stay with me at Lorenzo's. You *are* my girlfriend." When Zoë hesitated, it brought a devilish grin to Antony's face. "Can't trust yourself alone with me?"

Zoë's face flushed. "It's not that, it's . . ."

Antony leaned in and whispered, "One kiss, that's all it ever takes."

"You're right," Zoë straightened up in her chair. "I should stay with you. The paintings are at Lorenzo's, and I want the paintings."

"Use whatever excuse you'd like." His dimples deepened.

Victoria cleared her throat. "What do we do in the meantime? Stay locked in the house?"

"Until we meet with this guy," Sonny nodded, "yes."

Victoria took Sonny's hand. "I think you should go home and be with the kids. They sounded scared on the phone. They'll feel better if you're there."

"I hate to leave." He leaned over and kissed her. "But I think you're right."

She grabbed his neck and held him close. "Be careful walking out of here."

"I will." He sat on the edge of the bed. "Don't worry about me. I'll be fine." He wiped the tears that escaped her eyes and smiled. "I'll come get you tomorrow."

"Is that safe? If he's after you, you should stay home."

"I'll be here tomorrow to get you. I'll be fine." He kissed her again, his hand cupping her face. "You know I couldn't live without you."

She nodded.

He smiled. "I'm sorry this happened."

"I know."

Sonny caressed her cheek. "I love you."

"Tell the kids I love them."

"I will." He stood and backed away from the bed.

Zoë walked to her and squeezed her hand. "I'll see you tomorrow."

Victoria looked over at Antony. "Take care of my sister."

"Oh, I will." Antony winked. "Get some rest."

Victoria nodded, and they all left.

***

Victoria lay in the hospital bed, staring aimlessly at the TV. She flipped through the channels but never stopped on any particular one. She hoped the sounds of the incomplete sentences would muddle her nightmarish thoughts—the bullet, the pain, the gunshots, and the look on her children's faces.

Doc sat in the corner and leafed through a magazine. He periodically glanced at her, but he said nothing.

A knock on the door brought Doc to his feet with his gun drawn. Killing the power on the TV, she watched, her eyes wide and her heart pounding.

"Yeah?" Doc said through the shut door.

"It's Antony."

"Should've guessed that one." Doc slid the gun in his holster and pulled the door open. Antony walked in with a dozen red roses. "I'll wait outside," Doc said.

"You scared me."

"I can tell." Antony set the roses on the small table. "Stop worrying. Nothing is going to happen to you. I've got men at all the entrances, stairs, elevators, and on the floor. Two outside the door."

"But they don't know who they're looking for."

"My men know what to look for."

Victoria pushed a button on the side of the bed. The bed gave a loud grunt followed by a constant grinding, moving her into a better sitting position. She cupped one of the roses in her hands and smelled its sweet aroma. "Thank you."

Antony paced the small room, his hands deep in his pockets. When he stopped and stared at her, she searched his eyes. They looked different, strange. A mixture of anger and sadness.

"What's wrong?" Her heart pounded. "Is it Sonny or the kids?"

"No." He gave his hair a quick comb-through then sat next to her. "They're fine."

"Then what?"

"This is my fault."

Her jaw tightened. "If you're going to confess to knowing about the paintings months ago, I don't want to hear it."

"No. I had no idea Dimitri would bring this kind of trouble."

"Then what exactly is your fault?"

"You getting shot."

"What?"

His face hardened. "I should've stopped this."

She smiled deeply. His love and loyalty were as sweet as the roses he'd brought. "You had no way of knowing I'd get shot."

"I was right there. I should've protected you."

"You couldn't have done more than you did."

"I should've had tighter security, brought in more of my own men, pushed you out of the way."

She reached for his hand, hoping to extinguish the fiery guilt he was heaping on himself. "It's not your fault."

His face softened, and he stared into her eyes. "When I saw you get hit—and the blood—I thought I'd lost you." A single tear escaped from his eye. "I couldn't go on if anything happened to you."

A flutter ran through her entire being. She could see his unconditional love for her. "Antony . . ."

"Yeah?" He pulled her hand to his lips and gently kissed it.

Realizing what was happening, she pulled her hand from him. "You can't talk like this."

His softness immediately turned to cockiness as one corner of his mouth went up into a grin. His dimples taunted. "Am I coming on stronger than normal?"

"No." She laughed. "It's just . . ."

"You know I love you. I've always loved you." He touched her cheek. "There's nothing wrong with me telling you how I felt when you got shot."

"It's just when you talk like this, I mean, I'm married. I love Sonny."

His eyes softened. "You still have feelings for me, don't you?"

Victoria looked away. Feelings for another man were wrong, but she couldn't deny that he had a hold on her she couldn't explain. A hold that had begun the second they'd met years ago.

Antony touched her chin, forcing her to look back at him. "Answer me, please."

She couldn't lie but feared telling him the truth. "I love Sonny, you know that. I would never do anything to hurt him. I take my marriage vows very seriously."

"I know." He looked into her eyes. "Answer my question, please."

"How could I not have feelings for you? You profess your love to me every chance you get. Do you know how flattering that is? But it's not going to change anything. I love Sonny. I'm married to Sonny. My life is with him."

"So you do have feelings for me?"

When she didn't answer, he continued to stare at her, his eyes pleading. Finally, she whispered, "Yes."

His dimples deepened with his smile. "Man, I've waited so long to hear you say that." Then, as quickly as his smile rose, it diminished. "Why does it feel wrong?"

"Because it is. I love my husband, and I won't do anything to jeopardize my marriage."

He backed away, nodding. "I respect that more than you'll ever know." He stood. "I should go." He walked to the door.

"Antony?"

He stopped and turned to her. "Take care of my sister."

"Jealous?" He raised an eyebrow.

"Maybe a little."

He laughed.

NINETEEN

VICTORIA SLEPT RESTLESSLY and was thankful to see the sunlight inch its way into the room. She looked at the clock, which read eight in the morning.

After a change of clothes, she sat with her legs dangling over the side of the bed. Anxious to go home, she looked at her watch. "What time is Sonny coming?"

"Soon," Doc said. "Relax. You've been on edge since Antony left last night. What'd he say to you?"

"Nothing." She readjusted the sling. "The usual. Forget it."

Doc tossed the magazine on the chair and walked to her. "Listen, Mrs. L, don't let him get to you."

"It's not just him. It's this whole mess."

"If I'd known this was such a strong possibility." Doc shook his head. "If Sonny or Antony had filled me in—"

Victoria raised her hand to stop him. If one more person tried to take the blame in an attempt to make her feel better, she'd scream. What'd they take her for? A Southern Belle? Her dad was a cop. She'd heard the stories, and she'd seen what evil could do.

The tap on the door brought them both to attention. Sonny was in jeans and a t-shirt, his face unshaven. "I missed you last night." He took her in his arms and kissed her.

"Me, too. How're the kids?"

"Anxious for you to come home."

Sonny looked at the flowers. "Roses?"

"Antony brought them up last night."

"Of course."

Victoria grabbed him and pulled him close. "You know, you're the one I love."

Sonny kissed her deeply. "I know." He took her hand. "Let's get out of here."

Victoria walked in the center of a group of bodyguards. Sonny whisked her through the back of the hospital. Doc pushed her head down to clear the doorframe of the car, jostling her shoulder. She cried out as a jolt of pain shot throughout her body.

Sonny jumped in behind her. He said nothing. A fist struck the top of the car, and they immediately pulled away.

***

Antony peered over the newspaper as Zoë walked into the dining room of Lorenzo's estate wearing a pair of plaid flannel men's pajamas. Her short blond hair stuck up in the air in random spots. Antony sat in his usual attire, all black. He laid the newspaper down and scooted his half-eaten breakfast away. "You sleep okay?"

"As a matter of fact, I did." As soon as she sat at the large table, Consolata set a plate of food and a cup of coffee in front of her. Zoë nodded her thanks as the live-in housekeeper scurried from the room. "You got in awfully late."

"You noticed?" He picked the paper back up.

"I am your girlfriend. Don't make me look bad."

"I'd never do that." Antony turned the page. "Oh, we only made the fourth page?"

"They say anything good?" Zoë asked as she shoveled the food in her mouth.

"Nothing we don't already know." He laid the paper back down then sipped the last of his coffee. "Sonny called. We meet Ferdinand at noon."

Zoë's mouth dropped open, the half-chewed food almost falling out. "What? Where?"

"You know," Antony raised an eyebrow, "you'll need to wake up before nine if you want to be in on these things."

"Excuse me." She shoved another chunk of egg in her mouth, chewed it, then pushed it into her cheek. "First time in a real bed for almost two weeks. Forgive me if I overindulged."

"You're forgiven." He pointed to her chin. "You've got yolk dripping."

Zoë grabbed a napkin and swept it across her mouth. "First time in two weeks for real food, too."

"I can tell."

Consolata walked in with another plate of eggs and blueberry muffins. "You want more, Miss Stone?"

"Not too close, Consolata. She might bite you."

"Very funny." Zoë waved at Consolata to bring the plate closer. She slid off another egg and grabbed a hot blueberry muffin and ripped it open. Steam rose from it. "Oh, these look so good." She reached for the butter, slid some on her knife, and placed it on the muffin. It immediately melted. Licking her lips, she took a bite and relaxed in the chair.

Antony laughed. "I'll be in my office when you're done." She began to stand, but he stopped her. "Please, stay and eat. I like a woman with a good appetite." He grinned. "All kinds of appetites."

Her face flushed, and he walked out of the room.

***

The sweet aroma of perfume tickled Antony's nose. He looked up from his work. Zoë leaned against the doorframe of his office in a pair of jeans with a loose-fitting, casual shirt. Her deep green eyes were surrounded by the right amount of makeup.

He grinned.

She took a step into the room and did a spin. "Much better than a hospital gown, don't you think?"

Antony stood and began unbuttoning his shirt. He raised his eyes to meet hers.

She put her hands up. "Whoa! I don't look that good, do I?"

Antony stared at her as he pulled off his shirt and tossed it on the chair. His pecs swelled with solid muscle and the perfect amount of curly black chest hair. Muscles flexed as he grabbed her arms, leaned into her, and looked deeply into her eyes. Her heart raced as he cupped his hands around her waist, slowly moved them up her sides, then stopped and squeezed. He raised an eyebrow then flicked his finger on her abdomen to see if she was wearing her bulletproof vest.

"Oh . . . my vest." She breathed deeply. "Yeah, it's on."

Antony nodded, leaned over the couch, and picked his up.

Zoë opened her purse, pulled out the small Derringer, checked the gun for bullets, then replaced it.

Antony slid the vest over his head and pulled the Velcro tightly around his waist.

She opened her purse again and looked inside.

"You've done that twice now," Antony said. "The gun's still there."

Zoë glared at him while he replaced his black shirt over the vest and tucked it into his pants. Before putting on his black suit jacket, he checked to make sure his gun was loaded.

She applied a fresh coat of bright red lipstick.

Antony walked to the door. "Come on."

Zoë put on her pair of small black sunglasses and followed him to the car where Vince and two other bodyguards waited. They got into the black Durango and headed for Sonny's.

***

Victoria pulled the brush through her hair before setting it down on the dresser. Sonny emerged from the bathroom freshly showered and shaved. He wore khaki slacks, no shirt, and had bare feet.

Running his hand through his wet hair, he flicked the water from his hands at her.

"Hey." She smiled in protest.

He picked up the bulletproof vest and pulled it over his head and chest. Her left arm was safely tucked in its sling. With her right hand, she tightened the Velcro around his waist then helped raise the navy blue shirt over his shoulders.

"You're sure this is safe?" she asked.

"Yes." He took her in his arms. "We've got what he wants, and he's not going to hurt us. If he tries, I'm wearing this."

"I'm scared."

He pulled her closer and tucked her hair behind her ears. "We've got men inside the restaurant and surrounding it. We'll be fine."

"Okay." She melted in his strong arms and unwavering faith.

Sonny's dark eyes softened, and he smiled at her. "I'll call you as soon as it's over. It shouldn't take more than a couple of hours."

A lump sat in her throat. "Okay."

Rachel's voice floated up the stairs, "Hey. Uncle Tony. Aunt Zoë."

Sonny gave Victoria one final kiss. "I've got to finish getting ready."

They walked down the stairs to the constant pounding of a basketball on the carpet that rattled the glass figurines sitting on a shelf.

"Mom's gonna get mad!" Rachel yelled.

"I can handle your mom." Antony bounced the ball. "We play to ten." Antony looked at Christian. "White chair is the basket. Zoë is the ref. Rachel is the cheerleader." He tossed the ball at Christian, who caught it.

Christian bounced the ball toward Antony, who waved his arms in the air, limping, trying to defend him. Christian did a quick fake to the right then jerked to the left, pressed his back into Antony before he turned, and tipped the ball into the lap of the overstuffed white chair. Antony jumped on his good leg before falling to the couch.

"Personal foul, ref," Antony yelled.

"There was no foul on that play." Sonny smiled at Christian from the doorway. He walked into the room, grabbed the ball from the chair, and tossed it at Christian. "I'll step in for your uncle since he's obviously still out of commission."

Christian smiled and tossed the ball back at Sonny then waved his hands in the air at his father. Sonny dribbled the ball. Suddenly, Christian reached in and swiped the ball. Christian backed away, bounced the ball, and grinned.

"Yeah. Thanks for stepping in for me." Antony pushed himself up from the couch.

Sonny attempted to play defense, but Christian slipped past him. The ball was shot into the air and landed safely in the lap of the chair. "That's four!" Christian shouted. He turned to Zoë and gave her a high five.

Sonny pulled Christian into a hug then gently squeezed his shoulder. "We'll have to finish this later. Uncle Tony and I have to meet someone."

"With Zoë?" Christian looked up at his father. "You gonna be okay?"

"Of course." Sonny smiled.

"Why are you wearing a vest?"

Sonny leaned into Christian and said, "We're meeting with someone your aunt is trying to catch."

"The guy who had Mom and Nonno shot?"

"We don't know for sure. That's why I'm wearing a vest. Uncle Tony and Aunt Zoë are wearing them, too." Sonny smiled at Victoria then looked back as his son. "I'll be okay."

Antony's voice came from behind them. "Nothing will happen to your ol' man. Trust me. I won't let it."

"Mom, what are they talking about?" Rachel asked.

"Nothing," Victoria said. "Why don't you and Christian go down and pick out a game to play? I'll be down in a minute."

Victoria looked over at Christian. "Will you help her?"

"Yeah."

Sonny leaned over and gave Rachel a hug. "Don't beat your mom too badly."

"Okay." Rachel gave him a quick kiss then disappeared with Christian.

Sonny took Victoria's hand and led her to the front porch. Antony and Zoë followed. Sonny stopped and turned to Victoria. "Don't worry."

Her heart pounded, and she nodded. He walked down the steps.

"We'll all be fine," Antony said. "I'll make sure of it."

Sonny hit his arm playfully. "Let's get this over with. You know I like to spend Saturdays with my family."

Victoria gave him a wave as he climbed into the car with Antony.

Zoë got in a second car with Clay and two other bodyguards.

***

Sonny stared out the window as Vince pulled the Durango to the curb outside the Italian bistro. He and the other two bodyguards climbed out of the car and scanned all directions. Vince gave the brothers a nod. Sonny and Antony stepped out of the car, and Vince led them into the restaurant as the bodyguards followed behind.

Photos from Italy hung on the walls around three elaborate fireplaces. The smell of garlic, veal, and pasta danced in the air with the muted chatter of the Saturday patrons. Most of them worked for Sonny and Antony. Among them were Zoë and Clay.

Sonny walked to the host, whose hand was already extended, a large smile on his face. "Mr. Luciano," he said with a thick Italian accent. They shook. "So glad to see you again. I have your table." He motioned for them to follow, led them to the corner, and laid two menus down. "Tea?"

"Yes. Thanks."

Zoë sat at a corner table across the room. She took off her sunglasses and slid them onto the gold chain that hung around her neck. She picked up a menu and pretended to look it over.

Sonny stared as a tall, thin man with short brown hair, bushy eyebrows, and an overpowering chin walked through the front doors followed be a large, muscular man. The thin man's suit was black with a silver vest, black tie, and a scarf draped around his neck. His face appeared even longer than it was because his hair stood straight up. Rings covered his fingers.

Sonny leaned into Antony. "I think we got company."

The host led the two men over to their table. Antony and Sonny stood and extended their hands.

"Ferdinand Sirois," the man said with a heavy French accent. The larger guy took a few steps back.

"Something to drink?" Sonny snapped his fingers at the waiter.

"Water is fine." He turned to them and clasped his hands together. "You have some items in your possession that are mine. I'd like them back."

Antony reached into his suit coat. Ferdinand's man stepped forward, reaching for his gun.

"Relax." Antony opened his coat. "I'm just getting a toothpick."

Ferdinand shooed the man back as Antony placed the toothpick in his mouth and began chewing on it. "Our father was in possession of these items, and since his unfortunate death, we've been unable to track them down."

The table fell silent as the waiter set the drinks around them. Sonny looked up at the waiter. "We'll order later."

Nodding, the waiter left.

"So, you see, we have a bit of a problem," Sonny said. "If you continue to threaten our lives, we may be inclined to find these items and, oh, I don't know," Sonny turned to Antony and shrugged. "You think the police would like them? The Boston Museum is offering a five-million-dollar reward."

Antony leaned into Ferdinand. "What my brother's saying is if you try to kill any of us again, you'll never get your things."

Ferdinand stared at them, emotionless and apparently unscathed by their threat. "How do I know you'll give them to me?"

Sonny's chest pounded, and he could feel the heat creeping up his neck. "I can assure you when we find them, they're yours."

Silence fell over the table, but tensions were high as eyes glared. Sonny's eyes darted between Ferdinand's and Antony's. Ferdinand's were hard and cold. Antony's were riveting with revenge.

Ferdinand finally said, "You've got two weeks. Until then, you and your family are safe. You have my word."

Sonny leaned in. "You've already killed my father and shot my wife. What good is your word?"

"I've spent twenty years on the street making my word count." Ferdinand's eyes narrowed. "Don't sit there and tell me it's no good."

Antony tossed the toothpick on the table. "Dimitri said we'd be safe at the funeral, but you tried to kill my brother."

"Dimitri spoke without my authority. He'll pay dearly for that." He took a deep breath. "Two weeks."

Sonny nodded. *Like I have a choice.* "We'll have the items found and returned to you by then. Sooner, I hope." Sonny reached out his hand, and Ferdinand shook it.

Ferdinand moved his hand toward Antony. Antony looked at it then into his eyes. He crossed his arms.

Ferdinand stood. "I'll be waiting."

TWENTY

SONNY LEANED AGAINST THE DOORWAY of the master bedroom. Victoria stretched out on a white oversized chaise lounge, leafing through the latest *Vogue*. The French doors that led to a large deck were open and allowed a breeze to dance through the bedroom.

Classical music played softly, accompanied by the dull thud that came from Christian's room. After a cutthroat game of Hearts, Christian would retreat to his room, lay on his bed with his headphones on, and throw a tennis ball against the wall.

Sonny and Victoria tried to make their week-long confinement to the house more like a mini-vacation rather than a prison term, which was how Christian described it.

Victoria looked up at Sonny. "What?"

He walked over and gave her a kiss then grabbed her hand. "Come here."

The magazine fell to the floor as she stood and followed him out to the deck. He took her in his arms. "Antony just got here. He found the paintings."

"Really?"

"Yes." He ran his fingers through her hair.

"Thank God. Now what?"

"We make the drop. Zoë's working on the details." He kissed her. "How's your shoulder?"

"It's good." Victoria snuggled into him. "I love you."

"Me, too. More than you'll ever know. Can you do something for me?"

"Sure, what?"

"Would you talk to Antony? He's acting cold and distant."

"Worse than normal?" She laughed.

Sonny smiled.

Her forehead wrinkled. "You're serious?"

"He still acts like Papa's death meant nothing to him, but I know he's hurting inside. He won't open up to me, but I know he will to you."

"I worry about him, too, Sonny, but I don't know." She rested her arm on the deck railing as the breeze blew her hair. "The last time I brought up anything about Lorenzo he was pretty hateful."

"But he brought you roses at the hospital."

"That's because I was shot. He felt sorry for me."

"We both know the reason."

"And you still want me to try and get him to open up?" She shook her head. "I've spent the last fifteen years trying to get him to back off."

"I know, but he doesn't have anyone except us, and I'm partly to blame for that. I can never repay him for what he's done for me, but I have to start trying. Will you talk to him? For me?" When she was still hesitant, he grinned. "Do this for me," he kissed her, "and I'll be in your debt." He kissed her again, more passionately.

"Hmm." She grinned. "That is tempting."

"You'll try?" He pulled her close, kissed her neck, her cheek, then her lips. "He's downstairs."

"Now?"

"Yes, now." He laughed. "I've got a conference call in ten minutes."

"You'll owe me, right?"

"Yes."

"Okay. I'll try." She walked to the door.

"Victoria?"

She stopped and turned to him, her hand resting on the doorframe. Her auburn hair glistened, and her face was soft. "Yes?"

"Thanks."

"No problem."

He grinned, placed both hands in his pockets, and waited until she walked out the door before going to his office.

***

Antony had intentionally sat on the wicker loveseat that was in the rose garden, away from the French doors. He wasn't one to hide, but Victoria's confession made her consume him even more, and for the first time, he felt how wrong it was. His once hardened heart was being chipped away, and he didn't like it.

He sensed her at the same time he smelled her crisp, clean perfume.

"Can I sit?" She handed him a glass of iced tea.

"Sure." He took a sip then set it by his feet.

She sat across from him, and the wicker crunched under her weight.

"How's the shoulder?" he asked.

"Good. And your leg?"

"Can't complain."

He looked into her eyes then quickly away, feeling like a fool. He wanted something he could never have, yet there was the unshakable feeling that someday she'd be his. Was it a prophetic glimpse into his future, or a dream that he refused to let die?

He rested his arm on the back of the chair and tapped his fingers. "How are the kids doing confined to the house?"

"Not bad. We've had more family time than Christian would like, but it's good for him. He says he actually misses school. Rachel loves staying home. She says we should do it all the time."

"And the new store?"

"Sales are good."

Victoria tucked her hair behind her ears. The sun peeked through the heavy clouds and intensified her naturally tanned skin. His desire rose, and he was forced to look away. He crossed his legs and for the first time felt uncomfortable with the thoughts that ran through his head.

This is ridiculous. I shouldn't feel guilty. I've done nothing wrong.

He leaned over and grabbed the tea. *Get a grip.* He took a gulp and returned the glass.

"You doing okay?" she asked.

"Am I doing okay?" He tried to read her piercing gaze. Was she concerned about his undying love for her or the mess with Dimitri and Ferdinand?

"I was talking to Sonny . . ."

"Oh, you mean about Lorenzo's death? Tell Sonny I'm fine."

"What?"

"He's so obvious. He sent you down here to try and get me to talk about Lorenzo's death, right?" When she nodded, he grunted out a laugh. "I've already told him I'm fine."

Victoria opened her mouth. She looked like she was about to speak. Instead, she stood and began to walk away.

Antony grabbed her hand and looked up. "I know Sonny thinks I need to talk about this, but I'm okay, really."

Victoria nodded, gave his hand a squeeze, and then let it go. "Sonny said you found the paintings."

"Yep."

"Then this will be over tomorrow."

"We'll see."

Her smiled diminished. "If the cops catch Ferdinand when he picks up the paintings, we're out of danger, right?"

"I wish it were that simple."

She grew more serious. "You just can't believe that it might work?"

"We all can't walk around with our heads in the clouds."

"That's what you think?" Her jaw tightened. "I walk around with my head in the clouds? I've got a bullet hole in my shoulder to constantly remind me of our reality."

"A bullet hole in your shoulder." Antony stood and smiled. "There's probably nothing sexier than that."

Victoria rolled her eyes. "Only you'd think so."

"What? My brother doesn't think it's sexy?"

Victoria sighed, brushed past him, and went into the kitchen. Antony followed her. She opened the cupboard and reached up to grab the coffee can with her right arm. She winced and pulled it back.

Antony took the coffee can and filter from the cupboard. "Let me do this. Go sit down."

"I just reached too far." She held her arm across her stomach.

When the coffee finished brewing, he set a steaming cup in front of her. "What is it you want from me?" He poured himself a cup and sat down.

Victoria's eyes met his.

Antony grinned, giving her a questioning look.

Victoria looked away. "I hate the fact that you know me so well."

His grin widened.

"I want you to talk to me." She took a sip of the coffee. "Sonny's not the only one worried about you. Your father was killed, and you act like nothing happened."

"If I cried, would that make you feel better?"

"I just thought you might want to talk. I'm sorry. My mistake." She chewed on her bottom lip. "Can I ask you something?"

"Of course."

"Do you have nightmares about Lorenzo shooting you?"

"Are you having nightmares?"

Victoria nodded.

"It'll get easier."

"You say that with such ease."

"That wasn't the first time I've been shot." Antony sipped on the coffee. "The first time, I was nine. Carlo and I were messing around with his dad's new Colt, and it went off. Hit me right here." He pulled up his sleeve and exposed a small round scar on his lower arm. He lifted up his shirt and exposed a two-inch scar on his abdomen. "I got stabbed here one night on the streets. A guy tried to steal my coat."

"How do you live with it?"

Antony grunted out a laugh. "You mean with my wonderful childhood memories?"

"Yeah."

"I try not to think about it."

"Denial?"

"Why not?" He stood and refilled their cups then sat back down. "Alcohol dulls the pain when it gets too bad."

"I tried that after my mother disappeared. It never helped."

Antony stood and made a quick pace of the kitchen then leaned against the counter and crossed his arms. "What? You drank to forget that your mother walked out on you? If only Lorenzo would've been so kind." He rolled his eyes. "What a rough life you had."

"So because you had an abusive father, you're the only one allowed to feel bad about your childhood?"

"Abusive? I spent the first part of my life as a punching bag before getting kicked out. I slept in abandoned buildings and ate out of dumpsters. I saw things on the streets that would make your skin crawl. Don't sit there and tell me that your childhood was as bad as mine."

"I didn't say it was. I just said you're not the only one who grew up with problems."

"Problems?" He glared at her before turning to walk out.

Victoria grabbed his arm.

He stopped and turned back. "What?"

"What's wrong with you?"

"It's nothing, okay?" He ran his hand through his hair.

"I care about you, Antony. I want to help."

"There's only one way you could help, and that's not going to happen." He smiled. "I'll be fine."

***

As urgent as Martin's desire was to put Dimitri away forever, he couldn't complain about the last few days. Sometimes being undercover wasn't all that bad. Dimitri had assigned him to guard Elisa. Strict orders. No phone calls or visitors. Since she had no friends, the job was easy and vital. This was his chance to get information out of her, if she knew any, which he was beginning to believe she didn't.

They had made a quick lunch with a couple of reheated chicken breasts, carrots, and garlic bread. He wiped his mouth and looked over at Elisa who stared at her food and pushed it around on her plate.

"Aren't you gonna eat any of that?" he asked.

She stuck a carrot in her mouth and faked a smile.

"Come on. You need to eat."

"Why?" She dropped her fork on the table. "So you can report to Dimitri that I cleaned my plate?"

"You really think I'm like that?" Martin shook his head. "I thought you finally trusted me."

She looked away. "I'm sorry. I do trust you."

"No, I'm sorry. You're being held here like a prisoner, and I'm doing nothing to stop it." When her eyes met his, he studied her. "What can I do to help you?"

"Nothing." She turned away.

Martin reached out, placed his finger under her chin, and turned her back to him. He wanted to hold and protect her. He leaned in and kissed her lips. When she didn't recoil at his touch, he cupped her face in his hands. "Let's get out of here. I'll take you someplace safe."

"I can't tell you what that means to me, but I have to stay. Dimitri is planning something, and I have to try and stop him."

"Why would anything Dimitri does concern you?"

"It's not me I'm worried about. It's Antony."

Her confession made him cringe. Playing house over the last few days made him want her even more, and when this was over, he had no intention of losing her, especially to Antony Luciano. "I could tell at your grandmother's funeral that you once loved him. So this is about him?"

"Yes, but not in the way you think."

He let out a burst of air. "Then tell me what I can do to help."

"Can you get a message to him? I need you to tell him Dimitri's going to try and kill him."

Martin held her hands. "Have you heard Dimitri say that?"

"No."

"Then you'll have to come up with a reason. Otherwise, Antony won't believe me."

"There are too many coincidences."

"Like what?"

"When Dimitri moved in the night his house was bombed, he had two suitcases." She leaned in and whispered, "Why would he have things packed unless he knew about the bombing?"

"Maybe he was going on a business trip?"

"Antony said the same thing." She pulled her hands from his. "You don't believe me, either."

"I didn't say that." He watched the lines on her face deepen. He could tell she really believed Dimitri was that evil. "You honestly think Dimitri killed his own grandmother, the woman who raised him? Why?"

"I don't know." She shook her head. "Maybe so Antony will feel sorry for him. Maybe in some sick sort of way, Dimitri thought it'd gain Antony's trust. It doesn't matter why." Her next two sentences were spoken so quietly Martin had to lean in to hear her. "I always believed Dimitri killed Enrico, and I think he had Lorenzo killed. I think it was Antony he was trying to have killed at Lorenzo's funeral."

"You mean when Victoria got shot?" Martin asked the question even though he knew it was Sonny not Antony targeted that day. Evidence Elisa was unaware of.

"Yes, and I'm afraid he'll try again."

"Why?"

"Revenge. There was an accident a long time ago. Dimitri blames Lorenzo for the death of his parents and Antony for the death of his brother. With Lorenzo dead, all he has to do is kill Antony, and his revenge is complete."

Martin nodded. He remembered reading about the shooting and the car accident. "The paintings. Have you heard anything about them?"

"Paintings? Antony asked me the same thing." Her eyebrows wrinkled, and she backed away. "Why do you want to know if I know anything about paintings?"

Their eyes locked. He wanted to look away, afraid she would see he was a cop or, worse yet, think he was loyal to Dimitri, but he didn't. He couldn't take the chance when she finally trusted him. When she was falling in love with him. He let her search his eyes for the truth that wouldn't come, at least not yet.

"I work for Dimitri." He lied. "I overhear things. I like to know what's going on and how deeply I might get dragged into it."

Her face softened. She seemed appeased with the answer.

"Will you warn Antony?"

"Yeah." He kissed her. It felt perfect. Like they were made for each other, for this moment.

The front door opened and startled them. Martin released Elisa. He leaned against the counter and crossed his arms, a childish grin painted on his face.

Dimitri waddled into the kitchen. His hair hung free on his shoulders. He removed his suit jacket, exposing a shirt stained with yellowed rings of sweat. He pointed to Elisa's plate. "You gonna eat that?"

"No." She pushed the plate to him, her face still flushed.

"Good." He sat down, grabbed the plate and fork, took one bite, then gestured at Martin. "Get me a beer."

Martin handed him a Miller Lite, like the lite would do him any good.

Dimitri shoved the food inside his mouth then washed it down. "I got a job for you."

"Sure." He hoped this was it. The paintings. It was about to go down, and he was going to be in the center of it. This collar would make his career. "What about Elisa?"

"Hank will watch her. Justice will call you when he needs you." Dimitri turned to him, his eyes dark. "This is big, so don't let me down."

"You can count on me."

"Go, get outta here."

Martin tipped his head at Elisa. "Bye." He wished he could've said goodbye to her privately, but he felt somewhat good about her safety. She could reach him in a second by her cell, which he had returned to her.

As he drove, he grabbed his phone and dialed Zoë's number. "Where you at?"

"At my boyfriend's. You still at your girlfriend's?"

Her words cut through him. "Lay off. I think Elisa really is innocent in all of this."

Zoë chuckled. "I can't believe it. You've fallen in love."

He shrugged off his annoyance at her revelation. "You got the paintings?"

"Yeah, we make the drop tomorrow," Zoë said.

"That must be the big job I get to do tomorrow. We'll wrap up this case by tomorrow night."

"Then you can sweep Elisa off her feet, unless you already have?" His silence prompted her. "You have. Man, I forgot how fast you work."

"Shut up and stick to the case."

"Sure thing." He could sense her smiling while she spoke. "Sonny is getting in touch with Ferdinand to set up the drop."

"Ferdinand? Who's that?"

"The broker who's selling the paintings."

"Never heard of him." Martin pulled into a parking lot and threw the car into park. He was never good at talking while he drove. "Tell me about him."

"Ferdinand is the front man. Dimitri's just transporting the paintings."

Martin's eyebrows wrinkled. "Why wouldn't I have heard about that?"

"Maybe you've been preoccupied by a certain someone?"

"Ha ha."

"Okay. You're still a peon in the organization?"

"Then why would I be at the drop tomorrow?"

"They figure out who you are?" Zoë asked. "You didn't tell *her*, did you?"

"No. No one's on to me, not even Elisa."

"Then go to the drop tomorrow and let's finish the job."

Martin chewed on the inside of his cheek. Something didn't feel right. "Elisa says Dimitri's out for revenge. Do Sonny and Antony trust him?"

"I don't know about Sonny, but Antony doesn't. Why?"

"Elisa thinks Dimitri was behind Lorenzo getting killed and the fire at Genevra's."

"Why does she think that?"

"She says when Dimitri arrived at her place the night of the fire he had two suitcases. It's possible he planned a business trip I didn't know about."

"There was no business trip. He was supposed to meet me and Genevra to look at carpets." Zoë was silent for a moment. "You think he packed his bags then torched his place and his grandma?"

"I don't know what to think. All I know is Elisa is afraid of him. Heck, the guy is keeping her locked in her own house. She believes Dimitri's out to kill Antony."

"We'll keep our eyes open."

"Zoë?"

"Yeah?"

"Be careful."

He could sense her smile. "I will. You too."

"Sure." Martin tossed the phone on the seat, threw the car into drive, and headed to his rented house.

***

Zoë's arrival drew Christian from his room. He stood in the hallway outside his father's office and listened to his parents, Uncle Tony, and Aunt Zoë. His heart pounded. It sounded like something out of a movie. They talked about stolen paintings and some sort of sting operation.

He leaned closer to the doorway when a voice came from behind him. "Can you hear okay?"

Christian's heart raced. It was Doc. He turned his fear into cockiness. "As a matter of fact, no. I missed the part about where the drop was."

"Come on." Doc grabbed his arm and led him into the office. "Your son heard everything."

Victoria's eyes widened. "What?"

"Caught him eavesdropping." Doc slapped Christian on the back. "Good luck, man." He left.

Antony sat on the couch next to Zoë. Sonny walked to Christian, placed his hand on his shoulder, and led him to a chair. "Sit."

"You're not letting him hear the rest of this, are you?" Victoria asked.

Sonny raked his hand through his hair. "He already knows."

Christian sat for a moment then stood and placed his hands in the pockets of his jeans. "Can I get out of here tomorrow? Can I go to school?" His eyes darted from his father to his mother then to Zoë. "You said we'd be safe once the paintings were returned."

"Wait until we catch the guy before you go shooting out of here," Sonny said.

"Oh, come on." Christian crossed his arms. "I heard you. You said you talked to the guy. He said he wouldn't hurt any of us. Why can't I go? Have Doc go with me and Bruno or Clay. Heck, send them all. They got metal detectors at the school. No one will hurt me there."

"I'd wait," Zoë said. "Let us get the guy first."

Antony nodded in agreement.

"One more day," Sonny said to Christian.

"Oh, come on. You said yourself we'd be okay, that this guy wouldn't hurt us."

"No," Sonny said. "We play it safe."

"But Dad . . ."

"No. You can wait one more day."

Christian pursed his lips, his fists in balls. "Man, I hate this. Fine." He stormed out, slamming the door behind him.

Christian dropped on his bed, picked up the tennis ball, and threw it against the wall then caught it as it bounced back at him. A knock on his door interrupted him.

"What?"

Sonny walked into the room.

Christian rolled his eyes and threw the ball at the wall. As it sprang back, Sonny reached out and caught it. "You want to talk about it?"

"What? That some whacko is out there threatening our lives because you and Uncle Tony copped some stolen paintings? Naw, I'll just read about in the tabloids next week."

Sonny sat on the edge of the bed and squeezed the ball in his hand. "It's not like that. Someone planted those paintings in your mother's store. We're trying to help the police."

"Whatever."

"One more day, Christian. It's not that big of a deal."

"To you maybe, but it is to me."

"Why?"

Christian moved to the window and looked outside. "I'm sick of being in this house."

Sonny walked over to him and placed his hand on his shoulder. "I know." Sonny handed the tennis ball back to Christian. "One more day. After that, things will get back to normal. I promise."

Christian nodded and waited for his father to leave. He went to his desk, picked up the box, and opened it. He ran his finger over the small gold bracelet and sighed. Tomorrow was Liz's birthday. All he wanted to do was give her a present.

He put the lid on the box, plopped on the bed, and stared at the ceiling. What could he do? Wait another day? No way. They said he'd be safe. He grabbed his phone and called Russ. He'd snuck out before, he could do it again.

TWENTY-ONE

THE LATE AFTERNOON SUN BURNED away the clouds. Antony stared out the window, waiting for Sonny to finish talking to Christian so they could go over last-minute plans. Zoë and Victoria sat on the couch in Sonny's office.

Antony looked at his watch at the same time his stomach growled. He glanced at Victoria then turned away. He wanted to go home, to get away from her. She was consuming too many of his thoughts. The chirping of his cell phone was a welcomed interruption. It was Vince. Antony's heart raced. "I'll be right there."

"What is it?" Zoë asked.

"Nothing. I'll be right back."

"Wait a minute." Zoë stood and grabbed his arm. "If something's going on, I want to know."

"Nothing that would concern my girlfriend."

Narrowing her eyes, she cocked her head.

He smiled without humor. "It's nothing, okay?"

Antony walked to the hallway as Sonny came down the stairs. "Come on."

"What?"

"For once in your life don't question me. Just trust me."

Sonny nodded and followed.

***

Victoria and Zoë stared out the window as Antony and Sonny strolled down the drive.

Zoë rested her hands on her hips. "Where are they going?"

"Looks like the guest house where the bodyguards live." Victoria's eyes narrowed. "That's Vince at the door."

"Something's going on." Zoë shook her head and sighed. "I'm going down there."

"No, let me," Victoria grabbed her arm. "You betray Antony, and he'll never trust you again."

"What about you?"

Victoria laughed. "You and I both know he won't be mad at me for very long."

"True." Zoë grinned. "You can go."

***

The concrete basement was cold, dark, and eerie, and the only part of the guesthouse that was unfinished. There was a desk and two chairs. On top of the desk sat a lamp and a gun. A constant dripping from a large faucet echoed in the room.

A well-built man sat with his hands tied behind his back underneath a single hanging lamp surrounded by four bodyguards. He was dressed in a gray suit and didn't look much older than forty. His head hung forward, and a line of blood trickled from his bottom lip.

"What have they done?" Sonny whispered.

"Don't get soft on me now," Antony said. "We needed information. This man may have killed Papa."

Sonny nodded and walked around the guy then looked at Vince. "What have you found out? By the looks of him, I assume he's been helpful?"

"Oh, yes. He's been quite helpful." Vince rubbed his hands. "There's no Ferdinand. Just Dimitri."

"What?"

"Apparently Ferdinand works for Dimitri. He's a hired thug, not the guy running things. It's all a set-up," Vince said.

"The paintings?" Sonny asked.

"They're real and worth millions."

The man slowly looked up at Antony then Sonny, his face bloodied, his eyes swollen but fierce.

Vince picked up the gun. "Same gun type that killed Lorenzo."

"Did you kill my father?" Sonny circled him.

Antony saw the red creep up his brother's neck. Good, he was getting mad. He needed Sonny's anger if this was going to play out with them on the winning side.

The man spit blood at Sonny's feet.

Sonny's fists balled up, and for a moment, Antony thought he'd hit the guy. Instead, Sonny breathed deeply, his chest steadied. "Clean him up. He'll stay here until they catch Dimitri. Then we'll turn him over to the police. I'll go fill Zoë in."

Unbelievable. The guy who killed their father was sitting right in front of them, and Sonny goes soft. Revenge. It wasn't what should be done, it's what had to be done. It was their duty. Heat filled Antony's face. "What? He killed Papa."

"We don't know that for sure."

Antony pushed Sonny aside, grabbed the man by his shirt, and pulled him up. The jolt made the man's legs knock the chair over. Antony flung him up against the wall and punched his stomach. The man doubled over and slid to the floor. "Did you kill my father?" Antony stared down at him.

The man looked up with a slight grin on his face. "I just finished the job you couldn't do."

Antony kneed the man in the nose. His head jerked back then he fell limp.

Sonny lunged at Antony and shoved him against the wall. "Enough."

Antony panted, his eyes wide. He wiped the sweat from his top lip. He wanted to punish him for killing his father, but Sonny was right. It was Dimitri he should save his anger for.

The gasp startled both brothers. They turned to see Victoria standing wide-eyed on the stairs, covering her mouth.

Sonny turned to Antony. "Don't hurt him anymore."

Antony motioned with his head to one of his men, still trying to catch his breath. "You heard the boss. Clean him up and watch him." Antony turned and looked into Victoria's piercing eyes before she turned and walked up the stairs.

***

Back at the main house, Antony heard Sonny, Victoria, and Zoë arguing in the office. His anger still pounded through his veins. He went into the living room and fell onto the couch.

When he heard Zoë's voice getting louder, he took deep breaths. "Here it comes," he groaned.

"You just assaulted a man?" Zoë shouted.

"We got vital information."

"But you can't just beat it out of someone."

"Yeah, you can." Antony's eyes widened.

Zoë frowned and shook her head. "I'm going down to talk to him."

Antony flew off the couch and grabbed her wrist. "You'll do no such thing." When she tried to free herself, his grip tightened. "You are my girlfriend. How would that make me look?"

Red enflamed her face. "Let me go."

"Not if you're going down there. My men will watch him. You catch Dimitri tomorrow, and it ends." He pulled her closer, teeth clenched. "Understood?"

Zoë death glared him for a long moment then nodded, which brought a grin to Antony's face. He released her. "We'll go *home* shortly." His grin turned into a small laugh.

"I'm not going anywhere with you." Zoë rubbed her wrist.

"Then it looks like we're sleeping here."

"If your men lay one more hand on that man, I'll—"

"They won't touch him."

Christian's voice came from behind them. "We going to eat anytime soon?"

Victoria turned. "We'll be right there. Where's your sister?"

"She's coming."

"Take her into the kitchen," Victoria said. "I'll be in there in a minute."

Zoë took a deep breath. "I'll go make them something."

"I'll get Vince to help you," Antony said.

Zoë's eyes cut to him. "I don't need a babysitter."

"He'll help you anyway."

"I'll keep her company." Sonny touched Victoria's arm. "You coming?"

"In a second."

Sonny leaned into her. "Leave it alone, Vic."

"I want to know how he could do that and how you could stand by and let it happen."

"I don't condone how they got that guy to talk." Sonny rubbed his forehead. "But we got information that we needed to nail Dimitri."

"And he killed Papa," Antony snapped at his brother's lame justification. Sonny was too pious to admit that as Lorenzo's son, they had certain obligations.

"A father you detested until ten minutes ago," Victoria said.

"You don't understand anything." Antony shook his head and pursed his lips.

"Then explain it to me."

Explain loyalty? It was something beaten into them at a very young age. It never came without revenge. It didn't matter how

Lorenzo had treated them. Revenge was a duty. One that he planned to live up to.

"He *has* to pay for killing our father!" Antony shouted more for Sonny's sake than Victoria's. "I'm not sorry for what's happened to him. Once again, the burden fell on my shoulders. I succumb to the fact that I always have to do the dirty work." He paced. "You got a drink? I mean a *real* drink?"

"Why?" Victoria asked. "Is your conscience bothering you?"

He stopped and glared at her, his face hard. "No. You are."

Her eyes swelled with tears. Sonny reached for her arm, but she pulled away and stormed into the kitchen.

Sonny followed.

Antony hadn't expected Sonny to defend his actions, but it hurt just the same. He walked to the front porch where Vince stood. "I need alcohol. Check with the guys down at the house. Someone has to have something."

Vince nodded.

***

Zoë grabbed an orange Fiesta plate and placed a square of leftover lasagna on it. She put it in the microwave to nuke it. When the buzzer went off, she took the plate and handed it to Christian, who took it, a fork, and his pop and disappeared into the dining room.

Victoria heated up a plate for Rachel and handed it to her. She carried it into the dining room, too.

"You sure that man is safe down there with Antony's men?" Zoë put another plate of food in the microwave.

"Antony's men won't touch him." Sonny pulled the plate out, handed it to Zoë, and stuck the next one in. "I can't blame Antony for what he did. That man killed our father. He deserves more than what he got."

"Regardless of what he deserves, I'm still a cop." Zoë grabbed a fork and a napkin. "I could get into trouble for beating information out of someone."

"That's why Antony didn't want you involved." Sonny handed Victoria a plate. "Antony's right. We have one up on Dimitri now that we know the truth. We can use that to our advantage."

Zoë picked up a piece of garlic bread. "I should call this in."

"Will keeping him here overnight hurt the case?" Victoria asked.

"Probably not."

"Then let it go for tonight," Sonny said and pulled his dinner out of the microwave. He picked up a fork and a glass of tea. "I'm going to eat with my kids. After that, I'm going to watch a movie with them like I promised."

Victoria followed him into the dining room.

Zoë sighed, put another piece of bread on her plate, grabbed her tea, and joined them.

***

Antony stood at the top of the stairs and listened. Voices from the movie on the big screen TV floated up. Satisfied he wouldn't be disturbed, he found Vince in the kitchen with vodka.

"Finally." Antony reached into the fridge and grabbed a pop. Guess it would have to work. "I don't need your approval," he said aloud while he mixed a drink. He gulped it and let the alcohol wash away the guilt. He made another.

He paced the kitchen. Victoria was right, and he hated it. His conscience was bothering him. He was getting soft. He had allowed her goodness to creep in. It was an attribute that might get them killed.

A calmness soon washed over him. His stomach growled, and he realized he hadn't eaten any dinner. He grabbed a piece of garlic bread, headed into the living room, and sat on the couch. He ate the bread and washed it down with the alcohol.

Rachel came up the stairs. "Uncle Tony."

He hid the bottle behind his back and gave his head a quick shake to momentarily clear it as Rachel fell into his arms. He welcomed her love and wrapped his arms around her innocence. "Is it bedtime already?"

"Mom says so. Will you explain to her that I'm not a child and I can stay up later?"

He looked up at Victoria, who stood with her arms crossed. "Maybe tonight's not a good night to argue with her." He kissed her cheek. "You better go."

Antony gulped the last of the alcohol as they went up the stairs. His brother not defending him was nothing new, but it was Victoria's eyes that haunted him. Neither of their actions would stop him from protecting them at all costs.

He pulled out his gun and laid it on his lap. He was not afraid to use it. His head dropped then jerked back up. He put the bottle back to his lips before remembering it was empty.

Victoria took the gun and the empty bottle and set them on the coffee table. "You're drunk?"

"Get off my case."

"Come on. I'll put you to bed."

Antony stood, picked up the gun, replaced it in its holster, then followed her up the stairs. He flopped on the bed in one of the spare bedrooms, his body numb. "Don't look at me that way."

"What way?"

"That condescending way. I had a couple of drinks."

"A couple of drinks? You're drunk. Why?"

"Why not?" He pushed himself up and rested his head on the headboard. He widened his eyes and tried to focus on her face. "Down there you condemned me. I only did what had to be done." His head slowly moved around in a small circle, and the alcohol slurred his words. "Once again, I'm the bad guy." He licked his numb lips, grinned, and closed his eyes. "It's okay. It's a burden I've carried all my life."

She shook his arm until his eyes opened. "What if Dimitri comes tonight and tries to kill us?"

"He won't. He doesn't know we know there's no Ferdinand."

"Maybe this is part of his sick game."

He closed his eyes again.

"Antony." She shook him.

Antony raised his head and looked into her eyes, grinning. He patted her cheek with one hand and drew his gun with the other. "If he did come, I can still shoot."

Victoria put her hand on the gun, lowered it and his arm.

Antony licked his lips, spun the gun around, and returned it to its holster. He raised his eyebrows, grinned, and then passed out.

***

The morning sun was a welcome sight. Victoria had lain awake most of the night watching imaginary scenarios in her head of what might happen if Dimitri came.

She yawned, slipped a tan cardigan over her brown tank top, and sat on the chaise lounge. She looked up at Sonny. "Are you sure you have to meet with Dimitri?"

Sonny sat down next to her. He pulled her to him and wrapped his arms around her. "I'll be fine."

"I'm scared."

"I know, but it'll be okay." Sonny kissed her. "Now, I've got to go sober up my brother." He grinned. "Can't keep Dimitri—I mean, Ferdinand—waiting."

"I don't find this funny."

"I'll meet you downstairs." Sonny walked down the hallway, gave the guestroom door two pounds, then yelled, "Breakfast in thirty minutes. Get up."

Victoria walked behind him with a glass of water and two aspirins.

Sonny turned to her. "You're too nice to him."

"You want him at his best today, don't you?"

"Tell him to get downstairs."

She walked into the guest room and set the water and aspirin on the nightstand.

Antony lay face down. One arm and one leg hung off the bed. Something shiny lay on the floor under his hand. She bent down and picked up a gold chain with a crucifix on it.

It was Sonny's necklace. The one he got from his mother. She chewed on her bottom lip, clutched the cross in her hand, and let the chain dangle between her fingers.

Antony opened his eyes. "Are you stealing from me?"

"I was just about to ask you the same question. How did you get Sonny's necklace?"

Antony ran his hand over his face before he pushed himself up. He reached over, took the aspirin, and gulped the water. "Thanks." He reached for the necklace.

She clutched it tighter, drawing it close to her chest.

"That's mine." He shook his head. "Mama gave us both one."

"How come I've never seen you wear it?"

"Necklaces on men are out of style. Isn't that what you said once? I carry it in my pocket." He held his hand out.

Victoria dropped it into his hand. "I'm sorry. I didn't know."

He stood. "Tell me, Vic, what's it like to walk on water?" He slid the crucifix into his pants pocket. "You come in here still condemning me for a little drink then accuse me of stealing."

"I said I was sorry about that." She crossed her arms. "It's just— I was up half the night scared Dimitri would come, and you were in here drunk and passed out."

"You have my brother. Why were you so scared? Were you afraid I'd be killed or that I wouldn't be able to protect you?" When her eyes met his, he grinned. "You need me to do the dirty work, the work you know Sonny won't do?"

She turned to leave, but his voice stopped her. "You feel safer when I'm around. Why? Because I'm not afraid to kill? You can't have it both ways, love."

Victoria couldn't look at him. He was always right. She couldn't deny that she felt safer with him around. His confidence was not only overpowering, but it reeked of survival.

"Where's Zoë?" Antony asked.

"In the other room."

"This'll be over soon."

"Sonny wants you downstairs." She turned. "Antony?"

"Yeah?"

"Don't let anything happen . . ." She started the sentence but couldn't complete it.

"I'll protect Sonny no matter what the cost. You know that."

Victoria nodded, lowered her eyes, and left.

TWENTY-TWO

LYNYRD SKYNYRD'S "SWEET HOME ALABAMA" filled the black Durango. Antony's headache was gone, replaced by pure adrenaline. He tapped his fingers on the steering wheel as he drove Sonny, Vince, and Bosco to the small Italian bistro.

He knew the restaurant was filled with his men and Zoë's plainclothes officers. Cops were obvious, Antony had protested, but Zoë insisted, and he had backed down. It was the least he could do since Zoë had relented to the fact that neither brother would wear a wire, not that Antony had given her a choice.

He threw the car into park, killed the engine, looked in the mirror, and gave his hair a quick comb-through.

"You got your vest on?" Antony said to Sonny.

"Of course."

"Let's get this done." He had just grabbed the door handle when his cell phone chirped. He looked at the incoming number, raised an eyebrow, and brought the phone to his ear. "Dimitri?"

"Change of plans. I'm in the limo pulling in. Bring me the paintings."

"Give them to you?" Antony looked over at Sonny and smiled. "I thought we were meeting with Ferdinand?"

After a pause, Dimitri said, "I'll take them to him."

"Unless Ferdinand tells me himself, I don't release these paintings." Antony winked at Sonny. "Have him call me."

Antony ended the call. "Dimitri's in that limo. He wants the paintings in there instead of inside."

"You think he's on to us?"

"Doesn't matter. We got what he wants." Antony's phone chirped. "I guess this is would be Ferdinand." Antony rolled his eyes as he put the phone to his ear. "Yeah, sure thing."

Antony slid the phone into his pocket. "Stay here. Text Zoë and tell her what's going on."

Sonny grabbed his arm. "No way. You're not getting into that car alone."

"You're not going with me."

"You're not going without me."

"Listen, you've got more to lose."

"But—"

"But nothing. You stay here." Antony cocked his head. "He's big and fat. He couldn't pull a gun fast enough to shoot me."

"I don't care. You're not doing this alone."

"I'm taking Vince and Bosco."

"Man," Sonny said and hit Antony's shoulder. "When are you going to quit protecting me?"

Antony sighed. "I promised your wife."

"Oh . . ." Sonny rolled his eyes. "That explains it."

"Just let me do this."

"Whatever." Sonny's tone was dry and his arms crossed.

Antony didn't care how his brother felt as long as he stayed in the car. He got out of the Durango and opened the door to the limo. Leaning in, he glared at Dimitri. "Your driver gets out."

Bosco stood next to the driver, his gun in his hand. Vince pulled out his Glock, climbed into the limousine, sat next to Dimitri, and pressed the gun into his side. Vince reached around Dimitri's large stomach, pulled out two Smith and Wessons and tucked them into his jacket.

"Precaution." Antony climbed into the car.

Dimitri's cigar smoke filled the car, making Antony nauseated. Ashes fell onto Antony's pants. He brushed them away.

"Where are they?" Dimitri growled.

"I'll give them to you as soon as I get out of this car. Again, it's a precaution. You understand. You want them in the trunk?"

"No, in here. After I deliver these to Ferd—"

"Cut the crap, Dimitri." Antony's voice was cold and hard. "I know there is no Ferdinand."

His face emotionless, Dimitri took a long drag on the cigarette and then released it.

"Ferdinand is a front man you made up," Antony continued. "You needed the store to move your paintings—fine, you used it. What I don't get is why you would kill your own grandmother to make us believe Ferdinand existed."

"I didn't think she'd be in the house," Dimitri said without conviction or concern. "They were supposed to be out shopping for carpet."

Antony's neck burned. He pulled out his Colt 40 and shoved it into Dimitri's chest. "You killed my father?"

"He stole my paintings. Not to mention he killed my parents."

Dimitri looked down at the gun then deep into Antony's eyes. "We're just alike, aren't we? I'd kill you to avenge my family, and you'd kill me to avenge yours." He took a long drag on the cigarette and momentarily held the smoke in his lungs before allowing it to escape. "Go ahead and shoot me."

Antony resisted the urge to strike him down. He returned the gun to its holster. "I'm not like you. Not anymore." He glared at Dimitri. "Take your paintings and disappear."

"You'd just let me walk away?" Dimitri grunted a laugh. "I don't think so."

Vince shoved his gun harder into Dimitri's side. The left side of Antony's mouth went into a grin. "I'll let you walk away, but Vince works for me now, and I assure you, revenge runs as thick in his blood as it does in mine or yours. If he sees you again, he'll kill you."

"What about the beaker?"

Antony gave a derogatory laugh. "You've got your paintings and your life, and you're still worried about a beaker?"

"It's worth millions."

"We couldn't find it."

"You'd double-cross me?"

"I told you, I'm not like you. Some punks robbed the store before it opened and apparently stole your beaker. If I were you, I'd start checking the pawnshops."

"Some punks? Lorenzo, no doubt."

Antony grabbed Dimitri's shirt under his chin. "I'll forget you said that. I see you again, you're dead."

Dimitri pushed Antony's hands from him. "I guess I'll settle for the paintings."

"Yeah. A hundred million instead of a hundred and ten?" Antony used every ounce of energy he had to not make him pay for killing his father, for shooting Victoria, and for almost killing Zoë. He'd give the police one chance. If they didn't take care of Dimitri, Vince would.

Antony stepped out of the limousine and walked to his car. Once safely inside the Durango, he watched Vince place the black tube in Dimitri's outstretched hand.

Antony waited until the limo drove away then turned to Sonny. "That was the easy part. Let's see if the cops can do their job."

***

Zoë sat in her car miles from Dimitri's rented office building, waiting.

Chatter emanated from the security radios of cops in other cars that tailed Dimitri as they began their pursuit. There were six patrol cars on him, changing off so no one was seen behind him for too long.

Another five vehicles sat in strategic positions in parking lots and side roads, ready to take over if Dimitri got suspicious.

Dimitri had the paintings, and if all went according to plan, he'd be arrested in time for lunch. A voice announced over the radio that Dimitri had entered the office building carrying the tube. Zoë pushed on the gas and began weaving in and out of cars. She sped down the block, pulled up on the curb, jumped out, and burst into the office with her gun drawn.

***

Christian tucked Liz's birthday present into a pocket of his black leather jacket. The house was quiet. He wasn't too worried about Bruno, but Doc was good.

His heart pounded as he walked down the stairs and leaned closer to the office door. He could hear the muffled sounds of his mother and Doc talking. Good—with Doc busy, he just might make it.

He walked through the living room and out the back door. As he went around the pool, he heard a noise. He fell on a bench, pulled a pocketknife from his jacket, grabbed a twig from the ground, and ran the edge of the knife across the bark. He looked up, and there stood Bruno. Christian squinted from the sun. "Yeah? You want something?"

"Just seeing what you're doing."

"Back off, dude. I ain't stupid. Dad said to stay here until this guy is caught."

Bruno crossed his arms and leaned against the tree. "I'll hang with you just the same."

"Then I'm going inside." Christian plunged the pocketknife into the bench, stood, and walked around to the front of the house.

"The door's that way."

"What?" He turned to Bruno and waved his hands in the air. "I can't walk to the front door? Give me a break."

Bruno followed. Christian quickened his pace and after clearing the front of the house went into a dead run. He grabbed the metal bars at the front gate, jumped up, swung his legs over, and landed on the pavement on the other side. He looked both ways, his heart pounding. Where was Russ?

He ran down the road to the intersection, pulled his cell phone out, and hit Russ's number. "Where are you?"

"Right behind you." Russ gave a quick horn honk.

Christian turned to see Russ's truck. He grabbed the door handle, yanked it open, and jumped in. Trying to catch his breath, he looked in the rearview mirror. The gate was open. He hit Russ's arm. "Let's go, quick."

***

Sonny's phone chirped.

"We got him," Zoë said.

Sonny ran his hand through his hair and sighed. "Thanks." He looked over at Antony. "They got Dimitri."

Bruno shot through the intersection at the same time Antony did. Antony slammed on the brakes. His tires squealed, and the car skidded sideways, barely missing Bruno's car.

Sonny grabbed his phone and called Bruno as he watched him speed off. "Where you going so fast?"

"Christian ran off with that Russ character," Bruno bellowed.

"That kid!" Sonny slammed his hand on the dash. "Stay on him."

"What?" Antony glanced over.

"Christian's run off."

Antony threw the car in reverse, straightened it out, then threw it in drive.

"What are you doing?" Sonny asked.

"I'm following him."

"Let him go. Dimitri's been caught. Besides, Dimitri wouldn't have any reason to go after my kids. The family is sacred."

"To the mob, not to Dimitri." Antony sat with his foot on the brake. "It's your decision."

"Let me call him."

***

Christian's phone vibrated as he walked down the hallway. "Yeah?"

"You ran off?" His father's voice was strong and angry.

"I'm at school. You said it was safe."

"I told you to wait."

"But it's safe, right? You made the drop?"

"Yes." Sonny sighed. "The police caught Dimitri."

"Then I'm okay."

"You promised this wouldn't happen again."

Christian waved at fellow classmates as he walked. He stopped and faced a locker. "Dad, I ran out to go to school. You can't cut me a break for that?"

"I've cut you one too many breaks."

"Let me stay for a few minutes then I'll come straight home. I gotta do something."

"What? I want a straight answer or I'll come get you myself."

Christian looked around the hallway. Last thing he needed was to be teased by Russ or Ned. He lowered his voice. "There's a girl I like, and she likes me. Today's her birthday, and I have something for her. Just let me drop it off, and then I'll come straight home with Bruno. I promise."

"You have a girlfriend?" He could sense his father smiling. "Why didn't you tell me?"

"'Cause I don't want you making a big deal about it."

"Okay. Drop it off then straight home with Bruno."

"Yes." Christian raised his fist in triumph. "Thanks, Dad. I'll be home in half an hour."

***

Justice ran through the layout of the school in his mind. Dimitri had been right—Sonny was naive enough to think his family would be safe. Christian had arrived at school shortly after Dimitri had the paintings.

He pulled the pocket binoculars from under the seat and watched the man lean his tall, muscular body against the Jeep. "I see one bodyguard," he said to Jimmy, aka Ferdinand, who sat behind the steering wheel.

Justice pulled out a fake detective badge and tucked it into his dark brown suit jacket. He put on the black sunglasses and headed toward the school. He watched Bruno stand at attention. Deep breaths and a quickening of pace got him into the building, where he stopped abruptly. He scanned the metal detectors before looking over at one of the two security guards. Pulling out the badge, he opened his coat and exposed a Glock.

"What did you need?" The security guard handed him back the badge.

"Erik Nichols," Justice said in his raspy voice.

"What'd he do?"

"Nothing. I just have a couple questions for him." He tucked the badge away. "Can't catch the kid at home. Thought I'd talk to him here."

The security guard nodded.

"Which way to the office?"

"Down the stairs on the left. Can't miss it."

Justice took the stairs then turned right. When he hacked into the school computer last week, he found out that Christian should be in the gym. He'd start there.

***

Christian tucked the basketball under his arm. His plaid shirt hung over the white tank top, untucked and unbuttoned. He wiped the sweat from his forehead as the cop said something to him about a party, alcohol, and Erik Nichols. He half listened, nodded, and then tossed the ball to a friend who sat on a bench next to Liz. "Be right back."

He turned and walked out of the gym with the cop. They'd entered the hallway when Bruno held his hand out and pressed it into Justice's chest. "You are?"

Justice reached into his pocket and pulled out a badge. "I need to talk to this young man."

"Not without his parents' permission you won't."

Justice nodded. "We'll go to my car and call them."

"I thought you were looking for Erik Nichols?" Bruno's eyes narrowed.

"I was. He said to talk to this kid."

Justice pushed by him and walked down the hall. Christian shrugged. "He's a cop, man. I got nothing to hide."

Bruno followed them through the front of the school. "Call the police," he said to the security guards.

"I am the police." Justice gave the security guards an eye roll. "I'll take care of this."

Justice brushed past Bruno and walked with Christian to his car.

Bruno jogged in front of them, grabbed Christian's arm, and pulled him around. "Don't take another step."

Christian ripped his arm from Bruno. "What are you doing, man? He's a cop."

Justice opened the back door of his car. "Son, go ahead and take a seat. I'll call your father."

Bruno grabbed Christian's shoulder. "Do no such thing. Go sit in my car. I'll call your dad." Bruno pulled out his cell phone, but the shot was instantaneous, deafening Christian's ears. It came from inside the car and ripped through Bruno, splattering blood everywhere.

Christian reached for Bruno's limp body as it fell to the ground. Justice grabbed him, shoved him into the car, and struggled to close the door as Jimmy gunned the engine.

Christian's eyes widened, and his ears still rung. "You shot him?"

"Shut up." Justice grabbed Christian behind the neck and threw him face down on the backseat. He pulled both arms behind his back and tied his wrists together. Justice grabbed a handful of Christian's hair and pulled his head up. "You say a word, I duct tape your mouth." He dropped Christian's head back on the seat.

Tears flooded Christian's eyes, but he tried to blink them away.

It'll be okay.

The smell of stale cigarettes and body odor lingered in the cloth seat of the car, making Christian's stomach churn. He rolled his chin toward his chest which gave him relief from the stench, but it allowed him to see his white tank top splattered with Bruno's blood.

He closed his eyes tightly and knew *It'll be okay* wasn't going to be an easy sell, even to himself.

The car stopped with a jerk and almost sent Christian to the floor. Justice grabbed the back of Christian's shirt and pulled him out of the car.

Christian got his footing and looked around at the parking garage. He was pulled up four flights of stairs and finally shoved into a small, musty room, his hands still tied behind his back. He hit the floor hard, splitting his lip.

He pushed himself up to his knees, felt the blood on his lip with his tongue, then turned his head and wiped it on the shoulder of his shirt.

He crawled over to an old metal-framed bed, took a deep breath and held it as he pressed his head into the urine-stained mattress, and pushed himself to a standing position. A hand grabbed his arm, pulled him up, and shoved him onto the bed. It creaked under his weight.

The room had one window, covered in filth. The man sat down on the old wooden chair in the corner. He was the skinny one. The one who shot Bruno.

Christian looked over at him. If he didn't do something, he knew his heart would leap from his chest, or he'd pee his pants. Both scenarios were unacceptable if he was going to survive. "Can you untie me?"

There was silence.

"I'm not going anywhere. These ropes are cutting into my skin." He paused. "Come on, man."

Jimmy glared at him for a moment then nodded and tucked his gun in the front of his pants. He moved his jacket and exposed a large buck knife that hung in a leather case on his belt. He pulled the knife out, grinning.

Jimmy grabbed the ropes which twisted Christian's arms awkwardly. Pain shot through them. Christian clenched his teeth, refusing to cry out. He felt the cold steel against his wrist before it began sawing through the rope. After a long moment, his arms dropped free.

He rubbed his wrists then moved his arms in a circular motion, giving relief to his shoulders. "Did you kill him?"

"Hope so." Jimmy sat back down, replaced the knife, then pulled the gun out and laid it on his lap.

The door opened, making Christian's heart race faster. Another man walked in, looked at him for a moment, then nodded at Jimmy. "I'm supposed to take over. Boss wants you."

"Sure thing."

Jimmy left.

After the door closed, Christian stared at his newest captor. His shoulder-length blond hair was tucked behind his ears. He wore

Wranglers, a plaid shirt, and boots. A gun hung freely on his belt. He didn't look crazy like the other two.

"You okay?" the man asked.

"Why do you care?" Christian's heart pounded.

"You're Christian, right?"

"Who are you?" he spouted back, anger and fear running through him.

The man walked closer. "Martin."

"Yeah, sure," Christian grunted.

"You're going to be okay." Martin's face was calm, relaxed. "Trust me."

"Trust you? Right." Christian rolled his eyes. He pointed to the window. "Can I look out?"

"Go ahead."

Christian walked to the window and wiped the dirt off it. "You know my dad is rich." He squinted and tried to see where he was. "You get me outta here, he'll pay you."

"You won't get hurt. I promise."

"Sure." Christian silently prayed.

TWENTY-THREE

ANTONY, HIS HEAD BACK WITH A SMILE, stood in the backyard of Sonny and Victoria's estate. He could hear the birds chirping, and the heat from the sun cleansed his mind. He felt good. Breathing deeply, he paused then slowly released the air.

"Antony?" The voice was soft, and it came from behind him. It was Zoë.

He turned to her. She looked into his eyes momentarily and then away. A rush of anger ran through his body.

"Don't tell me . . ."

Antony shook his head and walked past her. She grabbed his arm.

He turned to her, his mouth curled, his body flooded with anger. "I can't believe you botched this."

***

Sonny slammed the phone down and threw the contents of his desk on the floor. His heart pounded, and he paced for a moment then sunk into the chair and buried his head in his hands. Tears seeped out.

Why hadn't he insisted that Bruno bring Christian straight home? Why hadn't he listened to his brother? Antony was right. Dimitri didn't hold anything sacred. It was evident the plan was revenge and Dimitri wouldn't stop at just killing Lorenzo. Dimitri planned on killing them all.

Antony ran into the office. Pens, pencils, and papers crunched under his feet. "What happened?"

Sonny wiped the tears from his eyes. "Dimitri took Christian." Sonny half expected an *I told you so*, but by the troubled look in

Antony's eyes and the hardness of his face, he knew his brother was just as angry and worried as he was.

"We'll get him back," Antony insisted.

Victoria and Zoë ran into the room. Antony held his hand up for them to stop at the doorway.

Sonny's temples pulsated, and he glared at Zoë. "You let him get away?"

"It wasn't my fault. We had him, but there was gunfire. I don't know exactly what happened. They're investigating now."

Sonny stood, walked past Antony, and glared at Zoë. "I just got off the phone with your office. A man disguised as a police officer went to the school, shot Bruno, and took Christian."

"What? No." Victoria shook her head. "Christian's in his room. You told him one more day. He promised."

Her voice drew his eyes to her, and his chest heaved. "He snuck out. Bruno followed him to school. When Zoë said they had Dimitri, I thought he'd be okay."

Victoria walked to the couch and sunk into it. She lowered her head and began to sob. Sonny went to her and held her. Her head shot up. "Where's Rachel?"

Sonny wiped the tears from her cheek and cupped them in his hands. "She's downstairs."

"What if?"

"What if, nothing. Clay!" Sonny shouted.

Clay appeared in the doorway.

"Take Rachel and Sean to Papa's. Use the safe house."

"Take Bosco and Vince and four other guys," Antony added. "Once they're settled, you and Vince get back over here. And Clay?" When Clay looked over at Antony, he added, "If anything happens to her, you better have died trying to protect her."

Clay nodded and disappeared.

Antony's phone chirped. He looked at the display. "It's Dimitri." He put the phone to his ear. "Yeah?"

"I suppose you heard. You tried. I'll give you credit. But now it's payback."

Antony's eyes locked with Sonny's. His heart pounded. "What do you want?"

"The beaker."

"I told you. We don't know where it is."

"My son!" Sonny yanked the phone from Antony. "Where is my son?"

"He's safe, for the moment. The beaker."

"What are you talking about?"

"Ask your brother."

The phone went dead.

"The beaker?" Sonny threw the phone at Antony. "You double-crossed him, and now he's kidnapped my son?"

"No." Antony's eyes darted from Sonny's to Victoria's.

"Don't look at her. She's through defending you." Sonny pushed him. "I want my son back."

"This is just like you to blame me." Antony brushed past Sonny and walked to the doorway. "He wants the beaker—the one Vic bought in the Bahamas—but it was stolen before the store ever opened."

"Why didn't you tell me he wanted the beaker?" Sonny asked.

"Because it's gone. Vic said you guys didn't know where it was or who stole it."

"The beaker?" Zoë's forehead wrinkled.

"Yeah," Antony said. "Dimitri switched them. The one Vic bought was an original worth millions." He turned to Victoria. "You said you recovered the other stuff from the pawnshop, but there wasn't a beaker." Antony's eyes narrowed, glancing at the three of them. "There was a beaker?"

"I don't know for sure," Victoria said.

"Do you know who stole the stuff?" When she looked away, Antony rolled his eyes. "I asked you about it the day Lorenzo died. You said you didn't know who stole it. You lied?"

"She didn't lie." Sonny's hand was in his pocket. He clutched the cross that hung from the rosary. "We don't know for sure who stole it, but we think it was Christian and his friends. They pawned everything but the beaker."

"What do you mean you think it was Christian? Did you confront him? Did you ask him if he did it?" Antony sighed. "No, you didn't, did you? You couldn't face the fact that your son isn't perfect."

Sonny's eyes cut to him. "If you hadn't filled his head with the past."

Antony shook his head. "You're not going to blame this on me."

"Would you two stop it!" Victoria yelled. "I don't care what Christian did or didn't do. I just want him back."

Zoë bent over, picked up the lamp, and set it on Sonny's desk. "If the beaker was never pawned, do you have any idea where it might be?"

"No," Sonny said. "But I know someone who might."

He picked the phone up off the floor and dialed Ned's cell number.

***

Martin punched in a text message that read, *Kid's safe.* He hit send, but nothing. "What?" He looked at the phone. *No service.*

"Shoot." He tucked the phone into his pocket then walked to the door.

He opened it and peeked outside. Justice stared aimlessly at a small TV that sat in the corner. He closed the door and turned to Christian who sat on the bed, his legs pressed tightly against his chest, his arms wrapped around them. He had no idea his big job would be guarding Zoë's kidnapped nephew. Christian looked up at Martin, his eyes dark and his face hard.

Martin went to him and sat down. Christian scooted away. Martin grabbed his arm. "Shh, listen. I want to tell you something if you can stay calm."

Christian held his head up. His face reeked of fear. "What?"

"How old are you?"

"Fifteen."

Martin leaned into him. "If I tell you, it has to be our secret."

Christian scooted farther away. "You touch me or anything, I swear . . ."

He grabbed Christian behind the neck and pulled him close. "I'm a cop."

"Sure, and I'm the Prince of Egypt."

Martin raised an eyebrow. Had he really expected Christian to believe him? "Your Aunt Zoë, she's a cop. She was my partner, my ex-wife. The last time I saw you, you were seven or eight. It was at the wedding reception your mother insisted on throwing for us."

Christian's eyes narrowed as he stared at Martin's face. "You're undercov—"

"Shh." Martin raised his finger to his mouth. "Or we're both dead."

The doorknob turned, and Martin jumped from the bed. He looked at Justice. "What's up?"

"We're supposed to let the kid call his dad."

"Sure thing." Martin turned and grabbed Christian by the shirt, winked at him, then yanked him up and pushed him into the other room.

Justice dialed the cell number, put it on speaker, then handed the phone to Christian. Christian pulled himself away from Martin's grip and waited for someone to answer.

"Yeah?" Sonny said.

Christian smiled when he heard his father's voice. "Dad?" A single tear rolled down his cheek.

"Oh, thank God!" Sonny shouted. "Are you okay?"

"Yeah."

They could hear Victoria's voice. "Tell Mom I'm fine. Bruno?"

"He's hanging in there."

"Good."

"Christian?"

"Yeah, Dad?"

"I love you," Sonny said. "We'll find you."

"I know. I love you, too"

Justice ripped the phone from Christian's hand and hung up.

"Take the kid back to his room." Justice sat down and rested his feet on the coffee table.

Martin took Christian back in and closed the door. He walked to the window and chewed on the inside of his cheek. There was service out there but not in here. He had to send a message.

He turned to Christian who sat on the bed, head down, feet crossed. Tears streaked his face. Martin knew he couldn't leave him.

***

Antony wanted to grab the phone and get the truth out of Christian, but he knew he couldn't. He'd have to figure another way to find his nephew and the beaker and get Dimitri out of their lives. He paced.

"They hung up on me." Sonny threw the phone.

Zoë placed her hands in her pockets. "We've got a guy on the inside. If we're lucky, he knows about Christian."

"A guy on the inside?" Sonny grabbed her arm, spinning her around. "You've had a guy on the inside this whole time and didn't tell us?"

"There was no need until now."

"Who is he?" Sonny asked.

"Martin," Zoë said. "He's been working for Dimitri for over a year now. He'll know about Christian. He'd have to."

"Can't you get word to him?" Victoria asked. "He could tell us where Christian is."

"I've been trying to reach him since Dimitri escaped. I'll keep trying." Zoë put on her cop face. "In the meantime, we find the beaker. Ned said he never saw it, but Christian told him he had it. It must be here." She looked around at them. "We tear the house apart, look down at the stables, in the old tree house, wherever you think Christian would hide it. You guys get started. I need to check in with the brass."

Antony waited until Sonny and Victoria left then grabbed Zoë's arm. "The cops aren't stepping in, not yet. When we get the beaker, we trade it for Christian first, then you do whatever you want to get Dimitri."

"We cops aren't imbeciles."

"Could've fooled me. You let Dimitri slip right out from under you, and now he's got my nephew."

"He's my nephew, too."

Antony released her. His eyes narrowed, and his head shook in disgust. He walked out of the office.

Antony went into the living room and found Victoria sitting cross-legged on the floor. Tears rolled down her cheeks. She pulled out books and CDs from the built-in wall cabinets.

Antony knelt down next to her. "You okay?"

"No, I'm not." She looked up at him and wiped her eyes. "I want my son back."

"We all do, Vic. I'll go start looking in the game room."

"No." She grabbed his arm. "I want you to do something for me."

Antony stared deep into her eyes. There was something different in them. Something distant and foreign. "I'd do anything for you, you know that."

"I want my son back and for this to end." She looked directly into his eyes, her face hard and her eyes pleading. "I don't care what you have to do, do it."

Antony's eyes narrowed, and he gave her a single nod. He stood and walked into the foyer. He pulled a toothpick from his jacket and bit down on it. Had he understood her correctly? She wanted him to get Christian back and for him to end this? To do whatever it took? He knew of only one way to accomplish that. Surely it wasn't what she meant, not Victoria. Her God wouldn't allow it.

Vince walked to him. His cold eyes glared deep into Antony's soul. He was patiently waiting for permission to avenge Lorenzo's death. Antony looked down at his outstretched hands and wondered if he could give the order.

The turmoil taunted him. He was born the oldest and was supposed to protect his family at all costs, to carry on Lorenzo's legacy. It was his destiny, so why was he doubting?

He knew why. In the depths of his heart, he had actually begun to believe Victoria, her God, and the idea that his life was worth more than what Lorenzo had deemed it to be. But even she didn't believe that anymore or she wouldn't have asked him to carry out this deed.

He narrowed his eyes and accepted his duty. He stood tall and brought his head up, his jaw tight and his eyes hard. "Get Bosco on the streets looking for Christian. Then do whatever it takes to find Dimitri and kill him."

Vince rubbed his hands together and grinned. "Gladly."

TWENTY-FOUR

ELISA STOOD OVER THE KITCHEN SINK. Hot water ran over a greasy pan, and the smell of fried hamburgers still lingered in the air. She reached for a book of matches, struck one, and lit the vanilla-scented candle.

She slid the last hamburger onto the plate in front of Hank, her brown-haired, average-looking prison guard. "I'm going out to the garden."

Hank stacked the second burger on the half-eaten first one, shoved a handful of chips in his mouth, and stood. "I'm coming." He took a gulp of pop.

She placed her hand on his shoulder and pushed him back into the chair. "I'll be fine for five minutes while you finish eating. I'm not going anywhere."

His eyes narrowed.

"You really think I'd shimmy over that fence?"

"No." Hank chewed the chips and swallowed. "I'm trusting you. You disappear, and it's my head."

"I won't. This *is* my house." She picked up the garden gloves and scooted one of the short-handled gardening shovels across the table. "Bring this when you're done, and you can help me dig up bulbs."

He rolled his eyes before taking a bite out of the hamburger.

Once outside, Elisa pulled out her cell phone to see if Martin had called. No missed call from Martin, but there was one from Antony. She dialed Antony's number then slid the phone to her ear and walked farther away from the house. "Hello."

"Hey. Thanks for calling me back."

Glancing at the house, she saw Hank looking out the window. She didn't know what he would do to her if he knew she had the phone, and she wasn't about to find out. "What'd you need?"

"We need to talk."

"Meet me in the corner of the backyard. Don't let anyone see you." She slid the phone back into her pocket.

She walked to the farthest corner of the yard where a large bulb garden was. The plants were dormant enough to dig them up and replant them on the other side of the garden.

A black iron fence surrounded by hedges, tall plants, and vines encompasses the property. She knelt down, pushed the shovel into the ground, wiggled it around, then pulled it and a bulb up. She placed the bulb into a bucket.

"Elisa?" Antony's voice came from the vines. He pushed them to the side and knelt down.

"Make it quick. You have to get out of here before someone sees you." She looked back at the house then at him. "Dimitri killed your father, and he wants to kill you."

"He tell you that?"

"No. I just know."

"Why are we hiding out here?"

"Dimitri has a man watching me. I can't go anywhere without being followed."

"Has Dimitri threatened you?"

Elisa touched her neck. She could still feel his large hands choking her. She brought her eyes up to meet his. "Yes."

"You're coming with me." Antony looked around at the vines. "You got a gate back here?"

Elisa looked back down and stuck the shovel into the ground, wiggled it back and forth, removed another bulb, then wiped the small amount of sweat from her forehead with her arm.

"Did you hear me?" Antony said.

"I heard you." She dug in the next spot. "I'm doing this in case Hank looks out the window. Meet me at the far corner, over there." She pointed with her shovel. "There's a gate hidden in the vines."

Elisa stood, picked up the bucket of bulbs, and walked to the far corner of the grounds. She glanced back at the house. Hank had not emerged. Her heart pounded harder when she heard Antony pull the vines from the gate.

As he opened it, the iron squeaked loudly. She knelt down and pretended to dig in the ground. "Is he coming?"

"He's looking out the window." Antony waited then slowly opened the gate, allowing the vines to hang to make it appear the gate had never been opened. "Now. Come on," Antony whispered.

Elisa didn't look back. She dropped the shovel and crawled through the vines to freedom.

Antony grabbed her hand as they ran to his Durango. Once safely inside, he floored it. "Dimitri's kidnapped my nephew. I need to know if he's got any warehouses or abandoned buildings. Any place where he could hide Christian."

"He owns an office building."

"Cops have been there. Anything else?"

"Enrico owned that abandoned building on First and Walnut. I don't know if Dimitri would use it or not."

"Thanks. I want you to stay with us at Sonny's until this is over."

"You'll keep me safe?"

"Yes." Antony squeezed her hand. "It'll be okay. I promise."

Elisa nodded.

**

Victoria found Sonny leaning over the last toy box in the basement. The one filled with toys the kids couldn't give away. He threw the pink Barbie convertible at the wall.

"No luck?"

"No, you?"

"Nothing. We've gone through every room," Victoria said.

"I'll start down at the stables."

"Remember when Christian took the autographed baseball card from your office at Renato's? When we started looking for it, he got scared and put it back. What if he did that? What if he took it back to the store?"

"You might be right," Sonny said.

"Let's go."

"You're not going anywhere. It's too dangerous. I'll send some men."

"I'm going," Victoria demanded. "I will not stand here and do nothing." Her jaw tightened. "That's my son. I know that store inside and out. If the beaker is there, I'll find it."

"No," Sonny's voice was hard. "I won't let you go. You could be next." He shook his head. "I can't let you go."

Fear engulfed her as much as determination did. "I have to do this for Christian. If the beaker is there, and I do nothing, I couldn't live with myself." Tears rolled down her cheeks.

Sonny brushed the tears away with the knuckles of his hand. "Okay, we'll both go." He kissed her. "I'll call Antony and have him meet us there."

***

Antony yelled over the phone as he swerved in and out of traffic. "Are you two crazy? Let the clerks look for it." He made a quick U-turn and floored it. He had wanted Elisa to stay at Sonny's, but his house was closer, and he couldn't waste time. He had to get to the store to protect Sonny and Victoria.

"Vic knows Francesca's better than anyone. If Christian took it back there, she'll find it." Sonny's frustration bled through his next question. "Will you meet us or not?"

"Of course I will." Antony slammed on his brakes, almost rear-ending a truck. He jerked the car into the next lane and glared at the driver as he passed. "Where's Zoë?"

"She left right after you did."

Antony's tires squealed as he pulled into his driveway. "I'm on my way." He tossed the phone on the dash, threw the car into park, and looked over at Elisa. "Come on."

He opened the front door of his house and motioned for her to go in. "The security code is 0403. Turn it on when I leave."

"I thought I was staying at Sonny's."

"I have to meet Sonny right now. It's important."

Elisa nodded.

"You are, too, but I gotta do this. I'll send over a couple of guys to get you and take you to Sonny's."

He ran back to the Durango, peeled out, grabbed his cell, and hit Zoë's number. "Where you at?"

"At the office."

"Check out the apartments on First and Walnut. Christian may be there."

"You going to meet me?"

"No, you're on your own. I'm meeting Vic and Sonny at the new store. They think the beaker might be there."

"You want me to send some police?"

"A couple of plainclothes would be nice."

"Consider it done."

"You want me to send Bosco over to help you?"

"I got it," Zoë said. "But thanks anyway."

"Don't go to First and Walnut with the entire force. If Christian is there and you can get him out quietly, we'll have one up on Dimitri."

Antony called Vince. "You got any leads on Dimitri yet?"

"No, nothing."

"Go to my place. Elisa's there. Take her to Sonny's."

"Sure thing."

Zoë tossed the pencil on her desk, pulled out her cell phone, and text messaged Martin again. "First & Walnut?" She waited. Nothing. Why wasn't he answering?

She called Jackson. "You and Garcia busy?"

"Depends."

As she walked through the police station to her car, she filled Jackson in.

"We'll be there," Jackson said.

Zoë hung up the phone and drove off.

***

Victoria stood in the middle of the store and looked up at the three stories. Doc stood next to her, his hand resting on the gun that hung from his belt. "Where do you want to start?"

"As soon as Stacie gets those pictures copied, Sonny will pass them out to each clerk. That will cover the store. I'm starting in my office. You check yours."

"Nope." Doc led her to the elevator. "I'm staying with you." They walked into her office, and Doc shut and locked the door. "Start looking."

"You're not going to help?"

"No way." He pulled the walkie from his pocket and began chatting with the security officers in the security room. She was thankful Doc had stayed. Her confidence was an act.

He pulled out his gun.

Her eyes widened. "What?"

"Two men in suits walked in and flashed badges."

Victoria began going through her desk drawers. "Zoë probably sent them over."

"Sure. Just like the one she sent to the school." He pulled the action back on the gun.

Victoria dropped the papers. Her heart pounded. The phone rang. Doc motioned for her to get it. "Hello?"

"You okay?" Antony asked.

"Yes. Where are you?"

"Stuck in a stinkin' traffic jam. Zoë said she was sending over a couple of plainclothes cops."

Victoria sighed and closed her eyes momentarily, allowing her heart to slow down. "They just got here. We weren't sure if they were real." She moved the phone to her chin. "Antony says Zoë sent them."

"I'll check 'em out just the same."

"Sounds like Doc's taking care of you," Antony said.

There was a knock on the door then a voice. "Mrs. Luciano?"

She motioned for Doc to open the door, but he shook his head, his gun near his face. He leaned into the door. Antony's voice drew her attention away from Doc. "Vic?"

"Yeah, I'm here."

"What's going on?"

"Doc insists on scaring me to death," she said loud enough for Doc to hear.

Doc turned to her, one hand on the doorknob, his eyes narrowed. "Just doing my job, Mrs. L."

Before Doc knew it, the door burst open. Two men bolted into the room. One grabbed Doc's shoulder, shoved the gun into his stomach, and fired. The muffled shot ripped through him, throwing him to the floor.

"Oh God!" Victoria screamed and dropped the phone as the man flew at her. He grabbed her and covered her mouth, muffling another scream. Doc held his stomach. Blood seeped through his fingers.

Victoria fought her assailant, and when she was finally free, she fell at Doc's side and laid her hands on his, pressing down to help stop the bleeding. Doc looked at up her, and his body shook. "Gun . . ." He motioned with his eyes to her desk then back at her.

She gave him a reassuring nod before a man grabbed her and pulled her away from him. She yanked her arm free then ran toward the desk where she could faintly hear Antony's voice through the phone. The man grabbed her arm, picked up the receiver, and hung the phone up.

Victoria's stomach churned. She looked back at Doc. His blue eyes stared back at her. He clenched his stomach, and the blood began to seep out from under him. She wanted to turn away from his piercing eyes, but she couldn't. He was telling her something. *Gun.*

The man shoved her. "Let's go."

Victoria defiantly ripped her arm from his. "Can I get my purse?" Before the man could answer, Victoria squatted down, reached under the desk, and felt around for the small Derringer Doc had mounted. Before she could reach it, the man grabbed her arm and jerked her forward. "Any tipoffs to anyone, and we start killing innocent customers."

Victoria nodded and fought the tears as she locked eyes with Doc. "You can't leave him there. He'll die."

The other man stood over Doc's limp body and held the gun over him. "Should I put him out of his misery?"

The man gripped her arm tightly. "Let him suffer."

The other man held the gun over Doc and laughed. He motioned with his gun. "Get her in the car."

The man's grip tightened. "We'll go out the back."

Trembling, she took a step then looked back. Doc raised his head, then it fell back down. She was pushed farther into the hallway. Tears filled her eyes. They led her to the service elevator. Her arms clutched her stomach, and she thought she'd throw up. Tears rolled down her cheeks as she prayed silently for Doc.

***

Antony pounded his fist on the dash and cursed. He dialed Sonny's number first then 911. He backed up the Durango, pulled out of the stopped traffic, went through the median, and landed on the shoulder. He drove against the oncoming traffic until he passed the accident then crossed back over the median into his own lane. Red lights appeared in his rearview mirror, but it only made him press harder on the gas.

***

Sonny dropped the phone and yelled at Clay, "They're here. They've got Vic." He ran toward her office and flew through the doorway. "Oh, man." He knelt down next to Doc. The blood had soaked through his pants to his knees. He felt Doc's neck. "He's still alive. Get help." Sonny leaned in and said, "Doc?"

Doc opened his eyes. His face was white, and his body tremored. "Back door . . ."

Sonny nodded then shoved past Clay as he ran down the hall. "They took her down the back."

Clay screamed orders into the walkie. When they reached the bottom of the stairs, Clay raised his gun and pounded it as hard as he could on the back of Sonny's head. "Sorry, Boss." Sonny took a tumble then slumped on the floor. "Gotta protect you, too."

Clay yelled at a security guard to watch Sonny as he ran to the loading dock. Jumping from the dock, he landed on the ground as the car sped out. Clay unloaded his gun in the tires of the car.

As it spun, he could hear Victoria scream. Then he saw her jump from the car, roll across the pavement, and dive into the bushes.

Police cars pulled up, and officers jumped out with guns drawn. Clay ran toward the bushes as shots filled the air. He landed on top of Victoria, her hands covering her ears.

TWENTY-FIVE

ZOË PACED OUTSIDE HER CAR. *Where were they?*

When she saw the Ford Bronco pull in, she walked toward them and opened the driver's door. "It's about time."

"Garcia needed to load his gun." Jackson laughed.

Garcia rolled his eyes. "You know how many men?"

"No, but Martin might be up there."

"And you don't want us to shoot him?" Jackson asked.

"Someone took his happy pill this morning." Zoë slapped his arm. "Let's just get my nephew."

They climbed the first set of stairs. She pulled the phone out and texted Martin.

Jackson leaned into her and whispered, "Personal calls on your own time."

"I'm trying to reach Martin." When there was no response, Zoë slid the phone back in her pocket.

They went up more stairs, searching each floor. When they reached the fourth, they heard sounds like a radio or TV. Jackson and Garcia stood on opposite sides of the door. Jackson held up three fingers and mouthed *on three.*

Garcia and Zoë nodded and watched Jackson count off. When he reached three, Garcia kicked the door in, and Zoë ran inside.

"What the . . ." Justice jumped to his feet, throwing the chair halfway across the room.

Justice was at least a foot taller and weighed a hundred pounds more than Zoë, but her years of training kicked in. She ran full force and threw all her weight on him, causing them both to fly across the floor into the wall. Zoë placed the barrel of her gun against the man's temple. She reached around and removed his pistol and tucked it in the back of her pants. She stood, her gun aimed at him as he stood.

When Justice lunged at her, she brought her knee up to his groin. The force knocked the wind out of him, and he crumpled to the ground with a moan and held himself.

Garcia laughed and pulled the cuffs from his belt. "Did you learn that at the academy?" His knee on Justice's back, he pulled his arms around and snapped the cuffs on him.

"Shut up," Zoë snapped. "Search the rest of the place. We've got to find Christian."

Zoë and Jackson walked down the hall then gently tapped on the door to a room. Nothing. Jackson tapped her shoulder and motioned for her to open the door.

Zoë slowly opened the door, and Jackson crept into the room, his gun drawn. He felt cold steel pressed against his temple. He turned his head and grinned. "Hello, Martin."

"Jackson." Martin slid his gun into its holster. "Glad you could make it."

"One guy? You couldn't take him yourself?" Jackson raised an eyebrow.

"And keep my cover, no."

"Your cover." Jackson pulled out his handcuffs. He grabbed Martin's wrist and slapped a cuff on it. "Yeah, we gotta keep your cover." He yanked Martin's arm behind his back and cuffed the other wrist. "I'll make sure to make it look real."

"You push me around, I cry police brutality."

Jackson reached around and took Martin's gun. "Good luck making that one stick." He grabbed Martin's arm as Zoë pushed past them, into Christian's arms.

***

"You knocked me out." Sonny's hand rested on the back of his head. He sat on the cement stairs just inside the loading dock, glaring at Antony. "Wipe that smug grin off your face. You probably ordered it."

"I wish I had." Antony tried not to laugh.

Sonny stood and turned to Clay, who fought a grin. "Don't stand there and laugh with him."

"He was doing the job you trained him to do." Antony winked at Clay. "You can't blame the guy for that."

Silence fell as Victoria walked toward Sonny with a bag of ice. "Have you heard any news about Doc?"

"He's alive." Sonny's eyes cut to Clay and Antony, who were still grinning.

"Vic," Antony said as Victoria placed the ice against Sonny's head. "I don't think I'd do that."

Sonny batted the ice away and glared at his brother.

"What?" she asked.

Sonny looked over at her. "We were discussing something here."

"You're mad at Clay?" Vic asked. "He just saved my life."

"He knocked me out."

"He hurt your ego more than your head." Antony laughed.

One of Antony's men walked up. "The cars are ready."

"Cars?" Victoria shook her head. "We're not leaving without the beaker."

"You're both going home." Antony stood.

Sonny rubbed his temple. "She's right. We need to find the beaker."

"No," Antony demanded. "I'm through with Dimitri's games. We go to your place and tell him we've got the beaker. When he comes to get it, we take him out."

Sonny couldn't deny that he'd rather see Dimitri dead than behind bars. His eyes fell on Victoria, her clothes stained with Doc's blood.

Antony's voice drew back his attention. "Fill your house with cops, I don't care, but we end it."

Sonny finally nodded. "Call Zoë then Dimitri."

"We should have the beaker," Victoria pleaded. "We *need* the beaker to get Christian back."

"Antony's right," Sonny said. "We don't have to have it as long as Dimitri *thinks* we have it."

Sonny's phone chirped. He put it to his ear. "Yeah?" His eyes widened. "Oh, thank God. Put him on."

He looked up at Victoria with a grin. "Zoë has Christian." He put the phone on speaker. "Christian?"

"You okay, baby?" Victoria said.

"I'm okay."

"Where are you?" Sonny asked.

"At some cop's house. They want me to stay here until this is over."

"Okay," Sonny said and wrapped his arm around Victoria.

They laughed as Christian told them Jackson's account of how Zoë laid Justice out.

***

Antony placed his hands in his pockets and walked out to the loading dock and fresh air. He couldn't deny the satisfaction of saving his nephew, but it was overshadowed. The fact that Dimitri was still on the loose and would stop at nothing to avenge his family loomed over them like a dark cloud.

Moments later, Sonny walked up behind him. "Zoë said you found out where Christian was. Thank you."

"No problem. It was an old building Elisa's husband owned."

"Elisa?"

"Yeah. She's going to stay with us until this is over. I don't trust Dimitri with her."

"Okay."

"Let's get you and Vic home safely. Then I'll call Dimitri."

Sonny pushed both hands deep into the pockets of his pants. "Is this what it was like when you lived on the streets and worked for Vito?"

Antony grinned. "Not even close." He hit Sonny's arm playfully. "How's the head?"

Sonny gently touched the bump where Clay had pulverized him. "Hurts." He stopped and turned to Antony. "Christian told me where the beaker is. It's in the stables."

"Good." Antony turned and motioned at Clay. "Take them home. I'll be there shortly."

He waited until they left then walked inside and dialed Zoë's number.

"Your info was right on," Zoë said.

Antony's chest filled with pride. "Wish I'd been there to help."

"We did okay without you."

Antony could tell she was smiling. "Yeah, I guess you did." He walked around the boxes of merchandise. "Sonny fill you in?"

"Yep, we're on our way over there now."

"We? Don't bring a truckload of cops. Dimitri will see right through it."

"Just me and Martin. I thought we proved we're not imbeciles."

Antony kicked the bottom of a box and smiled. "You did good, but I still have my doubts."

"I wouldn't expect anything less from you." She had laughter in her voice.

"See you shortly."

He snapped the phone shut and leaned against the wall. He rested his head back and closed his eyes. He used to get a rush from playing the game, but now the excitement was gone. Dimitri was like a rattlesnake that lay coiled in the bushes, waiting for his prey, ready to strike at any moment. Antony knew he had to stop him.

**

The pounding on the door startled Elisa. She froze until the voice yelled, "Elisa, open up."

Elisa looked through the peephole out of habit even though she knew she wouldn't recognize any of Antony's men.

"Hello?" he knocked again. "You in there?

"Just a minute." She walked to the security box, punched in the numbers, then opened the door.

"I hoped you'd come here."

Elisa gasped and pushed the door shut, but the man was overpowering. He grabbed her around the waist. She kicked and punched at him, but he was twice her size, and his grip was tight.

Hank, her prison guard, walked around them and stood before her with a gun in his hand. He brought it up and struck her across her face. "You broke your promise."

"I'm sorry," she cried.

"I don't think you are." Hank pulled a bottle from his coat pocket. Elisa's eyes widened as he slowly unscrewed the lid and poured some of the liquid onto a handkerchief. "Don't worry. You won't feel a thing."

Elisa tried to thrash her arms and legs, but the other man held her tightly. Her eyes widened, and she frantically shook her head as Hank brought the handkerchief to her face, completely covering her mouth and nose.

Everything went black.

**

Antony drove to Sonny's. Classic rock played softly in the background as he grabbed his cell phone and dialed Dimitri.

Dimitri's voice was calm. "You find my beaker?"

"Yep."

Dimitri gave a derogatory laugh. "I knew with a little pressure it'd turn up. I want you and Sonny to bring it to me."

"I'll bring it. Name the place."

"I never thought it'd come down to you and me. I thought I'd just kill Sonny then let this whole thing drop."

"Oh, I'll bet. Forgiveness? That would be a new emotion for you."

"I always liked you, Antony. I always felt Sonny should pay for making you live on the streets. I've seen how you look at Victoria. I can give you everything you ever wanted—the company, his money, his wife and kids."

Antony cringed. "You seriously think I'd sit by and allow you to kill my brother?"

The phone went dead.

TWENTY-SIX

ANTONY WAS DRAWN to the kitchen by the lemon-garlic aroma that floated in the air. It made his stomach growl. Victoria leaned over the sink and filled a large pot with water. He grabbed a handful of grape tomatoes, threw one in his mouth, and leaned against the counter.

Victoria shut off the water and wrapped her arms around him. "Thank you."

Antony backed away and grinned. "Tell me what I did, and I'll do it again."

"You found Christian. I knew you could."

"Anything for you." He winked and pointed to the chicken. "This looks good. I didn't realize how hungry I was. What are you making?"

"Chicken Alfredo." Victoria tucked her hair behind her ears.

"You got room for one more?"

"Yeah, who?" Victoria's eye widened. "Christian?"

"No. He's safely tucked at some cop's house." He tossed another tomato in his mouth. "It's Elisa."

"Elisa?" Victoria raised an eyebrow.

"It's not like that. I know Dimitri, and given the chance, he'll use her to get to me. She's at my place now. Vince should have her here anytime. You don't mind if she sticks around until this is over?"

"Not at all. Sonny's in the office with Zoë and Martin. Did you know he was undercover at Dimitri's?"

"Yep."

"Nothing gets by you, does it?"

Antony laughed.

Victoria picked up the pot and placed it on the stove. "I'm glad you're on our side."

Antony leaned into her. "You'll never get rid of me."

Victoria's face flushed.

Antony walked into the great room when he heard the squealing of tires and a quick horn honk. He rushed out the door.

Vince jumped out of the car. "It's Elisa."

Antony's pace quickened.

Vince wiped the sweat off his forehead. "When I got to your place, she was out cold, and two guys were carrying her to their car."

"Where are these two guys?" Antony grabbed the door handle.

"Around."

Antony's eyes cut to him.

"They ain't dead if that's what you're asking."

Antony opened the car door and squatted down, gently touching Elisa's face. A bruise on her cheek was the size of an orange and was turning shades of purple and yellow. The small gash on her lip still seeped blood.

"Elisa?" He caressed her hair. "Come on, babe, wake up."

Her eyes opened then quickly shut.

Antony scooped her up and carried her into the house. "Victoria."

Victoria walked into the living room. Her eyes widened. "Oh no. Lay her down. I'll get some ice."

Antony laid Elisa down on the couch, fell to his knees, and patted her hand. "Come on, hon. Wake up."

Sonny ran into the room, followed by Zoë and Martin. Martin shoved past them and knelt down by Elisa's head, his hands cupping her face and his lips to her ear. "Elisa, it's Martin. Wake up. You're safe. Come on, wake up."

Elisa's eyes opened. She looked at Martin with a faint smile. He leaned in and gently kissed her. "We need to get you to the hospital."

"No. I'm okay. It was only chloroform. Is Christian okay?"

"Yes," Antony said.

Her eyes were drawn to Antony's. "Good."

"You're safe now." Martin gently brushed his knuckles across her good cheek. "I won't let anything happen to you."

She looked back at Martin and held his hand. "Were you with him?"

"Yes." When she smiled, he leaned over her and kissed her. "You're going to be okay. I'm here now."

Antony stood up and placed his hands in his pockets. Despite the guilt he felt for leaving her alone at the house, he was angry that she was responding to Martin, a cop. As if sensing his turmoil, Zoë touched his back, but he jerked away from her.

"Don't." He walked into Sonny's office.

Moments later, Martin's voice bellowed through the office. "You used her for information then left her alone?"

"She was at my place. She should've been safe."

"How could you do that to her?" Martin tucked his blond hair behind his ears. "You had to know he'd hurt her again."

"Again?" Antony's face felt like it was on fire. "Dimitri hurt her before, and you left her?"

"I was busy saving your nephew."

"Saving him? I found out where he was and sent Zoë." Antony's eyes narrowed. "I saved Christian, not you."

"What are you really angry about?" Martin's mouth tipped. "That she loves me more than she loves you?"

Antony gave his head a shake.

"Lower the testosterone levels." Zoë walked between them. "You two are unreal. A killer is loose, and you're fighting over a girl. We need to decide what we're going to do about Dimitri."

"Dimitri is out for revenge," Antony said. "Sitting behind bars is not going to stop him."

"You haven't changed a bit." Martin took a step back. "You want to kill him?"

"Yeah, I want to, but—"

"What? You don't have the stomach for it anymore? KCPD said a body in a dumpster back in the eighties had your name written all over it."

Dimitri's handiwork, but Antony chose to ignore the comment. It would take him to an argument he couldn't win.

"If he comes in and we can't catch him, one of us," Martin gestured to Zoë, "takes him out."

"Legal murder," Antony scoffed. "I could live with that."

"That's always your solution, isn't it?" Zoë gave Martin a severe look. "Throw 'em in a body bag and wipe your hands clean."

"Excuse me." Victoria tapped on the opened door. "Antony, Elisa is asking for you."

"I'll be right there."

Antony gave Martin a slap on the back. "Still think she loves you more?" Not waiting for his response, Antony walked out of the office.

"Let's get you moved." Victoria leaned over Elisa. "Can you walk?"

"I'll get her." Antony scooped her up. She wrapped her arms around his neck and rested her head on his chest. "Which room, Vic?"

"Any of them. I'll be up in a minute."

Antony carried Elisa up the stairs, laid her down on a bed, and covered her with a blanket.

"I'm sorry." He sat on the edge of the bed. "I thought you'd be safe. What happened?"

"When I opened the door, I thought they were your men." She touched her swollen cheek. "He hit me with his gun."

"You hurt anywhere else?"

"No." Elisa shook her head. "I don't know what would've happened if your guys hadn't come."

"I always keep a promise, you know that."

Tears filled her eyes, and her chin quivered. "Then why didn't you come back for me in Kansas City?"

Antony sighed. "Do we have to do this now?" He began to stand, but she grabbed his hand and forced him to sit back down. Her eyes pleaded.

"I did come back for you." His voice was soft. "I saw you in the arms of Thomas Casteel, head jock. You had already moved on."

"I thought . . ." A single tear fell. "Dimitri said you had found someone else."

"Carlo hated us together. Why would Dimitri be any different?"

"So you hadn't found anybody?"

"No."

She looked into his eyes. "I'm sorry for all the pain I've caused you."

For a moment, Antony's heart softened, then pride overcame him. He pursed his lips. "It's okay."

"You say it's okay, but will you forgive me?"

He turned. She asked for something he couldn't give. He had carried anger and bitterness for so long he wouldn't know how to forgive her even if he wanted to.

She brought the ice pack up to her face. "Can you ask Martin to come up?"

"He's a cop. Did you know that?"

"No." Her eyes met his. "But that would explain a lot."

"And you still want me to send him up?"

"You think because you can't forgive me, I can't forgive him?"

"He lied to you."

"He tried to make me leave. He asked me to run away with him. He said he'd keep me safe."

"He was undercover. He'd say anything to gain your trust." Her eyes flooded with tears. He was sorry his words hurt, but it didn't stop him. "It was his job."

"Go away." She turned from him, and the tears rolled down her cheeks.

Antony stood and looked at her for a moment then left. His heart ached to comfort her, but he refused. He wouldn't allow her to hurt him again, ever.

Victoria stood in the hallway, her arms crossed. "Why'd you say that to her?"

Antony brushed past her, but Victoria grabbed his arm, forcing him to turn back. "You made her believe that Martin didn't care about her. I saw how he looked at her."

"He can't possibly love her."

"I believe he does. I don't think this has anything to do with Martin. You don't see what you're doing to her, do you?"

"I'm sure you'll enlighten me."

"You have the greatest ability to love. It's magnetic. That girl in there loves you so much that she can't move on until you forgive her. Forgive her, Antony."

Antony looked deep into her eyes. Despite his attempts to harden his heart, her words brought back pain he wasn't ready to face. "I can't."

"Can't or won't?"

Antony brushed past her and walked further down the hall. Victoria followed. He turned to her. "You don't know how many times I went to help her after her husband beat her, only to have her go back to that piece of scum. I was always there for her. I tried to protect her."

"It's okay to admit she's hurt you." Victoria took his hand. "You're allowed to feel pain."

Antony squeezed her hand, and a faint smile lit his face. "If I admitted to that, what's that make me?"

"Human." She grinned. "I always knew you were."

Antony ran his hand through his hair. "How do you do it?"

"Do what?"

"Make me want to change."

"Because I know you have a heart in there." She rested her hand on his chest. "Even if you don't like to admit it."

Antony placed his hand over hers and smiled. "You ever regret rushing into marrying Sonny? You never really did give us a chance."

"I was in love with Sonny." She pulled her hand from his. "I *am* in love with Sonny."

He conceded and gave her a single nod.

"You'll try to forgive her?"

"You know I'd do anything for you," Antony said.

"Then forgive her."

Forgive Elisa. It was something he wanted to do, but her betrayal ran deep. He had given her his heart and his soul, and she had trampled it. Forgiveness wouldn't come easy.

"I'll do my best." He bowed his head, his dimples deep.

"You're spending the night, aren't you?"

Antony raised an eyebrow. The left side of his mouth went up into a grin. "There may be hope for us yet."

"That's not what I meant."

Antony put his arm around her as they walked down the hallway. "Don't worry, your secret is safe with me."

She elbowed him in the stomach.

He jumped back and laughed.

"They want you downstairs," she said and turned back to Elisa's room.

Antony walked into the office to find Martin standing behind Sonny's desk shuffling through some papers. Antony pulled a toothpick from his shirt pocket, slid it into his mouth, and rolled it across his tongue. "Find anything interesting?"

"Not really." Martin looked and slid his hands into the pockets of his jeans. "How is she?"

"Why do you care?" Antony tried to ask honestly, but the words came out dripping with bitterness.

"Why is it so hard to believe that I do?"

"How long have you known her?"

"A few months." Martin walked around Antony and stood facing the wall, studying a picture of Sonny and Christian holding a large swordfish.

"And you love her?"

"You don't." Martin turned to him. "Not in a way that can make her happy."

Heat instantly flooded Antony's neck at the truth in Martin's statement. He did still love her. He always would, but it didn't mean he wanted to be with her. So why was it so hard to let her go?

"I'm going up to see her." Martin turned to walk out.

"She doesn't want to see you," he lied. He wasn't completely sure why. Could be pride, or maybe he just wanted to see if Martin loved her enough to fight for her. "Leave her alone. We've got a madman to catch."

Martin stood in the doorway and tucked his hair behind his ears. He looked up the stairs and sighed before he turned back to Antony. "Where's the beaker?"

"Sonny?" Antony yelled.

Sonny came into the office. "Yeah?"

"Martin wants to know where the beaker is."

Sonny walked behind his desk, opened a side drawer, and pulled out the ten-inch high, cone-shaped wine goblet and placed it on his desk. "The beaker."

Antony picked it up and ran his fingers around its smooth black rim. "Where was it?"

"Inside the hay feeder in the barn."

Antony set the beaker down and walked to the window. The sun was beginning to set, and shards of blue, orange, and red shot across the sky. "I got a bad feeling."

Sonny sat down in the chair behind his desk. "What do you mean?"

"Why hasn't Dimitri called? He knows we have the beaker."

"He's too busy trying to figure out how Christian and Elisa escaped," Martin said.

Sonny's eyes cut to Martin. "Let Antony talk."

Antony, doubt-consumed, turned to Sonny. Lies and pain, hatred and betrayal spun around him like a tornado. "I think we've played right into his hands."

"What are you talking about?" Martin asked.

"He knows we're here." Antony gestured to himself and Sonny. "He knows I'll keep Elisa with me to protect her. He probably thinks we have the kids here, too." Antony's face hardened. "I'll bet he knows you're a cop."

"Why would he think that? He just thinks I'm in jail with Justice for kidnapping."

"There's always ways to get information. If Dimitri wanted to know if you were arrested, he could find out." Antony looked around the room. "Where's Zoë?"

"She went to the office," Martin said.

"Why?"

"To fill Rollins in."

"By herself?"

"She is a cop you know."

"And my girlfriend." Antony pulled out his cell phone and dialed Zoë's number.

***

Victoria placed the chicken and pasta in a large plastic container then slid it into the fridge. She began clearing away the dishes. Most of the food had gone uneaten. Tensions were high even though she had tried to make it appear like a normal evening.

Sonny slid his arms around her. "It was a wonderful dinner." He tucked her hair behind her ears. "This will be over soon."

She looked in his eyes. "At dinner, you said you thought Dimitri might be coming here. When?"

"I don't know. Antony's trying to get in touch with him. I don't want you to go anywhere in this house without me or Antony, understood?"

She nodded, but he was unsure of her faith. It had been tested to the limits the last few months. He gently ran his fingers through her hair. "You know everything will be all right."

"I know." She chewed on the inside of her cheek. "But I'm still scared."

"I'm scared, too, but it'll be okay."

***

Martin tapped on the door to Elisa's room. He held the plate of food Victoria had made. When she didn't answer, he walked in, set the plate on the nightstand, and sat on the edge of the bed. The small light from the corner fell on her face. The swelling had gone down, and the bruise now covered most of her cheek.

When she opened her eyes, she smiled. "I wondered when you'd come see me." She scooted up and leaned against the headboard.

"How are you feeling?"

She touched her cheek. "Sore."

"Are you still groggy from the chloroform?"

"A little."

Her soft brown eyes made his heart pound and his palms sweat. "I have to tell you something."

"You're a cop."

He raised an eyebrow. "How did you know?"

"Antony told me."

"Figures." He stared into her eyes. He wasn't about to apologize for doing his job, but he was sorry she got hurt in the process. "I wish I could've told you the truth, but I was undercover."

"I understand. I wish I would've left with you."

"Me, too." Martin grinned. "But you're here now, and you're safe."

"Not with Dimitri out there. He's determined to kill Antony. He'll kill anyone who gets in his way."

"We'll stop him." Martin took her hand. "Do you still love Antony?"

"Part of me will always love him."

"I understand." Part of him would always love Zoë. "Can I ask you something?"

"Sure."

"Any chance you might love me?"

She smiled. "Yeah, there's a chance. A very good chance."

He leaned in and kissed her. "I think I love you, too."

TWENTY-SEVEN

ANTONY SLIPPED ON HIS JACKET.

"Where you going?" Sonny asked.

"I still can't get a hold of Zoë."

"So you're going to go find her?"

"Someone has to." Antony stood in front of Sonny's desk. "You still have the Derringer?"

Sonny opened the desk drawer, grabbed the small gun, and held it up. "Yes." He set the gun back in the drawer and closed it. "You can't just go running off. Dimitri could show up anytime."

"I can't sit around when Zoë's out there."

"We need you here."

Antony looked into his brother's eyes. They were the same eyes that had begged him to stay so many years ago. He looked away and rubbed the back of his neck. "I can't leave her out there."

"You really think she's in trouble?"

"Yes, I do."

Sonny nodded. "Be careful."

"I always am."

Antony walked out the front door. "Vince!" He climbed in the Durango and tapped his fingers on the steering wheel. He glanced in the rearview mirror, expecting Vince to be walking toward the car, but saw only darkness.

"Where is he?" Antony said aloud while he put the key into the ignition. He stopped and took a deep breath. Faint, powdery perfume floated in the air. He slid his hand under his jacket to go for his gun when cold steel pressed against his temple.

"Thought you could double-cross me?" Dimitri reached over the seat and removed Antony's gun.

Antony looked in the rearview mirror at Dimitri. "Where is she?" He half expected a response.

Dimitri slid his large body out of the car, the gun still in Antony's face. "Get out."

"I said, where is she?"

Dimitri gave Antony a shove, forcing him to walk. As he passed the car, he looked in the back seat. Zoë lay crumbled on the floor. Blood trickled down the side of her face.

"Is she dead?" Antony looked around. *How did Dimitri get on the grounds? Where the heck are the bodyguards? When this is over, heads are going to roll.*

Dimitri pushed the gun harder into his back. "Inside."

Antony opened the front door and yelled. "Sonny, Dimitri's here."

His words of warning didn't come without a price. Dimitri slammed the butt of the gun against the back of his head, which sent him against the wall. He shook away the pain and momentary confusion then turned to Dimitri, heat flooding his face.

Dimitri shoved the gun hard against Antony's cheek. "Try something like that again, I shoot."

The dull pain in his head only fueled his anger. "Just evening out the playing field."

Dimitri grabbed Antony's arm, spun him around, and shoved him into the foyer.

Antony saw Victoria frozen in the hallway, her face white, her hands shaking. He motioned with his eyes toward Sonny's office.

She ducked away without being seen.

Sonny came around the corner. "Antony did you just say . . ." His eyes widened. "Oh, God."

***

Victoria stood in Sonny's office, took a deep breath, and tried to slow down her pounding heart. She ran to the desk and grabbed the phone. No dial tone.

She set it down and slid open the top drawer. Her hands shook as she reached for the small Derringer. Sonny had reminded her that it was there if she needed it. She never dreamed she would.

She grabbed the small holster, lifted up her dress and strapped it to her upper thigh, then slid the gun into it. The metal felt uncomfortable on her legs, but no one would know it was there.

Victoria cracked open the door and looked around. The house was quiet and dark. She had just slipped into the hallway when a hand swiftly covered her mouth, and a gun came to her temple.

"Not a word," the voice whispered behind her.

She swallowed hard as her heart raced. The man was pushing her down the hall toward the great room when she heard a thump, and the weight of the man fell upon her. She moved forward and turned to see the man slump to the floor. Clay stood with a Glock in his hand.

Clay leaned into her and whispered, "Let's get you out of here."

"Not without Sonny."

"I'll get him." Clay grabbed her arm and pushed her back toward the office.

The lifeless body mesmerized her. She felt Clay squeeze her arm tighter, which brought her attention back to him. His eyes were hard.

"Go into the office, lock the door, and wait. This is my job—let me do it."

Victoria nodded and went back into Sonny's office. She turned and peeked back into the hallway. Clay had disappeared into the darkness. *I will not hide in here like a frightened child.* She went back into the hall to make her way toward the front door.

The distinct sound of action being pulled back echoed in the foyer. She froze.

A man grabbed her arm and threw her against the wall. "Got orders to frisk you." He grinned, his teeth yellowed and his breath reeking.

She batted at him as his hands wandered over her body. "Get your hands off me."

He grabbed her arms and shoved her harder against the wall, his elbow pushing into her chest and holding her. "Orders." He continued to place his hand on strategic parts of her body then stopped. Her heart pounded. He hadn't felt the gun.

He grabbed her arm and pushed her into the great room where five of Dimitri's men stood with submachine guns and Antony and Sonny sat on the couch.

Sonny jumped up, but Dimitri pushed him back down. He pointed the gun at Sonny's head. "Sit, or you'll be the first to die."

Sonny's eyes met Victoria's. "You okay?"

She nodded. He smiled. If he was scared, he didn't look it.

"Well, Dimitri," Antony said, as if the whole incident was an annoyance, "now what?" His leg crossed and his foot tapped to what looked like the beat of an imaginary song. One side of his mouth was in a deep grin. He winked at her then looked back at Dimitri. She couldn't believe his cockiness ran so thick when their lives were in danger.

Dimitri walked to the mantle, a gun still in his hands. His fingers brushed over the numerous pictures of the children until he stopped on one and picked it up. "Nice kids." He turned to Sonny, his eyes wide, demonic. "I'll take care of them later."

Sonny lunged at Dimitri, but one of the men pummeled a submachine gun into his gut and knocked him back onto the couch. He clenched his stomach. "You touch either of my kids, I'll—"

"You'll what?" Dimitri dropped the picture on the floor. The glass shattered. "You'll do nothing because you'll be dead."

"You know, Dimitri," Antony projected. "You'll never get away with this. You can't possibly kill all of us."

Dimitri raised one eyebrow then sat on the chair across from them. He brought up the tip of the gun to scratch his head while he laughed. "You were always so cocky, even as a kid. Carlo loved you like a brother."

"And you were always jealous of that, weren't you?" Antony's grin widened. He looked like he was actually enjoying himself.

Victoria's hands shook, and she locked eyes with Sonny. She couldn't imagine how she'd ever get the gun out, let alone use it. *Was the safety on? How do I flip it off? Think, think.* Sonny and Antony had both gone over it with her, but she hadn't really listened. She never believed she'd have to use it.

"Carlo and I had big plans," Antony said. "Plans that didn't include you."

Dimitri's neck turned red, and he flew out of the chair, aiming the gun at Antony. "Shut up and give me the beaker."

Sonny leaned into Antony. "Would you quit egging him on?"

"All right," Antony said to Sonny. He slapped his hands on the top of his thighs then stood. "I'll get the beaker."

Dimitri pulled the action back on the gun. Antony raised his hands. "Relax. You want the beaker or not?"

Dimitri's eyes narrowed, and he jerked his head at Hank. "He tries anything, kill him."

Hank grabbed Antony's arm and pushed him through the house.

TWENTY-EIGHT

MARTIN STOOD IN THE SHADOWS at the top of the stairs. He slipped back into the spare room where Elisa sat on the bed wringing her hands together.

"Is he down there?" Elisa whispered, her eyes wide.

"Yes."

Martin pulled his cell phone out, tried to hit a number, but nothing happened. *What? Great. The battery's dead.* He slid it back into his pocket. Zoë would love this. He'd hear a big *I told you so* when this was over. *Plug the phone into the charger every night,* she'd say, but he never listened.

Elisa stood and paced. Her tanned skin turned pale. "What are we going to do?"

Martin rested his foot on the edge of the bed, lifted his jeans, and pulled a small 9 mm Ruger from the ankle strap. He handed it to Elisa. When she didn't move, he pushed it closer. "Take it."

Her hands shook, but she took the gun.

"You ever shoot a gun before?"

"No."

"It's a semi-automatic." He hit the release button, and the clip fell into his hand. He pushed on the bullets. When he was satisfied it had all its rounds, he slipped it back into the gun. "You've got ten shots in that clip. Just aim and fire."

Martin grabbed her arm, led her into the bathroom, and sat her down on the side of the tub. "If anyone tries to hurt you, protect yourself. I'll lock the door behind me."

"Where are you going?"

"I'm going to go help."

Her eyes widened, and she shook her head. "No. Please don't leave me."

He knelt down on one knee. "I have to. You'll be okay." He leaned in and kissed her. "I'll be right back."

***

Antony's jaw was tight as he walked into Sonny's office, the gun pressed into his back. *Kill me? Kill me?* He laughed to himself. *Dimitri obviously doesn't know who he's dealing with.*

He took a deep breath and smiled. Perfume danced in the air. Antony turned to face Hank, his hands up, the gun now pointed at his chest. "You know you're not walking out of here with me."

"Just give me the beaker."

Antony shrugged his shoulders. "Don't say I didn't warn you."

Zoë slammed the butt of her gun on the back of Hank's head, dropping him to the floor. Antony took Hank's gun and tucked it in the front of his pants. He grabbed his feet and dragged him through the connecting door into Clay's office. He looked up at Zoë and grinned. "Glad to see you could join the party."

"Not a minute too soon, I see." Zoë cuffed Hank's wrists behind his back then readjusted his body so the door would close. "Where's Martin?"

"He's in love." Antony glanced up at her while pulling the door shut and locking it. "Far as I know, he's still upstairs with Elisa."

Zoë put her hands on her hips and cocked her head, her breathing fast. "You jealous?"

"Me, jealous?" He grinned. "Not of Martin." He moved the hair away from her forehead, exposing a two-inch gash. "You okay?"

She reached up and gently touched the cut. "I'm a super cop, right?"

"That you are."

"You got a plan?"

"To keep everyone alive." He walked around Sonny's desk, pulled open the top drawer, and felt around for the small Derringer. He stopped and smiled.

"What is it?" Zoë asked.

"Vic's got a gun."

"You sure?"

"Yeah." He walked to the door.

"How do you want to play this?"

"I'll take care of it."

"Antony . . ."

He gave her a wink then disappeared into the darkness of the hallway.

***

Martin snuck down the stairs and slipped into the dining room. He felt the barrel of a gun in his back. He raised his hands then turned. "Clay."

"Finally decide to join us?" Clay sounded annoyed. He lowered the gun. "Where's Elisa?"

"Locked in the bathroom. Where are the rest of the men?"

"I don't know. Hopefully not dead."

Martin peeked out the doorway. He couldn't see into the great room, so he turned back to Clay. "Can you get around back, to the French doors?"

"I could, but I'm not going to."

"What?"

"You want to shimmy out a window, go ahead, I'm going into that living room to save my boss and his wife."

Martin pulled out his badge. "You see this? It gives me the right to tell you what to do. Get out that window and cover me at the French doors. Now."

Clay glared at Martin, his face hard. After a long moment, he walked to the window, unlocked it, and slid it up. Pulling out his pocketknife, he slit open the screen then climbed out.

Martin slipped into the hall and looked down the corridor. He saw a figure. It was Zoë.

She pointed to herself then to the east entrance then motioned for him to go to the west entrance then made a fist. He nodded and walked along the hallway until he got a few feet from the doorway then leaned against the wall and waited.

***

Elisa sat in the bathroom, staring at the gun. Dimitri. He had destroyed her life. She hated him. She stood and took a deep breath. She had no doubt—she knew what she had to do. She walked into the hallway and down the stairs.

***

Victoria's heart pounded as Dimitri waved his gun around the room.

"Who should die first? You?" Dimitri brought the gun around to Sonny then turned the gun back on her. "Or your lovely wife?"

"You'll have to kill me first." Sonny's face flamed.

Dimitri pointed the gun back at him. "That can be arranged." He grabbed Sonny's arm, pulled him up, and pressed the barrel against his temple.

"Wait." Victoria stood.

Dimitri's eyes cut to her. "Sit down."

She obeyed. Her eyes locked with Sonny's. His appeared calm and steady. "Please." Tears escaped and rolled down her cheek. "We're giving you the beaker. Just let us go."

"The beaker isn't the only thing I want. I must avenge my brother."

When Dimitri turned back to Sonny, she reached under her dress and pulled out the small gun. It was completely concealed in her hand. She rested it between her legs and felt around on the gun until she found the safety.

Up is on or up is off? Oh, God, I can't remember.

Antony strutted back into the great room as if Dimitri, his men, and their guns didn't exist. He laughed and brought the gun up before anyone even noticed it was in his hand.

"Hank had a little accident in the office." Antony had the barrel of the Glock aimed directly at Dimitri's face.

Dimitri clutched tighter to Sonny's arm, his gun at Sonny's head. "I'll kill him. I swear."

Antony glanced around at Dimitri's men, their guns raised, then looked back at Dimitri. "You may shoot Sonny, but you'll be dead before he hits the floor."

"My men will shoot."

"Not before I shoot you. Let my brother and his wife go, and I'll get your beaker."

"He killed Carlo!" Dimitri yelled. "You know he has to pay."

"Sonny was only protecting me."

"Man, you are unbelievable. You really think Carlo would've shot you?" Dimitri pressed the gun deeper into Sonny's temple. "Father always said, an eye for an eye."

***

Martin glanced down the hallway to see Elisa walking toward the great room. He waved at her, but she either ignored him or didn't see him, he didn't know which.

***

The first shot triggered a small arsenal throughout the room.

The small force of the gun made Victoria's hands shake so badly she dropped it, fell to the floor, and covered her ears. Bullets sprayed over her head.

Antony lunged at Dimitri and Sonny. Dimitri fired aimlessly as his large body fell to the ground with Antony on top of him.

Sonny threw himself on top of Victoria as gunshots continued to blast throughout the room.

She turned her head to see Antony and Dimitri fighting. Dimitri had a definite advantage in size. When Dimitri landed on top of Antony, he groaned as the air was thrust from his lungs. Dimitri grabbed Antony's hand and slammed it on the floor, causing Antony to release the gun. It spun across the floor.

Dimitri raised his gun, pointing it at Antony's chest, but Antony grabbed it with both of his hands. She wasn't sure how, but Antony flipped Dimitri over, and they rolled out of sight. She heard a muffled gunshot over the now short, sudden bursts of gunfire, and then silence.

Sonny pushed himself off her. "You okay?"

"Yeah." Tears flooded her eyes. "I thought he was going to kill you."

Sonny touched her cheek. "I'm okay." He looked around the room. Martin lay on top of Elisa, a gun in both of their hands. "Where's Antony?" Sonny yelled.

Victoria brushed the hair from her face. She saw Antony leaning against the fireplace, his elbows resting on his knees. His head fell forward, and he had blood on his chest.

"I'm okay." Antony sounded out of breath.

"Stay down!" she heard Clay yell.

"Are we secure?" Zoë yelled.

Martin stood. "Clay, check the grounds. Zoë and I will check the house." Martin tossed Sonny a gun. "Call nine-one-one."

"Phones are dead," Victoria whispered.

Sonny looked down at her. "I'll use my cell." He kissed her. "Stay down until we know it's safe."

She waited a few seconds then crawled to Antony who had blood all over his shirt. Tears ran down her face, and her hands shook as she reached for his arm. "Oh, God. You can't die."

Antony rubbed his forehead, Dimitri's gun still in his hand. He looked into her eyes. "Are you okay?"

"I'm fine." She felt his forehead. "Sonny's calling an ambulance. Stay still."

"Where are you hit?" Sonny knelt down.

"I'm fine." Antony stood and pointed to Dimitri who was lying on the floor, blood seeping from two gunshot wounds in his chest. "It's not my blood, it's his."

Victoria pounded her fists on Antony's chest. "You scared us to death."

Sonny grabbed her from behind. "It's okay."

When she began to relax, he let go of her. She brushed his hands away. "Let go of me."

Sonny backed away.

Antony laughed, which made her turn and smack him one more time in the chest. "What? I save the day, and this is my thanks?"

Victoria looked over at Elisa, who sat in a chair, hypnotized by Dimitri's body.

Victoria felt Sonny's hand on her shoulder. She turned to him and his open arms, and tears escaped and rolled down her cheeks. "Come on." Sonny led her out of the room. "You don't need to see all of this."

She glanced over her shoulder at the bodies riddled with bullet holes and soaked in blood. She wondered how many times her father had witnessed such a scene. Looking over at Martin and Zoë, they appeared unaffected, like it was just another day at the office. How did they deal with it? The dead bodies seemed to scream at her, asking her to second-guess herself. Her shot had started it all. Could there have been another way?

A chill ran through her entire being.

***

Antony stood over Dimitri's body. "I think that went very well." He leaned over and felt Dimitri's neck. No pulse. He moved the long strands of black hair off his face then closed Dimitri's eyes. "It's finally over for you, old friend."

"Brass is going to kill us." Zoë stepped closer to Dimitri's body.

"But we got the bad guy." Martin ran his hand through his hair.

"In a body bag—again."

"You got the beaker." Antony grinned. "It's in the office."

"We still need the paintings." Zoë chewed on her bottom lip.

"They shouldn't be that hard to find." Antony put his arm around her. "You *are* a super cop."

Zoë laughed. "I am, aren't I?"

***

Victoria sat on the bed. The moonlight shot through the trees, making strange shadows on the walls. She had prayed for the images to go away, but they flooded her mind and made her stomach churn. One question haunted her. Had she killed Dimitri?

She walked down the stairs and stood in the doorway of the great room. Crime scene investigators had invaded the house like cockroaches. Flash bulbs randomly lit the room, and endless chatter between detectives floated through the air.

She watched one detective squat on the floor over Dimitri's large, lifeless body. He shook his head. "Man, this guy is wanted by everyone. We'll be here all night just calling all the agencies involved."

"Zoë's lucky she bagged this one." Another detective squatted next to him. "What a collar."

Victoria turned away as Antony came out of Sonny's office. "Hey." He touched her arm. "You need something?"

"I was just looking for Sonny."

"He's talking to a detective. Come on." Antony led her back up the stairs. "They'll want to talk to you soon enough. Stay upstairs until they get the bodies moved."

Victoria nodded and numbly walked into her bedroom and sat on the edge of the bed. She looked up at Antony. "Did I kill him?"

"Dimitri?"

She nodded. "You were wrestling with him. You had a gun, and he had a gun. There was another shot, right?" Victoria's hands shook.

"I can't remember how it happened." She wiped her eyes and looked deeply into his. "I know all about self-defense, but it still doesn't change the fact that I might have taken a man's life."

"The cops have the guns. They'll have to match bullets. But if you killed him, you did it to save our lives."

"But you shot, too, right?"

He nodded. "So did Elisa."

"Did I kill him?"

"I shot him after you did. If anything, it was my bullet, not yours."

Victoria nodded and took a deep breath. Her chest shuddered, and the tears fell.

"It's over now." Antony took her in his arms. "You're going to be okay."

"Victoria?" Sonny sat next to her.

She pulled away from Antony into the open arms of her husband.

"She's having a hard time." Antony stood.

"Thanks." Sonny's arms tightened around her, and he rubbed her back.

They lay on the bed. He kissed the top of her head. "He's right, you know. It'll be okay."

"I can't stop seeing his face. The blood. The sounds." She looked up at him. "How do I make it stop?"

"It'll take time." He pulled the comforter over her. "Try to sleep. It'll make you feel better."

Victoria closed her eyes and nodded, clinging to him, silently praying sleep would come.

TWENTY-NINE

ANTONY DROVE TO LORENZO'S ALONE.

Vince stood on the porch, rubbing his hands. "You want me to get Rachel?"

Antony looked at his watch. It was close to midnight. "I'll get her in a little bit. How's your head?"

"Not bad. It's better than a bullet hole."

Antony nodded. He lost four good men that night in their attempt to alert the other bodyguards who had stood their posts, oblivious to what was going on until the shots were already flying.

Antony walked to his father's bedroom. The empty wheelchair sat in the corner, and the bed was made perfectly, just like he liked it. He walked to the dresser, opened it, dug underneath the t-shirts, and pulled out the picture of his mother. He carried it into the spare bedroom he had moved into a few weeks ago.

The picture sat on the dresser, making him smile. He unbuttoned his shirt. Dimitri's blood was dried on his chest, and it was making him itch.

He went into the marble bathroom and stepped into the shower. The hot water turned red as it rushed over his body. Resting his hands on the wall, he let the water beat against his chest. Tears of anger flooded his eyes.

"Why God?" he said aloud. "Why did Victoria have to shoot? I was there. I was willing."

Moving his face under the water, he allowed it to wash his tears away. They were useless.

Thirty minutes later, dressed in black stonewashed jeans and a gray t-shirt, he climbed into his car and drove to Elisa's. Victoria had asked him to forgive her. He didn't know how but knew he had to try.

Antony stood on Elisa's porch and looked up at the countless stars. He knew God was up there, somewhere. "Help me get this right." He took a deep breath and knocked.

Martin opened the door. "I thought you might show up."

Antony held back the condescending words that sat on the end of his tongue. He placed one hand in his pocket and felt the crucifix his mother had given him so many years ago. "I'd like to talk to Elisa."

"She's in the living room." Martin pulled the door open. "I'll be in the kitchen."

"Thanks." Antony stepped into the living room.

Elisa sat on the couch with her legs tucked under her and a pillow on her lap. Her brown eyes were bloodshot, and her face was streaked with red. Her eyes met his.

"Can I sit?"

"Sure."

There was an awkward pause. His heart pounded, and his confidence disappeared. "I loved you so much. I was so hurt when I came back and you had moved on."

Her eyes met his.

"Then you married Enrico."

"But, I thought—"

"Please, just let me finish." He rubbed his hands together. "I was excited every time you called and said you still loved me. You said you were leaving him, but you never did." He tried to push the pain and humiliation deep within his soul. He closed his eyes. *I can't do this, God. I need help.*

Suddenly, the anger evaporated, and a peace rushed through him.

He smiled and looked back at her. "I understand why you stayed with him. You were trying to protect me because you loved me. I'm sorry for being angry about that."

Tears filled her eyes.

He kissed her cheek then pulled her into his arms and held her as she cried.

"I've waited so long for this," she said.

Martin stood in the doorway of the kitchen. Antony's eyes met his, and they stared at each other for a long, uncomfortable moment.

"That stuff I said about Martin just doing his job, I was wrong. I think he really loves you." Antony pulled away. "Do you love him?"

She nodded and lowered her head.

"I'm happy for you." He placed his finger under her chin and raised it until her eyes met his. "I'll always love you. And you know you can call me if you ever need anything."

"I'll always love you, too."

Antony leaned in and kissed her cheek. "I gotta go."

As he walked to his car, he heard Martin yell thanks. He didn't acknowledge the statement aloud, but it made him grin.

Fifteen minutes later, he walked into Lorenzo's and opened the basement door. The wooden stairs creaked under his weight. He walked to the farthest corner where the fake electrical box sat, pulled the box open, punched in the code, and a hidden door opened.

The glow from a TV lit up the small living room. Sean walked toward him, giving his short brown hair a quick comb-through. "Rachel's asleep."

"Dimitri's dead. It's over." Antony walked across the living room. "I'll take her upstairs."

Antony opened the door to Rachel's room and grinned. She clutched a stuffed teddy bear she'd had since she was a small child. Her brown curls fell across her face. When he scooped her up, her eyes opened slightly. He kissed her cheek. "It's Uncle Tony."

"Do I get to go home?"

"Tomorrow."

Rachel's arms wrapped around his neck. "Can I sleep upstairs tonight?"

"Of course."

He carried her up the stairs, pulled back the covers, and laid her down in the bed of one of the spare rooms.

She opened her eyes. "Where are you sleeping?"

"I'll be right next door."

"Love you." Her eyes closed.

"Love you, too, Rach."

THIRTY

SONNY WAITED FOR VICTORIA in his office. He tapped his foot as he drew small circles on the notepad, his mind going in five different directions. Mr. Swift, the family attorney, had set up numerous meetings—estate readings, wills, the final legalities of Renato's and its shares.

Upper management was nervous about all the publicity over the killing of Dimitri Romeo. It had not only made the headlines nationwide, but the tabloids ran with it like it was a two-headed baby.

The crisp, clean scent of Victoria's perfume filled the room. Sonny smiled and looked up. Victoria stood in the doorway, her face relaxed.

He stood. "You ready?"

"I hope you're taking me to see the kids."

"They're meeting us." He pulled out his car keys and grabbed her hand.

Sonny held the car door for her. Victoria stood, closed her eyes, and leaned her head back, the sun beating on her face. "I forgot what it's like to be outside and not be afraid."

"Come on." Sonny tapped his thumb on the hood of the Escalade. "I'll open the sunroof if you like."

Victoria put her sunglasses on and got in.

Sonny peeled out with his finger on the button. As the overhead window slid open, the wind flung her hair out of the car. She reached over and grabbed his hand.

He drove up the coast to a private beach just north of Ventura and parked next to Antony's Durango.

Antony watched Rachel on the beach, running at the waves as they rolled out to sea then running away from them as they rushed back at her. He faintly heard the car doors slam. He turned. "Rachel, they're here."

Rachel waved while she ran up the beach to her mother's open arms. "Mom."

"Man, I missed you." Victoria hugged her.

Sonny kissed Rachel on the top of her head. "How are you?"

"Good, now. I hate the safe house. There was nothing to do. I couldn't even use my cell phone."

"I know. I'm sorry." Victoria smiled then looked up at Antony. "Thank you for bringing her."

"Christian should be here soon." Antony looked at his buzzing phone then let it go to voicemail. "I'll be by the car. Sonny, we meet the attorney in an hour."

Sonny nodded. "Thanks."

Antony walked to his car, pulled out his briefcase, and placed it on the hood. He clipped the phone's small earpiece in his ear and shuffled through papers, beginning with the first message on the pile.

His heart pounded as he watched Victoria on the beach holding Rachel's hand. The color had returned to her face, and she looked happy. Her hair fell loosely around her neck. He forced himself to look away.

His heart ached for a love like hers. He wondered if he'd ever find someone as special as her. One thing he knew—he had to get rid of these feelings for her. They weren't right.

When his cell phone chirped again, he answered it. "Yeah . . . I told you I'd get back to you, and I will. I'm busy . . . Yes, I will." Antony hung up and yanked the earpiece out as Zoë's silver PT Cruiser pulled into the drive. His phone rang. He looked at the caller ID. It was Lauren again. Ignoring her, he walked to the car as

Christian and Zoë got out. Antony took Christian in his arms. "It's good to see you, kid."

"Yeah." Christian pushed Antony away.

"What, too big for hugs?"

Christian laughed. "Where's Mom and Dad?"

"On the beach."

Christian ran off.

Antony turned back to Zoë. "How are you this morning? Buried in paperwork?"

"Yep. You got one of those hugs for me?"

Antony cocked his head and playfully raised an eyebrow before he grabbed her and hugged her tight.

"You get the ballistics report?" he asked.

She took off her sunglasses and looked up at him. "It wasn't your bullet that killed Dimitri. It was Vic's."

"How? He was still fighting me when I shot him."

Zoë shrugged her shoulders. "I've seen perps fight after being shot more than once. Report shows Vic's bullet perforated the sternum and the lung. Yours perforated the spleen."

Antony sighed heavily and rubbed the back of his neck. "You can't tell her this."

"She can handle it."

"I know she can, but why make her?"

"Antony, you can't ask me to lie to her."

"You won't have to lie. Neither one of us will. Let me handle it."

"I don't know, Antony."

"You ever kill anyone?"

"Yeah, more than once. I'm a cop."

"Then you'll agree. It doesn't matter what the circumstances are. Taking someone's life still affects you. I'm just asking you to spare her that."

Zoë placed her hands in her pockets. "I've already sent you a copy of the report."

"That's alright. She shouldn't ask for it, and if she does, I'll dummy one up. Just don't tell her it was her bullet."

"You're always protecting her, aren't you?"

Antony stared into Zoë's eyes and waited for an answer.

Zoë took a deep breath and let it out. "Okay, but you owe me."

Antony grinned. "I owe you. Hmm." He raised his eyebrows. "This could be fun."

Zoë's face flushed.

Victoria's voice interrupted them. "Zoë." She pulled her sister into a hug. "Thanks for bringing Christian over."

"No problem." Zoë looked over at Antony then back at Victoria. "Preliminary ballistics report came in."

"Did I?" Victoria asked.

"Oh, come on," Antony laughed. "You know I shot him after you. You didn't really think he could've fought me like he did if your bullet was the one that killed him."

Antony and Sonny locked eyes. By the slight grin on Sonny's face, Antony knew his brother was aware that he wasn't lying, but he wasn't telling the truth, either. Sonny gave Antony an approving nod. The left side of Antony's mouth went into a grin.

Victoria looked over at Zoë. "So it wasn't me? I didn't kill him?"

"Like Antony said, guys with fatal gunshot wounds don't usually fight like he did."

The color returned to Victoria's face.

Sonny rubbed her back. "We should go. After the estate reading and the meeting at Renato's, I thought we'd fly up the coast to Monterey for a few days."

"Really?" Christian said. "Can I surf Carmel?"

"Of course." Sonny rested his hand on Christian's shoulder.

Rachel grabbed Victoria's hand and tugged her toward the car. "Come on."

"How about if we go visit Doc and Bruno in the hospital while Dad goes to his meetings?" She looked up at Christian, who nodded.

Rachel's head tilted. "In the hospital? What's wrong with them?"

"They got hurt." Victoria caught her hair and tucked it behind her ears. "But they're going to be okay. Why don't you wait for us in the car?" Victoria hugged Zoë. "Thanks for everything."

"No problem. You guys have fun."

Victoria turned to Antony. "Thank you. Without you . . ." Her eyes filled with tears.

"You know I'd do anything for my family." Antony gave her hand a squeeze. "Have a good trip."

Antony outstretched his hand to Sonny. Sonny pulled him into a hug. "Love ya, man. Thanks for everything."

"No problem. I'll see you at the office in an hour."

Sonny climbed into the car. The back window rolled down, and Rachel's head popped out of it. "Bye, Uncle Tony."

Antony grinned. "Bye, Rach."

THIRTY-ONE

LAUREN SAT IN THE RESTAURANT, drumming her red dragon nails on the table and sipping on a martini. Her long, thin, straight blond hair hung over her shoulders. She picked up a small handful and checked it for split ends.

"Hello." Antony's hand brushed across her back and stopped on her shoulder. "What was so important?"

"Nice to see you, too." She pointed to his drink. "I ordered for you."

"Thanks." Antony sat down, moved the whiskey to the center of the table, and sipped on the water. The waiter approached. Antony handed back both menus. "I'll have the filet, and nothing for the lady."

Lauren's eyes narrowed. "Salad, your house dressing on the side."

Antony raised his eyebrows. "Eating, I see. I thought you looked like you put on a few pounds."

Lauren sighed. "Fat is more like it. David's got me on a diet and is killing me with all the new exercises."

"What do you need, Lauren?"

Lauren used the tip of her fingernail to swirl the olive around in her almost empty drink. "I wanted to see you. I'm tired of being ignored. Only time I'm around is when you want something."

The waiter placed their salads in front of them.

Antony looked over at her. "Oh, come on, it's been months. No games. You need money?" He ran a napkin over his mouth. "I'm sorry."

"You? Sorry?" Lauren laughed as she drizzled the vinegar dressing on her salad. "For what?"

"I treated you badly in the past."

Lauren waved her fork in the air as she talked. "You grow a conscience all of a sudden? Something you've conveniently lived without over the past sixteen years?"

Antony tilted his glass and let the water roll along the side of it. "What do want from me?"

"Companionship. Love."

Antony laughed.

"Oh, I forgot." She rolled her eyes. "You only have eyes for your brother's wife." When Antony said nothing, she pouted. "I want you to be around more."

"No."

"No?"

"My father just died, and I have a company to run. I don't have time for a relationship." He pulled out a wad of money, threw a fifty on the table, and put a couple hundreds in her hand. "I gotta go."

"Call me."

"Don't hold your breath."

"Then I'll call you."

Antony stared down at her. "Now why would you do that?"

"Because I have something you might be interested in." She raised her eyebrows.

"I can't think of anything you have that interests me anymore."

"This will." She gently patted the napkin on her lips, being careful not to remove any lipstick.

Antony shook his head and walked out.

Lauren waited until he was gone then sauntered to the back of the restaurant where her mother sat with a fifteen-year-old boy.

Her mother looked up. "I thought you were going to tell him about the kid."

Lauren glanced at the boy then clicked at the waiter and ordered another martini and asked him to bring Antony's filet to them. "Get off my back, Mother. I'll tell him, now just wasn't the time."

"That was my dad?" Julian's shoulder-length black hair hung in his face.

"Yeah, that was your dad." Lauren picked up Julian's untouched water and drank it. She could feel his glaring eyes. She curled her nose up at him. "I don't need a lecture from you."

"Oh, no." Julian's eyes narrowed. "I wouldn't dream of that, like it would help. Why don't you just disappear again? We don't need you around. We never have."

Julian's grandmother smacked his arm. "Speak for yourself. It's me who has to pay for everything."

"You drink our money away. Only thing you give me is a roof over my head, and even that's a dump."

"Would the both of you stop it?" Lauren looked around. She had to decide how to play this. *Think. Think.* Spencer had been fierce on the phone. He wanted his hundred and twenty-five thousand dollars, or she was dead. Antony owed her for having his child, for using her like he had over the years. All she needed now was enough to pay Spencer off, then she'd get what was due her . . . Antony's millions. Her son was the means to the end.

***

Julian sat in the high school library. His dark eyes narrowed as the web page loaded. One of *The Kansas City Star's* archived articles finally appeared. *Antony Luciano Wanted for Murder.* Six months later, the charges had been dropped. Missing evidence.

"Antony Luciano is my father," he whispered. Pride filled him with a vengeance. He didn't know which intrigued him more, the vast wealth his father had or the devious lifestyle that made him who he was. Julian's grin deepened. He was worth millions. He could finally kiss his sordid past goodbye.

Tucking his hair behind his ears, he arrowed back to the thousands of hits on the Luciano name. His eyes widened as he continued to read about his family, past and present.

He hadn't known his last name was rightfully Luciano until he saw his mother talking to Antony at the restaurant in Ventura a few hours ago. He recognized him because his picture was plastered on the front page of all the newspapers. Big shootout. Killed four men in self-defense, one of them the notorious Dimitri Romeo. Uncovered three priceless works of art from the Boston Museum heist. His father. A hero.

Heat filled his face as Lauren Bauman's name come up on a page. The article claimed that the semi-famous fashion model denied all rumors that she had given birth to a child. His heart pounded, and he cracked his knuckles. Why had he expected anything less? His mother thought of only one person, herself. She even claimed her own mother was dead. Well, he couldn't diss his mom for that. He only admitted grandma was alive when the school insisted on speaking to his legal guardian. Grandma was an embarrassment and a drunk.

Clicking on web page after web page, he searched for a phone number. "Figures," he said out loud. "No listing." He continued to search and finally found the number of his father's company, Renato's, and jotted it on a scrap piece of paper.

Looking over the computer screen, he saw a small gang of boys come through the doors. Their pants hung baggily, and the brims of their hats turned left, both signatures of who they were. Kids quickly shut books and left. Julian's mouth went up into a grin. "What's up?" Julian jerked his head.

"Heard you were dissin' us?" Sal said, his Latino accent strong.

"Me, dissin' you?" Julian smiled. "Never."

Sal shooed the others away, rested his arm on the computer monitor, and leaned into Julian, his voice soft, "You really out?"

"Yeah, I'm out." Julian closed the window on the computer before standing up.

"You ain't scared, man?" Sal's brown eyes were sympathetic. It had only been a few months since Ace Nunzio killed Sal's older brother. The Bonnie and Clyde style drive-by shooting was Ace's signature.

"Naw, I got you watchin' my back." Julian and Sal clasped hands, then Julian pulled him closer and lowered his voice. "I'm getting out of this place. There's gotta be something better." Julian released Sal, grabbed his black leather jacket, and slipped it over his T-shirt.

"When you find it, come and get me."

"Don't worry." Julian grinned at his best friend. "You know I will."

Sal gave Julian a single nod then motioned with his head to the other boys as he walked out of the library.

Julian walked down the street until he reached a rundown apartment building. "Hey, Mac." Julian stepped over the permanent drunk that lived in the doorway. Mac said nothing. His eyes opened momentarily then closed.

Walking down the hallway of the apartment building, Julian ran his fingers along the outline of a word written in graffiti. A word he never could read. A stream of cuss words bellowed from a neighboring apartment, and an object slammed against a wall. He quickened his gait until he reached the small, dingy one-bedroom apartment he reluctantly called home.

Empty beer cans and trash littered the wood floor. A hole in one of the walls proudly showed off a rotting two-by-four. Circular water rings stained the ceiling, and when the people above them fought, paint chips fell like snow.

His grandmother lay on the worn-out rust-colored couch, home to more mice then Julian wanted to know about. The brown sweater his grandmother wore had made numerous moths fat before she had found it in the dumpster along with a pair of black polyester pants embellished with random bleach stains.

Her pale, wrinkled face was framed by long, gray, matted hair that gave the appearance of a large spider web as it rested on the side of the faded, flowered pillow. An empty vodka bottle was tucked under her arm.

She was either passed out or dead. He couldn't tell which. He gave her a quick shove and waited. Holding his breath, he wondered if today was the day she had drunk herself into her grave.

The loud grunt startled him. Her eyes closed more tightly. She rolled over and dropped the empty vodka bottle. He jumped back, the bottle just missing his worn high tops. They were a Christmas gift from his mother last year. He grabbed the telephone from the empty milk crate that served as an end table and ignored his growling stomach. There was never any food.

He walked into the bedroom, the phone cord overturning numerous old newspapers and the latest tabloid magazine. His father's hard, indifferent face was immortalized on the cover. He leaned over and picked up the tabloid, staring at Antony.

Julian's eyes narrowed before rolling. He dropped the magazine on the mattress that sat on the floor, his blood pounding furiously through his veins. He'd wasted fifteen years in this dump while his father was a multi-millionaire.

He picked up the receiver and placed it to his ear. No dial tone. He repeatedly pushed the button then threw the phone against the wall. It was disconnected again. Mom must've conveniently forgotten to send the check.

Leaving the small apartment, he walked to the payphone. The sounds of neighbors fighting played like background music in the dark, dingy hallway. He picked up the receiver, wiped the ear and mouthpiece against his shirt before putting it to the side of his head.

Dropping a quarter and a dime in the slot, he pulled the crumpled piece of paper out of his pocket and dialed the number. When the receptionist answered, he said, "Antony Luciano, please."

"May I tell him whose calling?"

"Yeah. Julian . . . Julian Luciano."

ABOUT THE AUTHOR

DANA K. RAY has been writing gutsy, true to life stories since her early teens. A full-time children's minister, she and her husband reside in the Midwest with their four children and four dogs. *Absolution* is her second published novel and the first in the *Luciano Series*. She loves to connect with her readers. Find her on Facebook.com/danakray, DanaKRay.com, or danakray@yahoo.com.

Also by Dana K. Ray:

A Second Chance

Made in the USA
Middletown, DE
09 December 2017